THE HARDY BOYS CASEFILES (TM)

FRANKLYN W. DIXON

THE HARDY BOYS
CASEFILES(TM)
3 STORIES IN 1

THICK AS THIEVES
THE DEADLIEST DARE
WITHOUT A TRACE

AN ARCHWAY PAPERBACK
Published by SIMON & SCHUSTER
New York   London   Toronto   Sydney   Tokyo   Singapore

THICK AS THIEVES, THE DEADLIEST DARE and WITHOUT A
TRACE first published in Great Britain by Simon & Schuster, 1992
First published together in this combined edition in 1997
by Pocket Books
An imprint of Simon & Schuster Ltd
A Viacom Company

Simon & Schuster Ltd
West Garden Place
Kendal Street
London
W2 2AQ

THE HARDY BOYS CASEFILES is a trademark of Simon & Schuster
Inc.

Simon & Schuster Australia
Sydney

A CIP catalogue record for this book is available from the British Library.

ISBN 0 671 00487 5

Printed and bound in Great Britain by
Caledonian International Book Manufacturing, Glasgow

THICK AS THIEVES

Chapter

1

"GO AWAY," said the thin man who stood between Frank Hardy and the single open entrance to the darkened Bayport Museum.

Caught off-guard, Frank took a step back and blinked in the harsh artificial light from overhead. The man in front of him folded his arms and smirked, almost begging Frank to try to push by.

Frank knew that look, from other bullies he'd run across. At first glance, this one didn't have the usual bully equipment—he was almost a head shorter than Frank, who stood just over six feet tall, and much older, with dark, thinning hair that had worked back on both sides into a widow's peak. His thick glasses magnified his eyes, making them look far too large for his head. An ill-fitting suit hid his physique. The man might have been athletic once, but had long since let himself go—a small potbelly spread out from under his thin chest. Frank had no doubt he could push past the guy without any effort.

But there was that smirk, the smug grin of a man who had a rule book behind him, if not muscle. It was the look of a clerk who could use the power of a large company—or government—to make himself feel big.

"Who does this guy think he is?" an angry voice burst out from the darkness behind Frank. It was his younger brother, Joe. He was seventeen, a year younger than Frank, with blond hair and a powerhouse build, in contrast to Frank's brown hair and lean frame. Joe's approach to problems was different from Frank's too.

"We're supposed to be here," Frank explained. "Chief Collig hired us to handle security for one of the museum exhibits."

"Who cares?" the man snapped back.

Joe moved into the light beside his brother, clenched his fists, and glared at the guy.

One look at Joe's angry, flashing blue eyes and the man's smug mask cracked. With a frightened gasp of breath, the guy stepped back, opening his hands in front of his chest to ward off any possible punches.

Frank put an arm out to hold Joe back. "Cool down," he said to his brother. Then he turned his attention back to the man and stared coldly into his eyes. "Mind telling me *why* we can't go in?"

The man returned his level gaze, his confidence returning. From his pocket he drew an ID card. "Elroy Renner, American Insurance Investigators. You're interfering with official business. Now move off."

Joe snatched the card from Renner, glanced at it, and grinned. "I guess you're here with the new exhibit."

Angrily Renner grabbed the card back and slid it into his pocket. "Listen, kid. I'm in charge of security around here, and if you know what's good for you—"

"Who's in charge?" a deep voice boomed from inside the museum. Chief of Police Ezra Collig stepped through the door, his face red with rage. "Renner! What have I told you?"

Renner glared at the chief, the two men locked in a duel of stares. "The insurance company left operations in my hands, not—"

"This is *my* town," Collig interrupted. "No one tells me what to do in my town. The insurance company sent you to work with me, not to run the show."

Renner's jaw dropped. "I'm not going to

leave the protection of valuable gems in the hands of some hick-town cop."

"Hick town!" Joe yelled, and Renner spun toward him. The thin man's eyes darted from Joe to Frank to Chief Collig, then back to Joe. Sourly rolling his eyes, he gave up the argument and slunk into the museum.

Collig chuckled. "He's a good man, really—but a real pain in the neck to work with sometimes." In a grand gesture, the chief swept his arm toward the open museum door and winked at the Hardys. "After you, boys."

Frank drew a deep breath and looked up at the front of the building before entering. He always found the museum inspiring. An old mansion, it had four spires rising to the sky like corner towers on a castle. The spires were being rebuilt as part of a plan to renovate the museum. Scaffolding rose up around them, making the museum look like a castle under siege. The building was set back from the street and separated from other houses by woods and a huge lawn.

Inside, a short foyer opened into a parlor the size of a normal house. The walls were lined with heavy gold-framed paintings, and in the center of this main room was a giant sculpture of bronze and chrome. Frank wasn't exactly sure what it was supposed to be. The last time he'd been in the museum, a statue of a Greek warrior had stood there.

He remembered it well—the statue had fallen and almost killed Tessa Carpenter back in *The Borgia Dagger* case.

"Could use your help," he heard Chief Collig say as they left the room and walked down the carpeted hall. He realized Joe and the chief had been talking while he'd been deep in thought.

"I don't know," Joe was saying. "I thought the Bayport police didn't like working with us amateurs."

Collig smiled apologetically. "Sure, I prefer not having to look over my shoulder for you two whenever a crime happens in this town. But this is different. We need security guards to watch the Star of Ishtar exhibit. I don't have the manpower to staff a special detail like this twenty-four hours a day."

"I read about the exhibit in the paper," Frank said. "The Star is one of the largest sapphires in the world."

"Right. And I need people I can trust."

"You can trust these two?" Renner had reappeared almost magically and was leaning in a doorway, his arms tightly crossed.

"I'd rather trust them than all your electronic gadgets," Collig snapped back. "I've known these boys for years. They're smart, honest, and they've got great instincts."

"Electronics don't need instincts," Renner replied. He pushed open a door, and the four of them walked through it. The relatively dark space on the other side was large. It was a corner room, and one of the spires rose a hundred feet above it. The floor was a rich marble, and exhibit cases lined the brocaded walls. In the center, surrounded by electric eyes and vibration alarms, was an eight-sided glass case.

"There," Renner said proudly, "is the Star of Ishtar!"

Frank's eyes widened.

There was nothing in the case.

"It's empty," Joe said. For a moment Frank thought Renner was going to collapse like a balloon with the air let out. His face went chalk white, and his mouth flopped open, then shut without a word coming out.

Chief Collig stepped forward with his usual no-nonsense attitude and tested the defenses. When his fist passed through the electric-eye beam and pounded on the glass, alarms began to shriek.

"Well, that ought to bring reinforcements," Collig muttered, his eyes darting around the room.

"This is your fault!" Renner screamed.

"There was supposed to be someone in this room at all times!"

"There would have been!" Collig answered. "If you hadn't been playing drill sergeant and stopped the Hardys from coming in. I had to come find you to see what was taking so long."

"So you admit it!" Renner bellowed. "The loss is your responsibility."

"Let's worry about getting the stone back before we decide who's to blame," Frank suggested. "How could anyone manage to steal the Star without tripping the alarms?"

He studied the case, and then the room. Nothing seemed out of place. Puzzled, he glanced up into the darkness of the spire.

About sixteen feet up a flicker of motion caught his eye.

"A rope!" Frank cried. "Someone hit the lights. Joe, come here."

As Collig hit the switch that lit the spire, Joe reached his brother's side. "Get me up there," Frank said. Joe cupped his hands together, and in seconds Frank stepped from Joe's hands to his shoulders and was leaping for the rope.

It was just within his grasp. Quickly Frank started to work himself up hand over hand. As his eyes adjusted to the lights, he looked straight up.

Almost at the top of the spire, also climbing the rope, was a woman in a black jumpsuit.

When she glanced down at him, Frank saw she was young and beautiful, with reddish blond hair sweeping over her shoulders.

"I don't believe it," Joe said when he caught a glimpse of the woman's face. "It's Charity."

"Who's Charity?" said Collig, bewildered.

"Don't ask," Joe muttered, shaking his head. The beautiful young jewel thief had made a fool of him once. Could Frank even the score?

"Get outside and have the building surrounded," Frank called down. "I'll keep climbing. Let's give her nowhere to go." Already he could hear the sirens of reinforcements arriving outside. They had Charity trapped.

For what seemed an eternity, Frank continued to pull himself up. He was almost within reach of the woman dangling above him. She was peering out through a skylight at the top of the spire as if she were waiting for something or someone.

"Why, Frank Hardy," she said, finally deciding to acknowledge him. "I haven't seen you since when? San Francisco? Is your brother still as cute as ever?"

"Give it up, Charity." Frank's voice was gravelly from the exertion of the climb. "We've got you surrounded."

"That may be," Charity admitted, the lovely

smile never leaving her lips. Her hand slipped into her jumpsuit and came out a second later with a glint of silver.

Charity moved so fast, Frank hardly saw the knife as she slashed the rope.

Frank sucked in a last breath and pictured with horror the long plunge to the marble floor below.

Chapter

2

AFTER A COUPLE of inches Frank's fall stopped. The shock jarred the rope from his grasp. He desperately grabbed for it and tightened his grip around the heavy cord.

Swaying one-handed in midair, he was holding on for dear life.

After he had caught his breath, Frank looked up to see why he hadn't plunged all the way to the floor below. Charity hadn't cut the rope all the way through. A single strand had him dangling in the air. If he remained perfectly still, the strand might support his weight until help came. If he moved, the strain on the rope would snap it, and he would plummet to the hard floor.

But if he stayed where he was, Charity would escape, and Frank couldn't let that happen.

Slowly he eased himself up, putting as little strain on the strand as he could. The rope slipped another inch, and he froze to stop its swaying. After a moment he started working his way up again, but the strand kept untwining.

Frank knew he wouldn't make it.

From above he heard a metallic creaking, and looked up to see Charity opening one of the glass skylights at the top of the spire. A blast of cool night air gusted in, sending the rope swaying again. Another fiber popped loose from the strand.

Frank closed his eyes and took a deep breath. He had to make his move and get up past the raveled strand.

He gathered his strength. Then, in a flurry of movement, he pulled himself up in a couple of rough, rapid motions. The rope dropped by another inch. His hand was almost past the split when the last fibers pulled loose and the strand broke.

Frank lashed out, his fingertips grazing the top rope, but he couldn't get a grip on it. His fingers slid along the rough fibers, then closed on empty air.

No! They'd caught on the tail end of the frayed strand. Frank's fingernails dug into his palm as he clung to it. The pain in his fingers blotted out all thought. By instinct he threw his free hand up and caught hold of the rope. Ignoring the burning in his shoulders, Frank pulled himself the rest of the way to the window in the spire.

As he crawled out the window, the pain caught up to him, and Frank collapsed on the scaffolding. The cool air washed over him, and he opened his eyes to see what looked like a giant bat standing over him.

Frank shook the pain from his head and stared. It was no bat.

Charity smiled down sweetly at him and blew him a kiss. Before Frank could reach her, she leapt off the scaffolding. The wind caught the hang glider she had strapped herself into, and she was gone, a shrinking, winged dot vanishing into the dark.

A spotlight hit Frank, blinding him, and from the ground came a voice through a megaphone: "You're surrounded. Give yourself up." It was Elroy Renner. Frank yelled back and pointed to Charity, but they were too far away to hear him and in the wrong location to see Charity's flight. Frustrated, Frank began the long climb down the scaffolding.

"Where is she?" Chief Collig asked as Frank reached the ground.

"Gone," Frank said on the run. "She took

off in a hang glider." He had Joe by the arm now. "Come on."

"Wait!" Renner shouted. "You can't just run out! You have questions to answer!"

"Later," Frank shouted back as he and Joe raced to their black van in the museum parking lot. "When we catch Charity, we'll have all the answers."

"How are we going to catch her?" Joe asked, climbing into the passenger's seat. He yanked the seat belt around him. "If you lost sight of her, she could be anywhere."

The van had roared to life, and with a screech peeled out of the parking lot and onto the street. They headed for the west end of Bayport.

"She took off over the west woods," Frank said. "If she plans to make a safe landing—and there's no guarantee of that—there's only one place she can do it."

Joe snapped his fingers. "The old Miller farm. It's the only clear, flat land for miles."

"Right," replied Frank. "I can't wait to bring her in."

"You?" Joe said. "*I'm* the one she made a fool of in San Francisco."

"She did a pretty good job of that with both of us, brother."

Joe grinned. "That'd really be something, wouldn't it? Us capturing the greatest jewel

13

thief of the decade—'' He stopped as the gates to the old Miller place appeared in the headlights.

The Miller farm had been one of the many in the Bayport area, but times had changed. Farmers had moved out, and more and more of their land had been built up with new housing developments. Yet, even as the city swallowed up so much land, this old farm remained untouched, even after the last Miller died. Now it was a slowly collapsing monument to a way of life that had all but vanished from that part of the country.

The lock that should have been on the gate wasn't there. Frank killed the headlights as Joe got out of the van and pulled open the barrier. The van rolled onto the farm.

''There's a light on at the house,'' Joe said. He stood on the step of the van, hanging out the open door. Something dark spread out across the road in front of them. ''Watch it.''

Frank brought the van to a stop. ''Charity's hang glider,'' he said, getting out of the van. ''If we run over that, it'll make so much noise that she'll know we're here. Let's leave the car and not move the glider. It'll be quieter approaching on foot.''

Joe grinned. ''I can't wait to see the look on her face when we burst in on her.''

Quietly they crept through the tall weeds and

then across the grass to approach the house. The curtains were drawn, but a woman's shadow fell on them, moving back and forth. Frank squinted. There was something odd about the silhouette, but he couldn't put his finger on what.

"Let's hope she's alone," he said. "I'd hate to run into someone toting a gun."

Joe reached the house first and flattened his back against it. Inside, the shadow still walked back and forth. "If she's got the Star, she'll have already dumped any partner she might have had. Charity uses people, but she never splits the loot with them."

"Looks like she's waiting for someone," said Frank, who had flattened himself against the wall next to Joe. "Let's not disappoint her."

They reached the door. It was solid wood, but years of decay had splintered and weakened it. It gave slightly against Joe's testing shove.

"Ready?" he whispered. Frank nodded.

Joe threw down one finger, and then a second. On the third finger, the Hardys stepped away from the door, then hurled their shoulders into it.

The door cracked open with a sound like a sudden thunderclap. It fell away, and the Hardys rushed into the farmhouse. All the furniture was still there, covered with a thick layer of dust. There was no sign that anyone had lived there in recent months.

Frank didn't hang around to check out the decorating. They ran for the living-room door and rushed into the lit space.

In the middle of the living room was a lamp, trained on the window. Between the window and the light was a record player, its turntable moving round and round. Riding around was a cardboard cutout shaped like a woman's head and shoulders. The shadow cast by the light seemed to move back and forth across the curtains. Cords from both the light and the record player ran to a small portable generator in a corner of the room.

That was it—there was no sign of Charity.

"A trick!" Joe roared. "She's not here at all."

"What's that noise?" Frank cut across Joe's yelling. From somewhere came a low hum, like that of a giant electric fan that was growing louder and louder.

"Outside!" Joe dashed for the front door.

"I've got a bad feeling about this," Frank said, following on the heels of his brother. "Remember old man Miller, back when we were kids? How he used to entertain at fairs?"

"Barnstorming," Joe recalled. "He did flying tricks in an old biplane."

16

"And his barn is built to store a plane," Frank said, leading the way now, to the barn. "That's how she's going to get out of here! She has a plane stashed here."

They flung open the barn doors, and a blast of air hit them in the face. The single engine of a biplane roared in their ears. The boys rushed in, raising their arms to keep the blowing dust out of their eyes. They could just make out a woman sitting in the pilot's seat.

"Charity," Joe yelled, but his voice was drowned by the engine noise. There was a grinding of machinery behind him, and he turned—too late—to see the barn doors closing. There wasn't enough space for them to get out.

"Frank!" Joe shouted. "The doors!"

They rushed over and pressed their hands against the doors, struggling to keep them open, but strong motors forced them shut. Charity stuck a remote control out the side window, and on her lips she plastered a smile.

Bits of straw were sucked into the propeller and were shredded. As Frank and Joe pressed back against the barn door, the plane began to move forward.

The propeller, slicing everything in its way, was aimed straight at them.

Chapter

3

"SCRAMBLE," FRANK YELLED, diving to the ground to avoid the whirling blade. Joe rolled under a wing as the plane passed over him.

With a laugh, Charity aimed the remote control at the barn doors again and pressed a button. They swung wide open, and the plane rolled away from the Hardys and out into the night.

"Stop her!" Joe yelled. He leapt for the tail of the plane, which rolled along on a single wheel. He was too late. The biplane was already in the air.

Charity was out of reach.

"It figures she'd be able to fly a plane," Joe said, brushing himself off after his hard landing. "She's an expert at everything else. We'll never catch her."

"Maybe," Frank said, every bit as annoyed as Joe by the escape. "That doesn't mean we shouldn't try. She's obviously been using this place as her base of operations. Maybe she left something behind to trace her by." They went back to the house.

A search of the bedrooms and kitchen turned up nothing. Neither did a check of the record player.

As Joe moved the lamp that had shone on the window, a tiny scrap of paper fluttered out from under the bottom of it and settled near his shoe. He picked it up and studied it. It looked like a duplicate from an order form, with serial numbers on it.

"I think I found something," he called to Frank.

Frank walked over to Joe and took the paper from him. "I'd say it was a piece of a receipt. It looks vaguely familiar, but I'm not sure why or where it's from."

Joe sighed. "One thing I *am* sure about is that there's nothing else to find here. We'd better get back to town and give them the bad news."

The mood back at the museum was bleak. A line of police officers barricaded both ends of the street that the museum was on, keeping reporters and TV camera crews out. Frank and Joe were let through the barricade and shortly found themselves in the museum curator's office, where Chief Collig sat on a couch, with Officer Con Riley nearby, leaning against a wall. Both sets of eyes were on Renner. Renner was speaking on the phone, but he talked too quietly to be heard across the room. Though good friends, Collig and Riley didn't speak. Right then there was nothing to say.

Riley's eyes rolled up as the Hardys entered the room. Unlike Chief Collig, he had never minded the Hardys helping out on cases, but he also knew that wherever Frank and Joe were, trouble was sure to follow. "Your father know you're here, boys?"

The Hardys' father was Fenton Hardy, a former New York police detective who had become a world-famous private investigator. It wasn't unusual for him to take off across the globe at the drop of a hat—which Frank and Joe sometimes did as well.

"Mom and Dad are in Boston for the week," Joe said. "Dad recommended us for this security gig because he couldn't be here."

Riley grinned. "I suppose he thought it would be easy."

"Wipe that stupid grin off your face," Renner growled as he slammed the phone down.

He pointed to the chief. "I want this man arrested."

All four stared at Renner, stunned. Chief Collig bounced to his feet, angrily asking, "And what am I to be arrested for?"

"You stole the Star," Renner said, glaring at Collig. "You stole it while I was out front talking to these kids." He waved a hand in the direction of the Hardys. "Then they concocted this story about a jewel thief to cover your tracks."

"She was there!" Frank protested.

"Says you," Renner said bluntly. "I didn't see anyone. Suddenly you three were tripping alarms and pulling stunts, till I couldn't tell what was what. But the thief had to be someone who knew how to turn the alarms on and off and who could get to them. That means Collig or me. And I was with the boys."

"It was Charity," Joe said. "We have proof." He held up the scrap of paper. Renner snatched it, studied it for a moment, then crumpled it into a little ball and tossed it back to Joe.

"Stray garbage," the insurance man said. He pointed a finger at Collig again.

Con Riley glared at Renner, his hands on his hips. "There's no evidence against the chief, and he's too fine a man for you to accuse."

"I should have figured you hick-town cops

would stick together," Renner snarled back. "But I know what my report is going to say."

"If you think you've got something on me, do whatever you have to," Chief Collig said. "But don't you speak to my officers like that. And don't forget that I'm still chief of police in this town."

"You won't be much longer if I have anything to say about it," Renner said. "And I will. The insurance company I work for has lots of pull in this state. No yokel cop is going to make fools of them. Collig, you can kiss your job goodbye." He eyed the Hardys. "Now, what about these two?"

"They're free to go," Riley said.

"No, we're not free." Joe gave Renner a look so menacing the insurance guy jumped a step back. "We're going to find Charity, bring back the sapphire, and wreck this little frame you're trying to put around the chief and Frank and me."

"I've got it!" Frank cried. "Joe, where's that scrap of paper?"

As Joe handed him the numbers, Frank went behind the curator's desk and dug out a phone book. "Airlines, airlines . . ." he mumbled, running a finger down a column in the Yellow Pages. He picked up the phone and dialed a number.

"Hi," he said in a cheery voice. "I'm afraid

I've destroyed my plane ticket, and all I have left of it is the order number. I think it was with your company. Could you check? . . . Thank you." He rattled off the number on the paper.

"Oh. Transcontinent Air. . . . I see. Thank you. And that flight was to . . .? Sorry, but my appointment book was destroyed at the same time. I go so many places on business, I can't keep track of them. . . . Thanks.

"Of course. Thanks. And the flight is leaving . . . It just left. Oh, dear. Is there any other flight I can— When? . . . Tomorrow morning? That'd be great. Two tickets, please. . . . Hardy. . . . Yes. You've been very helpful."

Frank hung up the phone, cold determination on his face. "Let's go, Joe. We have some packing to do."

"Where do you think you're going?" Renner snapped.

"San Diego," Frank said, trailing Joe out of the room. They slammed the door behind them.

Joe Hardy woke the minute the plane touched down on the runway in San Diego. He and Frank both knew that that might be the last time they'd have to sleep in days. They had drifted off as soon as they left New York.

Joe almost wished he hadn't. His rest had been constantly interrupted by nightmares of Charity.

He nudged Frank awake. "I've been thinking—" he began, as the plane rolled up to the terminal, but Frank interrupted him.

"Me, too. Something's not right here." Frank yawned and stretched. "It strikes me that Charity could've escaped from us several times. Why was she so slow?"

"Slow?"

"Sure. First, she dangles on that rope until we see her, then she stays on the scaffolding outside until I get there."

Joe nodded. "And she was way ahead of us in the barn. She could have flown away before we got anywhere near her."

"But instead she closed the doors and played with us," Frank agreed. "Sounds a little like she was trying to make sure we stayed on her trail, doesn't it?"

"You think she left the number for us to find?"

"I don't know. There's only one way to find out."

"Right," Joe said. "Catch Charity." The flight attendants opened the doors, and the passengers started filing out of the plane. Trapped in their seats until the flood of people passed, Frank and Joe watched each of them move by. Finally, when the plane was almost empty, the Hardys got up.

"Here's something else that's funny." Joe lowered his voice. "I just recognized about half a dozen of the people on this plane."

"Me, too," Frank said, frowning. "We've seen their faces in those investigator's updates Dad gets. They're criminals."

"Thieves," Joe added. "Just like Charity. What are they all doing in San Diego at the same time?"

"Do criminals have conventions?" Frank asked jokingly. Then his face grew serious "Something's going on. The question is, what, and what are we going to do?"

They stepped into the terminal. Already the passengers were dispersing, but just ahead Joe saw a familiar hairless head, polished to a shine. "That's a second-story man out of Baltimore, named Chrome Lasker. Why don't we ask him what's going on?"

The Hardys pushed through the crowd, closing in on Lasker. The bald man didn't notice them. He was busy speaking to a guy in a white suit. In profile, the second man had a thick mustache and what looked like tiny, ratlike eyes.

"Lasker," Frank said, clamping a hand on the bald man's shoulder. Without missing a beat, the mustached man clipped Frank with a massive hand, knocking him down. The two men took off running.

"They're heading for the exit," Joe said as he helped Frank to his feet. Frank looked down the corridor where the two men had gone. It ended in double doors.

"That's not an exit," Frank said. "It leads to a service area. We've got them cornered. Come on."

They pushed through the double doors into darkness. As the doors slammed shut behind them, each of the Hardys felt something thin and cool wrap around his throat. Frank and Joe felt hot breath raise the hairs on the backs of their necks. The men behind them were taller than they were, and, if they could go by the grip the men had, they were a lot bigger too.

Wires held in strong hands tightened and began to bite into the Hardys' throats, slowly squeezing the life out of them.

Chapter

4

JOE HARDY RAISED a foot and brought it down as hard as he could on the toes of the man strangling him. The man howled and loosened his grip on the wire. Joe rammed an elbow into the man's stomach.

Pain shot through Joe's arm, as if he'd just smashed into a rock. With a grunt and a laugh, the man rapped Joe on the side of the head, knocking the younger Hardy off his feet. The wire caught him around the neck again and tightened.

Joe dangled there, trying to brace his feet again, feeling his weight drag him into the strangling wire. His pulse pounded in his ears, and his lungs burned for air. Nearby, he watched Frank struggle, with no more success than he was having.

Something—a foot, Joe figured—smacked into the back of his knees, knocking his legs out from under him. He knew the man holding the wire wasn't about to let him get his balance again.

There was a click, and instantly light streamed through the darkness and widened. A woman's shadow fell across them, but Joe, almost unconscious, could see nothing. He heard two dull thuds, and air rushed into his lungs as he fell to the floor and the wire slid from his neck.

"Frank!" Joe called as he wobbled to his feet. "You all right?"

Next to him, Frank rolled over and sat up, coughing and rubbing his neck. "I'm okay. What happened?"

Joe looked at his and his brother's attackers lying at their feet. They weren't the men the Hardys had been following, but rather tan, muscular giants. One had a tattoo of an anchor on his forearm. Both were unconscious now, sprawled on the floor.

"Sailors of some sort, I'd guess." Joe's voice croaked out of a throat that still stung from the bite of the wire. "When the doors opened, there was this shadow, and—"

"Charity!" they said at the same time.

"I'm starting to get real tired of her." Frank fumed.

But Joe wasn't listening. He was out the door and back in the main terminal, looking for any sign of Charity. Other planes had unloaded passengers, and the terminal was filled. If Charity was there, Joe realized, she would be well hidden by the crowd.

"Kid!" a voice nearby called out, followed by murmured protests from the passersby on Joe's left. He turned to see what the commotion was about.

A heavyset man with a round face was pushing against the flow of the crowd, jostling people in his hurry to get to Joe. He smiled and waved, and Joe thought about turning tail and running. But it was too late. The cheery man clasped Joe's hand and shook it fiercely. Joe stared at the man, puzzled.

"Kid!" the man cried. "Don't you recognize me? It's Jolly!"

"Jolly?" Joe replied.

The man named Jolly nudged him in the ribs and lowered his voice. "Sure. You remember. That job we pulled on the French Riviera?"

"Oh," Joe answered, smiling nervously. "The French Riviera job. How've you been?"

Jolly winked at him. "I don't blame you for not recognizing me. We only met once, and that was a good ten years ago. But I never

29

forget a face, kid." He ran a finger along Joe's cheek and nodded admiringly. "Great lift job. I can only just make out the scars.

"As for how I've been, well, it's been slow. I was thinking of getting a real job when this came up." For a moment Jolly's face fell into a frown, but then the smile returned. "A score like this should put us both on easy street for the rest of our lives. You want to ride with me to the meet?"

Joe glanced over his shoulder. Frank stood against a wall, watching them with the same puzzled expression that Joe felt he must have. Joe shrugged slightly and caught Frank's eye. Nodding, Frank faded back.

"Sure," Joe said.

Jolly led him out of the airport to the taxi stand, talking about old times and old scores. Joe decided to let Jolly do the talking, since Joe didn't have the slightest idea what he was talking about.

He settled back in the cab, listening to Jolly and wondering where they were going.

The cab pulled up in front of a warehouse along the docks on San Diego's Embarcadero. "Sure this is where you want to go?" the driver asked. "This place has been shut down for years."

"Sure I'm sure," Jolly said, handing the

driver a twenty-dollar bill. "Keep the change, pal."

As the taxi drove off, Joe looked around. The street was all warehouses, but to the northwest Joe could see the tall buildings of downtown San Diego. Behind the warehouses was the shining blue of San Diego Bay; he could smell the ocean in the air.

"This way," Jolly said, gesturing toward a warehouse with a steel door painted red. "Didn't they give you instructions?"

"Let's just say I had to leave the dump where I was staying in a hurry," Joe lied. "Everything got left behind, including my luggage and the instructions."

"Well, that's one of the hazards," Jolly said. He pulled open the warehouse door.

Joe was expecting darkness inside, but instead the warehouse was filled with a soft blue light. "Come in," said a deep voice. They went in, letting the door close softly behind them.

A tall man stood just inside. He wore an expensive gray silk suit, white-on-white shirt, and a deadly gleam in his eye. A razor-thin scar, dead white, traced a line on his tanned face from the bottom of his left ear to the corner of his mouth. As he turned to face the newcomers, the outline of a large gun in a shoulder holster showed in the fabric of his suit coat.

"Names?" he asked with a faint Hispanic accent.

"I'm Jolly," Jolly said. He clapped a hand on Joe's shoulder. "This is my main man, the Kid. We're expected."

The scarred man nodded but didn't smile. "You're the last. Go in."

Joe and Jolly stepped past him, and the man followed them into the warehouse. A dozen or more men stood there, or sat on crates. No one spoke. Their eyes were riveted on a five-foot projection television screen that hung from the ceiling. The screen, empty of any picture but still on, was the source of the blue light.

The scarred man stepped in front of the screen and clapped his hands twice. All eyes were on him. "Greetings," he said. "I am Chavo. Your host, my employer, will join us shortly.

"You, gentlemen—and lady—are the world's finest thieves. Perhaps the best that ever were. You all know why we are gathered here. If we are successful, we will all be rich beyond our wildest dreams. This means that we must work together, without fear of betrayal. Is there anyone here who feels he can't do that?"

A short man with red hair piped up. "I don't trust anyone I've never met. The name's Brady."

"Everest," the man next to him said.

The next man stood up, the blue light bouncing off his shiny skull, and Joe swallowed hard. It was Chrome Lasker. But Lasker stared straight at Joe and identified himself. There was nothing in his face. Their two-second encounter at the airport hadn't been enough for him to recognize Joe.

" 'Cat' Willeford," said the man sitting on the crate with him, and Joe recognized Willeford as the mustached man who'd been talking to Lasker at the airport.

It went on and on, until everyone had identified himself.

Then Jolly stepped forward, bowing to the crowd as if they were an audience. "The name's Jolly," he said, "specialist in all things crystal and silver. And this"—he pointed at Joe—"is the Kid."

Everyone was growing bored by then, but at the mention of the Kid's name, all heads popped up, eyeing him.

"You got to a score just before I did," Everest growled.

"Sorry about that," Joe said, clenching his fists. He could feel a fight coming on.

"Forget it," Everest replied, and his scowl turned to a smile. "Just don't cut me out of this one, or . . ." He ran a fingernail across his throat, leaving a bright red streak. Joe nodded.

"Don't let him throw you, Kid," Brady said admiringly. "You're a legend. We study your capers.

"Now," Chavo continued, "if there's nothing else . . ."

"Don't forget me," said a melodic voice, and Joe's blood ran cold. From the shadows stepped Charity, dressed now in a blouse and skirt. Calmly she strolled across the room, moving toward Joe.

He stood still, not knowing what to do as she said, "Someone here is hiding something."

The rest of the thieves in the room began to move, some nervous, some scowling. Several slipped things out of pockets—knives, blackjacks, brass knuckles—the weapons of their trade. Joe knew that when Charity fingered him, the others would descend on him and tear him to pieces. She kept walking, moving steadily toward him.

"I know," she said as she put her arms around Joe's neck, "who you really are."

Chapter

5

JOE'S STOMACH KNOTTED as if a fist had been driven into it, but to Joe's surprise, Charity leaned over and kissed his cheek. Putting an arm around his waist, she swung back to face the others. A shiver ran through him, and he tried to breathe, but he couldn't. He could feel the hot breath of death on his face.

"The Kid and I pulled a caper together once. We got very close. I even learned his *real* name." She flashed him a catlike smile.

"You can't," Joe muttered, but he knew she wouldn't listen. He flexed his fingers, determined to take as many of them with him as possible.

"The Kid's real name is Crawford Laird Pulansky."

For a moment Joe couldn't understand what he had heard. She had lied for him! Why? Relief and shock washed over him, and his legs grew rubbery, but he locked his knees and forced himself to stand.

"*Crawford*." One of the thieves let out a guffaw. Then everyone in the room was roaring with laughter, until Chavo clapped his hands again. "If we are done with the entertainment portion of our program . . ."

Joe leaned over to Charity and whispered, "Is that the Kid's real name?"

"How should I know?" Charity whispered back. "I never met the guy."

Chavo hit a switch. A tiny dot of light formed in the center of the video screen and spread out until it formed a picture. It was a head and shoulders, but Joe couldn't tell if it was a man or a woman. The face on the screen was covered by a brown hood. Joe guessed that eyeholes had been cut into it, because the brown hood had dark glasses over the eyes. The voice was scrambled electronically, so it came out sounding like a robot's voice.

"Welcome," it said. "Welcome to the perfect crime. You may call me the Director."

The crooks began to murmur, but Chavo shouted, "Silence!" and they turned their attention back to the screen.

"For reasons of security, I can't tell you

where we are going to strike, or when. The operation will be divided into sections. Chavo will tell you who is needed, and for what.

"I want to thank everyone for being here. I can guarantee that if you follow instructions, this venture will be satisfactorily profitable for everyone.

"Now, go have a good day, see San Diego if you wish, stay out of trouble, and be back here at nine this evening. That is all."

The light blinked out, and the screen went dead.

Joe stood there for a moment, staring at the screen in bewilderment. What *have* I stumbled into? he wondered. He decided that, for the moment, it wasn't important. The first thing he had to do was bring in Charity. She was right beside him, and he could walk out with her now and she wouldn't be able to say a word. If this band of cutthroats ever got the idea that she had lied to them, she'd be dead. He had a hold on her.

But when he turned to grab Charity, she was gone.

He joined the others as they filed out into the street and looked all around. Again, no sign of Charity.

But he did notice something he'd missed before. On top of the warehouse was a satellite television dish.

"So, want to hang out with me today?" he heard Jolly say.

"Thanks," Joe replied. "But I've got a lot of things to do. Buy some new clothes, rent a room—"

"Yeah," Jolly agreed. "I understand. That would take up a lot of time. Well, I'll see you again tonight." He walked off.

Joe hoped Frank had managed to follow them. He wished he could talk to Frank now, but the others were still too close. If Frank contacted him now, it could be fatal for both of them.

He walked down the street, heading for the buildings in the distance. No sign of Frank on the empty streets. Here and there he passed other people, but they paid no attention to him.

Only one man nodded at Joe as he passed, a man in slacks and shirtsleeves, with his coat draped over his arm. Looking at the guy, Joe realized for the first time how hot he was himself. The weather had been cooling off in Bayport, but in San Diego it was just like summer.

Joe continued looking for any sign of Frank but saw none. He did see the man with the coat over his arm again. There was something strangely familiar about the guy.

No one I've met, Joe decided. The guy was blond haired and blue eyed, just over six feet tall, broad and muscular. From a distance he looked like a teenager, but as he came closer, Joe saw the man's looks could be the result of cosmetic surgery. Joe knew he was much older than his unlined face would indicate.

"Excuse me. Do you have the time?" the man asked, stopping next to Joe.

Joe raised his arm to look at his watch, and started to say, "A little after—" when he felt a heavy nudge in his ribs.

"That's a Smith and Wesson persuader in your side," the man said in a low, deadly calm voice. Out of the corner of his eye Joe caught the dark polished glint of gunmetal. "Walk."

"I don't have much money on me," Joe began, but another nudge shut him up.

"This isn't about money," the man said. "Make a move and I'll blow you away. Just do what I tell you." The man shoved Joe toward a car parked at the curb.

"I'll make any move I want," Joe threatened. "You wouldn't dare shoot me in front of other people."

The man sneered. "I'm a little crazy, see? Someone takes my name, I don't care *what* I have to do to deal with it."

Joe's heart jumped to his throat. It was the real Kid!

"You drive," the Kid said as they got into the car. "It's a nice day for a trip to the zoo."

Joe studied the Kid as they drove off. The Kid was good-looking, but Joe couldn't understand how anyone would mistake the two of them.

Frantically, Frank Hardy flagged down a cab after his brother had been forced into a waiting car. Frank had been tailing Joe since the airport, but he hadn't been able to get close enough to figure out what was going on.

"Follow that car," he told the driver as he got into the cab. He bit down lightly on his tongue when he heard himself say it. He pointed out the Chevy.

When the driver heard Frank's order, he cried, "Far out, man! I've been waiting to have someone say that all my life." The cabbie had long, stringy hair and a set of beads around his neck. Frank thought he looked like something out of the 1960s.

The San Diego Zoo was one of the largest in the world, set in the middle of the twelve hundred acres of Balboa Park, just north of downtown San Diego. The zoo contained more than thirty-two hundred animals, separated by moats and fences from the thousands of people who visited the park daily. Much of the environment looked like a tropical jungle.

Joe Hardy wasn't interested in the animals.

The Kid had herded him through the main entrance, toward the aerial tram ride that ran above the park from this side to the other, a third of a mile away. The trolley cars held only two people each. The cars were so light that they swayed on the thin cable they hung from.

"Get on," the Kid muttered in Joe's ear as he handed their tickets to the young woman who loaded the trolleys. She opened the car door and closed it after them. Then, with a jerk, the cable pulled their car up into the air and out over the zoo.

"Nice view, isn't it?" The Kid brought the gun out into the open, his finger still wrapped around the trigger. The nose was pointed at Joe.

"Are we up here for my health?" Joe asked.

"Yeah," the Kid replied. "Time to improve your physical fitness. You're going to practice high dives."

Joe looked down, his stomach pulling tight. They were at least seventy-five feet up, swaying between the concrete path below and the animal pens on either side of them.

"You're crazy," Joe said.

"Never say that to the man with the gun," said the Kid. "The way I figure it, you're big, but not too big for me to toss into a bear or tiger cage as we go over. The fall will probably kill you, but if it doesn't, the animals will get to you before help can.''

Joe gripped the safety bar and held on tight. ''What if I just promise never to use your name again?''

The Kid shook his head. ''Too late.''

The butt of the gun suddenly smashed into Joe's jaw. Hold on, he told himself as a gray cloud fogged into his mind. Hold on!

Strong hands gripped Joe diagonally around his waist and shoulders. He tried to move his arms to fight, but they wouldn't work. The gray cloud moved in, swallowing all thought.

Standing up in the trolley, the Kid lifted Joe over his head as if he were a doll, ready to heave the younger Hardy into the bear pits far below.

Chapter

6

FRANK HARDY GOT OUT of the cab and followed his brother and the blond guy. He'd been trying to catch Joe's eye, but the other man always got between them.

The stranger looked more like Joe's brother than Frank did, Frank realized suddenly with a shock. They obviously weren't identical, but in the right light, facing someone who knew neither of them very well, they could easily be mistaken for each other.

The two of them got into a tram car and lifted off, heading for the other end of the park. Frank jogged along the walkway beneath the trolley line, keeping his eyes on the car overhead.

"Joe!" he called out, but the trolley was too far up. There was no way Joe could hear him.

The car began to sway too violently to be caused by the wind. Something was happening up there, but Frank couldn't tell what. He sprinted ahead of it, turning and looking up to get a glimpse of the inside of the car. The angle was all wrong. He couldn't see.

Then a dark mass tipped over the lip of the car. It struck the pavement with a dull thud and rolled over once, landing in a position impossible for a living man.

All the color drained from Frank's face. He recognized the body.

It was Joe.

Frank sank to his knees next to his brother. He didn't care about anything, not Charity, the Star of Ishtar, Chief Collig, or the people gathering around them. All that mattered was that his brother was dead.

As tears filled his eyes, he froze, startled. There were little marks next to Joe's ears, tiny, almost invisible scratches he assumed were caused by the fall. He looked at them more closely, and his heart raced.

The marks were old—scars. Joe never had any scars around his ears.

It was the other man, he realized with a thrill. It *wasn't* Joe!

His eyes darted up at the trolley car that was

vanishing into the distance. Frank sprinted past the people coming to stare at the body, shaking off hands that reached out to stop him.

"You can't go," someone shouted. "What happened?"

"He fell," Frank yelled back over his shoulder. He didn't want to talk. He needed the air for running. "Call the police."

He reached the trolley car as it was coming to a stop at the far end of the line. Joe, still woozy, staggered out of the car, and Frank, still running, threw his arms around Joe and hugged him.

"You sound a little winded," Joe said as Frank tried to keep his legs from buckling under him.

Puffing, Frank said, "I've just run three hundred-yard dashes back-to-back, and I think I set records. What happened? Who *was* that guy?"

"That was the Kid—the crook that guy Jolly took me for. He was about to throw me off the car, but I managed to get a grip on the roof. I held on. He lurched forward, but I stayed where I was, and he pitched off the car. I barely made it back into the seat before I blacked out."

"We don't have to worry about the Kid anymore," Frank said. "But we'd better get out of here before the police arrive."

"Good idea," Joe said. Hiding behind bushes, they scaled the tall back wall and dropped down to the street behind the zoo. As police cars roared past, sirens blaring, they walked calmly down the sidewalk, heading back downtown.

Relaxing, Frank asked, "So how did you get mixed up with the Kid?"

"A gang I ran into at the warehouse thinks I'm him," Joe said. "He didn't like that." He looked over his shoulder, checking for the police before continuing. There was no sign of them.

"So what did you learn? What's going on?"

"It's all pretty confusing," Joe replied. "Apparently all those thieves we saw at the airport have gotten together for a big heist. It's being planned by someone calling himself the Director, but I don't know who he—or she—is. He wears a mask and talks to us on television." Joe's face brightened. "Hey! You're good with computers and electronics. Is there any way we could trace where the TV signal's coming from?"

Frank shook his head. "Only if it's a direct cable feed. If he's using a satellite dish, he's bouncing the signal off a satellite. It could be coming from anywhere."

"Then the only way to crack this scheme is for me to keep pretending to be the Kid."

"No," Frank said. "It's too dangerous. You'd be completely on your own."

"You'll be nearby," Joe protested. "Besides, Charity's in with them."

When he heard that name, Frank gave his brother a look. He let out a weary sigh, and, after thinking a long time, said, "All right. But be careful." He thought a moment more. "Let's get a hotel room and some food. Then later we should go to the warehouse and check it out before the gang gets back."

"Outside of this TV projection screen and the cable leading to the dish on the roof, it's an ordinary warehouse," Frank said. He and Joe had been there for several hours, scouring the place from top to bottom. It was clean. "We'd better get out of here."

Joe stiffened just then, listening. A dozen pairs of footsteps were headed their way outside. "Too late," he said. "They're here. Better hide."

Frank glanced around. The only place to hide in the warehouse was behind the crates, and Joe had told him that the gang would be sitting on them. He needed a hiding place they wouldn't find, somewhere they wouldn't go.

Moments later the gang entered the room, with Chavo bringing up the rear. Chuckling, Jolly walked up to Joe as the others seated themselves around the projection TV. "I take it we're about to embark on our little project."

Charity pressed herself between them and slipped her arm into Joe's arm. "Mind if I borrow him?" she asked Jolly, batting her eyes sweetly at him. Then, before the heavy man could answer, she pulled Joe away. They sat down together in front of the screen, his arm firmly locked in hers.

"Mind yourself and don't say a thing," she whispered in his ear. "There's a big surprise coming." Joe clenched his jaw angrily but kept quiet.

Chavo switched the screen back on, and once again the covered face of the Director appeared on it. "We are about to begin," the electronic voice droned.

"By tomorrow morning you will all be millionaires. Half of you will receive instructions from Chavo for later tonight. The other operatives, whose names I am about to read, will assemble at the boat moored behind this warehouse. On the boat, you will get your orders for an invasion of the Point Loma Naval Station."

Several of the criminals stood up, yelling in disbelief. Chavo stepped in front of the screen and stared at them with those cruel, piercing eyes. His hand slipped into his coat pocket and pressed the shape of a pistol against the fabric so everyone could see. The criminals quieted down.

"Now," the Director continued, "the assault group will be co-commanded by Charity and Willeford. It has been carefully planned, and if all the instructions are followed to the letter, no one will be hurt." He rattled off a list of names, and, after a long pause that sent a shiver down Joe's spine, ended the list with "the Kid."

"Go now," he said. "And good luck."

Charity pulled Joe out of the warehouse toward the mooring, with the rest of their crew following them. Joe still said nothing, but now his silence sprang from anger.

"Cheer up," she said as if she had read his mind. "It'll be fun."

They climbed onto the boat, a small cabin cruiser.

Behind the screen, Frank listened and waited for all the footsteps to die away. He realized he'd been sweating. All through the meeting, he had been pressed up against the screen, hoping not to be noticed. But what he had heard alarmed him. He had to warn the police and the navy of what was about to happen, and he hoped Joe would be able to protect himself. Cautiously Frank stepped to the front of the screen.

It came on with a loud click, and he found

himself face-to-face with the TV image of the Director. A gun barrel nuzzled against the back of Frank's neck.

"You're caught, spy," the Director said.

"Hands up," Chavo said. Frank put them up.

"I thought you were on tape," Frank told the man. "You sure fooled everyone."

"They think what I want them to think," said the Director. "What's your connection with the other spy?"

"I don't know what you're talking about," Frank said.

"The one who claims to be the Kid," the Director replied. "The real Kid was found today in the San Diego Zoo. I'm afraid he's in no condition to help our little operation. The impostor, I'm afraid, will be in for a rude surprise—after he has outlived his usefulness."

"Why, you—" Frank began, but before he could move, Chavo punched him in the small of the back, doubling him over. The scarred man waved the barrel of a silenced .45 in front of Frank's nose.

"Take him out back," the Director told Chavo, "and shoot him."

The boat pulled away from its mooring and sped out into the dark night. Moodily Joe leaned against the back rail of the boat, staring back at the well-lit dock they had just left. I've got to figure a way out of this, he thought. But he could think of nothing except leaping overboard, and then he'd never be able to stop the caper that was going down.

Joe's jaw dropped and a tiny cry burst from him. From out of nowhere, Charity appeared.

Joe shouted, "We've got to go back. Right now. Look at the dock!" He turned his eyes back to the land, but he knew he would be too late already.

Chavo had marched Frank to the end of the pier, overlooking the water. "Turn around," he ordered. Frank turned, his heels over the edge of the pier.

With a chuckle, Chavo pressed the silenced gun against Frank's chest. A noise that sounded like a loud sneeze erupted twice from the gun.

Frank toppled backward, hit the water, and slowly sank beneath the waves.

Chapter

7

JOE WOULD HAVE SCREAMED, but Charity had clamped her hand over his mouth. He felt like leaping off the boat and swimming to his brother's side, but Charity whispered to him, "It's too late for Frank. There's nothing you can do to help him."

He tore himself free, wanting to strike out at something, anything, to avenge his brother. Joe clenched his fists, calculating how many men were on board and what chance he'd have against them if he took them all on.

None, he realized. He might take down one or two, but the rest would get him, and they'd have no qualms about killing him as Frank had been killed. Joe had to stay in the game if he wanted to nail the ones really responsible for Frank's death.

Beside him, Charity was shaking, a look of horror on her face. Like Joe, she was still staring back at the one brightly lit dock, at the last place they had seen Frank.

"I'm so sorry," she said. "It wasn't supposed to go like this."

"What did you have in mind?" Joe snarled, not really interested.

"We can't talk here," she said. "Things aren't what they seem." Almost as an afterthought she added, "You'll have to trust me."

On a boat full of killers and thieves, Joe knew he had no other choice.

Frank Hardy struggled woozily, spitting water from his mouth. He had a dull ache in his chest, and he was soaked to the skin. Where was he? His hands were clinging to something round and wooden, so damp that the wood was flaking off in wads of soggy pulp. He opened his eyes.

He remembered the pier, and the last words Chavo had spoken as they walked to the end of it. "This will hurt, but go along with it. Act like you've been shot. Stay under the pier until I can come for you. You'll have to trust me."

Now Frank was under the pier, hidden by it, clinging to one of the poles holding it up, water up to his ribs. Above, he heard slow, deliberate footsteps, then a cold Hispanic voice. "Frank Hardy?"

It was Chavo.

Frank thought about hiding there, waiting until Chavo had gone. What did he know about the man? Nothing. Why should he trust him? There was no reason.

Except Chavo had saved his life. Why? What was Chavo's game?

Frank climbed up the rough planks that had been nailed onto the pole as a makeshift ladder. As he reached the top of the pier, Chavo reached down and offered him a hand.

"Are you all right?" Chavo asked as Frank knelt on one knee and caught his breath.

"I've been better," Frank said. "You didn't need to use the rubber bullets. If you weren't going to shoot me, you could've aimed a little to my left."

Chavo laughed. "Yes, but it wouldn't have been as convincing. The Director had to be convinced."

"Do you have some special reason for double-crossing your boss?"

Chavo produced a badge. "Don't you want to thank me for saving your life?"

"Thanks," Frank said as he studied the badge. "Federales. Mexican National Police.

Does our government know you're working out of San Diego?"

"No. You understand my position. I infiltrated the Director's gang months ago. I must go where I am sent, and no one knows who I really am."

"Pretty good infiltration job," Frank said. "You made it all the way to number-two man."

"*Sí*. I recruited the others on his orders. But he does not trust me. Like the others, I receive my orders in pieces. No one but the Director knows everything he is planning."

Frank stared at the Mexican lawman. "How do you know who I am? You called me by name."

"The other one was identified as Joseph Hardy," Chavo replied. "I don't think you could be your illustrious father, so who else would you be but Frank?"

"You know Dad?"

"I know of him," Chavo said. He led Frank toward the land. "Come. The others have been sent to Tijuana, in Mexico, to wait for more instructions. We must hurry."

"I'm soaking wet!" Frank protested.

Chavo looked grim. "You'll find a change of clothes in my car. We must warn the Naval Station of the coming attack. There is no time to waste."

Frank studied the face of the scarred man,

but it told him nothing. Was Chavo an undercover agent, trained to keep himself a closed book? Or simply a clever crook looking to double-cross his boss?

Frank had no way to tell, but he agreed with Chavo on one thing: the navy had to be warned. With doubts he followed Chavo up the pier to the waiting car.

Willeford stepped onto the deck as the boat cruised in toward the rocks under Point Loma Naval Station. The entire area was fenced in, and from high towers, spotlights swept across the water. The cabin cruiser came to a halt just outside the range of the lights, and Willeford cut the motor. The boat drifted silently on the waves.

"How are we supposed to crack that place?" someone asked.

Instead of answering, Willeford took a sealed envelope from his pocket and ran a thumbnail through the seal. Pulling a paper out, he whispered, "Everyone quiet. Want the whole navy to hear us?" The criminals sat in silence as Willeford carefully read the instructions.

"There are two inflatable rubber rafts being dragged behind the boat. They're fitted with outboard motors, and are small and quick enough to dodge the spotlights." He held up a small photograph and passed it around. "This is where you go ashore."

The photo reached Joe, who saw that it showed the rocks under the base, with one area marked by an arrow drawn with a felt-tip pen.

"Climb up those rocks. You'll find specially drilled hand- and footholds. At the top, you'll meet a sailor." Willeford rubbed his fingers against his palm and grinned savagely, and Joe got the idea. Someone had been paid off to get them into the base.

"What happens then? What are we doing?" one of the guys asked.

"You'll learn more as you need to know it," Willeford answered, staring the guy down. "Everyone ready?"

There was some murmuring, but it wasn't long before everyone was set to go. If this operation worked out the way the Director planned, it would be a cinch, and even Joe knew it.

The rubber rafts cut the water like speedboats, leaving nothing but waves for the spotlights to light up. Their motors were specially muffled to keep the sound to a minimum, and it wasn't long before they were at the rocks. The holds were exactly where the Director had said they'd be, and one by one the gang climbed the rocks to the base.

A guard stood there, glaring down at them, aiming his rifle. "Who goes there?" he asked menacingly.

The criminals froze, faced with the gun muzzle.

Willeford piped up, "Blackjack."

A nervous smile crossed the guard's lips, and he lowered his rifle and stepped aside. "Pass." The guard had his shirtsleeves rolled up, and Joe recognized the anchor tattoo on his forearm. He was one of the two men who'd tried to strangle him and Frank at the airport.

The guard stepped back to the fence and pulled out a section.

In a line, like commandos, the raiders scrambled onto the sleeping base. They clung to the shadows as the occasional jeep went by, but they met no one.

"The fleet's out on maneuvers," the guard explained as they approached a gray metal hut with No Admittance stenciled on the door in huge letters. "The base is working with a skeleton crew." He jangled keys, then put one in the lock. The door swung open.

Swiftly they swarmed inside and shut the door behind them and flipped the light switch to on. "What you're looking for is over there," the guard said. Following the beam from the guard's flashlight, Joe saw racks and racks of metal drums.

"Some of this is poison gas," Joe said, dread creeping into his voice. "You breathe this long enough and you're dead."

"We need some of that poison," Willeford replied, looking at his orders. "This stuff has been stored here because no one could figure out what else to do with it. Everyone grab a canister and let's move out."

The criminals scrambled through the hut, lifting the drums off the racks. Joe was worried. Nerve gas was something he didn't want to fool with. In the darkness, he looked for another way out. There was none but the door, where the guard now stood.

"Where's Charity?" Joe asked, realizing she wasn't with them.

"Forget her," Willeford ordered, but he scowled as he spoke. "Do your job."

Joe spotted a different canister, one marked Knockout Gas. Quickly he plucked it off the rack, covering the name with his arm, and carried it on his shoulder.

"Come on!" Willeford barked, checking his watch. "We're running behind schedule. Move it." As one, they started for the door.

It swung open suddenly, and there stood a sailor. He was young and bewildered by the activity. "What's going on here?" he asked.

The guard grabbed him and punched him once in the stomach, doubling him over. As the guard twisted the sailor's arm behind his back and dragged him into the hut, Willeford came forward and put a gun to the back of the sailor's head.

"Too bad you stumbled into this," Willeford said, and cocked back the trigger.

"You can't!" Joe shouted, before he realized what he was saying.

All eyes were on him, and Willeford's eyes turned to dark, murderous slits in his face. "Going soft, Kid?" He pulled another gun from his belt and tossed it to Joe. "I think you'd better take care of him."

Joe hesitated, staring at the pleading eyes of the sailor.

Angrily Willeford aimed his gun at Joe. "I don't think you understand me, Kid. You don't have a choice. We can't afford to have this sailor boy running around to tell about our business. Kill him."

His eyes were icy cold. "Or *I* kill *you*."

Chapter

8

"Of course he has to die," Joe growled angrily.

Willeford hesitantly lowered his gun.

"But a shot might bring the whole base down on us. How about we run a little test on him?" Joe raised the canister he held, keeping the label against his chest. He knew the gas wouldn't cause severe injury to the sailor. "How about we give him a sniff of this?"

"Please, no!" the sailor pleaded. "I won't say anything. I swear."

"I like your style, Kid," Willeford said. "Everybody out."

Joe handed the gun back to Willeford as he passed and lifted his canister so the nozzle on it was aimed at the sailor. Turning his head away, Joe opened the valve, and a thin spray of white gas rushed into the sailor's face.

"Close that thing," Willeford said from outside, fear in his voice. His eyes were on the sailor, who gasped and clawed at his throat, trying to get words out. They stuck in his throat.

The sailor toppled forward, to land facedown on the floor. Willeford walked back in and nudged the body with his toe: the young seaman didn't move.

"Good work, Kid," Willeford said, going back out. "I misjudged you."

Cautiously the guard led the criminals from the hut. Before he left, Joe looked back at the sailor, who still hadn't stirred. In the dark, Joe could just see the sailor's chest steadily rise and fall. The man was breathing, and Joe felt a wave of relief.

Now all he had to do was keep himself alive and figure out what had happened to Charity.

"The admiral's not available," the military policeman at the front gate of the naval base said.

Chavo held up his badge, and the MP grinned. "This isn't Mexico, pal. Come back tomorrow."

"You don't understand," Frank said. "Your base is being robbed."

That raised the MP's eyebrows. He rested his hand on the automatic in his holster. "I think you two had better wait here. The officer in charge will want to talk to you."

The MP went into the little booth at the gate and spoke briefly on the phone, keeping his eyes on Frank and Chavo. Moments later a jeep rolled up to the gate, and two MPs leapt out, followed by a white-haired man in a uniform marked by the silver-eagle insignia of a navy captain. The MPs stood at ease as the captain approached the gate.

"Let them in," the captain said, and the MP on guard swung the gate open. Chavo and Frank tensely walked in. "I'm Captain Hammond. You were saying something about a burglary on base?"

"There's a gang of men stealing something here," Frank said, but Chavo stepped between him and Hammond and held up his credentials again.

Captain Hammond shook him off. "You understand that I'll have to call your superiors and learn if you're who you say you are. There are procedures to follow."

"There's no time," Frank insisted. "The heist is happening right now."

"I cannot permit you to check with my superiors," Chavo admitted. "I am on special undercover assignment. It is essential that my cover not be blown. This matter must remain strictly between us."

"That's not possible," Captain Hammond replied. "Frankly, I don't believe either one of you. There's nothing on this base worth stealing. We have no real money, and all the weapons are stored over on North Island." His eyes widened slightly. "Unless—"

"Sir?" an MP said, noting the look of concern on the captain's face.

"Into the jeep," Captain Hammond suddenly ordered. He pointed at Chavo and Frank. "You too." They clambered in.

"Where to, sir?" the MP who was driving asked, shifting the jeep into low gear.

"The gas depository," the captain said gravely. "If someone got his hands on that . . ."

"Nerve gas?" Frank said. "I thought the government didn't make that anymore."

"This is old, but just as dangerous as it was when it was created," Hammond replied. "We store it here because there's no safe way to get rid of it." He turned to look at Frank. "Who are you, anyway? You don't look Mexican."

"I'm American, sir," Frank replied. "I ran into this business from a different direction than Chavo."

"And you don't want to identify yourself either," Captain Hammond interrupted.

"Plenty of time for that later, I suppose. You two aren't going anywhere."

The jeep approached the hut where the nerve gas was stored, and the captain's face turned to stone. The door to the hut was wide open, and just inside, lit up by the jeep's headlights, a sailor lay flat on the floor.

Frank leapt from the jeep and ran into the hut. He crouched and laid a hand on the sailor's neck. "I'm getting a pulse." Gently he patted the sailor's cheek. As Captain Hammond, Chavo, and the two MPs entered and stood above them, the sailor's eyes fluttered open.

"What happened here, man?" Captain Hammond demanded.

The sailor told the story as if he couldn't believe he was alive.

"They couldn't have gotten far," Captain Hammond said. To one MP he said, "I want the entire base on alert. Do a full perimeter check. Well, what are you standing there for? Go!"

He scowled as he looked at Chavo and Frank, and as he faced the other MP, he waved his thumb at them.

"Place these two under arrest."

* * *

Joe had barely climbed back in the rubber raft, setting his cargo on his lap, when an alarm sounded on the base.

"We've been discovered," Willeford shouted. "Move it." The man handling the outboard motor pulled on the crank and brought it to life. The raft zipped across the bay, heading back to the cabin cruiser. Nearby, Joe could see the other raft, keeping pace with them.

Then a spotlight caught the other raft, and Joe looked over his shoulder at the shore. All along the cliff, men were lining up, and in the moonlight Joe caught the glint of rifles in their hands.

"Stop those craft immediately!" commanded a booming voice over a loudspeaker. "Do not move. This will be your only warning!"

"Keep going," Willeford shouted.

Joe ducked down as a hail of bullets rained down around them in the water. In the other raft, still caught in the spotlight, one man clutched at his shoulder, screamed, and tumbled into the black water. Suddenly there was a blast like a gigantic balloon popping.

A shot had punctured the other raft. One whole side had blown open, and the raft began to sink. The desperate criminals threw their canisters overboard and abandoned ship. They swam off the sinking raft and moved toward Joe's raft.

"We don't need them," Willeford said, and they took off, leaving the stranded criminals behind. Joe realized the raft had moved out of firing range.

Moments later the raft reached the cabin cruiser, and Willeford climbed aboard while everyone else stayed in the raft. One by one, the others climbed the rope ladder leading to the boat, leaving only Joe in the raft. He handed the canisters up to them, and they handed them man to man like firefighters handing off buckets of water, until all the canisters were on board.

"Stay there," Willeford called down to Joe, as he pulled the ladder up.

"What's going on?" Joe asked, and Willeford popped his head over the edge of the cabin cruiser and beamed a friendly smile down at him. Joe shivered.

Willeford held out a package. "This is the last of the Director's orders for this operation. Catch." He dropped the package, and Joe caught it.

It was small, about the size of a roll of film, and tightly wrapped in brown paper. "Take it back to the warehouse and give it to Chavo," Willeford continued. "You'll get your next order there. We're heading out."

Joe acknowledged the order with a brief nod, then turned the raft away from the boat and sped off into the night toward the dock. He was glad he'd finally gotten away from the others. Now he'd have a chance to face Chavo and make him pay for what he had done to Frank.

The cabin cruiser sped out of the bay and into the Pacific Ocean. Back at the base, the shooting had stopped. The night was quiet now, as if nothing had happened.

The outboard motor hummed a deep staccato tune, uneven enough to keep Joe from being lulled to sleep. As he listened, he began to notice a second, higher-pitched whine of another motor.

Someone was following him.

"Joe!" a woman's voice cried. He looked over to see Charity pulling alongside, piloting a speedboat. Between the noise of the two engines, nothing else could be heard. Charity signaled for Joe to shut off his motor. He did.

"You have to get off the raft!" she yelled.

"What?"

She gritted her teeth and waved at him to jump. "They know who you are. You have to get off that raft—"

"They're gone, Captain," the MP told Hammond, and Hammond frowned. He stood on the cliff, looking down at the frantic scene below. Half a dozen men were splashing in the water below, waiting for help.

"Call the Coast Guard and have them search for the boat," Hammond said. "Fish those men out and have them arrested."

A sailor with a pair of binoculars waved them at Hammond. "There's something else out there, sir. Some kind of a raft."

Captain Hammond reached for the binoculars, but Frank, who had been brought there with Chavo so Hammond could keep his eye on them, stepped forward and grabbed them. Hammond started to give another order, but Frank explained, "My brother's out there somewhere. I have to know what happened to him."

He scanned the sea. Joe wasn't among the men in the water, and Frank turned his gaze on the raft. He grinned with excitement.

Joe was standing up in the raft.

"It's Joe," he said happily, and handed the binoculars to Hammond.

A few minutes later there was a thunderous explosion, and when Frank looked through the binoculars again, the raft was a ball of fire, flying apart above the waves.

When the smoke and debris settled, Frank studied the water in horror. Joe was gone.

Chapter

9

"JOE!" FRANK SCREAMED, starting for the edge of the cliff. Two MPs grabbed him and dragged him back.

"Take them both to the guardhouse," Captain Hammond commanded, pointing to Frank and Chavo. "I want some questions answered."

"Joe!" Frank screamed again, still struggling as he was pulled to the jeep. It was no use. The guards had him in an unbreakable grip, and he was shoved roughly into the jeep's backseat as Chavo quietly took the seat next to him.

"Stay there and be quiet," an MP growled. The guards climbed into the front seat and started up the jeep.

"I'll get him," Frank muttered as they sped through the base. "I'll get the Director if it's the last thing I do."

"Didn't I tell you to keep quiet?" the MP barked.

Chavo raised a finger to his lips, signaling Frank to stay silent. With his other hand he jabbed a finger three times at the MPs and nodded slowly to Frank.

After a long moment Frank nodded back. This was their only chance, he realized. Chavo held out three fingers and started flashing the count.

On the third count, Frank and Chavo jumped into action, clipping both MPs on the back of the neck. The men pitched forward, unconscious.

Chavo stood and reached over the driver, grabbed the steering wheel, and switched off the ignition. The jeep rolled on even after the power had been cut, sideswiped a hut in a shower of sparks, and then slowed to a halt. Frank and Chavo pulled the MPs out and propped them against the hut.

"They'll be all right when they wake up," Chavo said. He climbed behind the steering wheel.

"Let's get out of here," Frank said, seated in the passenger seat.

They sped for the main gate. The MP there

stepped into their path, his rifle ready. "Stop!" he yelled. He dived to one side, though, as the jeep zoomed past him and smashed through the gate.

Once outside, Frank and Chavo scrambled to Chavo's car. As the MP started firing at them, the car roared off into the night.

"Now what?" Frank asked.

"We dump this car," Chavo said. "The police will be looking for it, and for us. I'll leave you in San Diego and rent a new car."

"Forget that," said Frank. "Where you go, I go. Where are we going?"

Chavo gave Frank a long look, then said, "Tijuana."

Joe woke on the floor of Charity's speedboat and wondered what he was doing there. Then it all came back to him.

He had jumped from the raft just as the night exploded in a shower of flames. But the shock waves that had pushed the still speedboat away from the scene of the blast had tossed Joe down, and he smashed his head on the wooden deck.

How long had he been out? he wondered, and decided it had been only a few seconds. Charity hadn't started the motor yet. Joe stared at the thick column of black smoke that was all that remained of the rubber raft.

"That could have been me," he said, trembling slightly as the realization caught up with him.

Charity looked at him oddly, as if surprised to see him moving. "It wasn't."

"Thanks to you," Joe replied. "Where did you get the boat?"

Charity smoothed her hair. "I borrowed it from the U.S. Navy. I figured it might come in handy."

"And here I thought you'd run out on me."

"Joe, I had to do something. They found out who you really are," Charity said.

Joe frowned. "How?"

"Well," Charity said, flashing her cat smile, "I told the Director."

"I knew it!" Joe raged. "I knew it!"

"Calm down," said Charity. She took a deep breath. "It's time I told you everything."

Joe fumed but said nothing. He stared at the misty sky and waited skeptically for her explanation.

"Oh, don't look like that," she said. "I *had* to turn you in, to establish my credibility."

"Sure. Your credibility. I suppose you stole the Star of Ishtar to establish your credibility."

"As a matter of fact, I did." She pulled a small wallet from her pocket, flipped it open, and held it up where Joe could see. "I'm a federal agent."

Joe read the card without interest. "No, you're not. You're a thief. This is another one of your tricks."

Charity shrugged and put the wallet away. "I know you have no reason to believe me, but I'm telling you the truth. I'm an undercover agent. I've worked for years at establishing a reputation as a master thief. It's the sort of rep that comes in handy when you're dealing with crooks."

"You were sure operating as a thief when we met you in San Francisco," Joe said, his voice still full of doubt.

"Whom did I steal from in San Francisco?" she asked.

"That was government property."

"Right," she said. "I work for the government. They set up things for me to steal, and I steal them. Then I give them back."

Nothing changed on Joe's face to indicate he believed a word she said.

"Don't look at me like that, Joe. I'm telling the truth. You could check it out yourself if we were going back to land, but we have to catch up to that cabin cruiser."

"The government didn't own the Star of Ishtar. Thanks to you, a friend of ours has his reputation and maybe his freedom on the line."

Charity lowered her eyes as if ashamed. "Yes, that's true. But I had to steal it. The

Director gave each of us an assignment to prove we were qualified to take part in his caper. I had to steal the Star and give it to him, but we'll get it back when we capture him."

She looked at Joe. "When I realized you and Frank lived in Bayport, I knew I could bring you into it. I needed you for backup. Why do you think I made sure you had a trail to follow? Everything's going to work out fine. Trust me."

Frank's name stirred up Joe's anger all over again. He had, for a second, forgotten about his brother. *I shouldn't trust her,* he told himself, *but she's the only one who can lead me to the Director and Chavo, and she might be on the level.* If he was going to get his revenge, he'd have to go along.

"What was the Kid's assignment?"

"Pretty impressive," Charity replied. "He managed to get into the Soviet Historical Institute and get out of Russia with some of the czar's crown jewels. Not all of them, but enough to convince the Director he had what it took."

"So who's the Director?" Joe asked.

"I don't know. It's my mission to find out. He stays away from everyone, communicating only by television or radio."

"What's he up to?"

Charity dug under her seat and came back with a map of North America.

"Ever hear of Puerto de Oro?" she asked.

Joe thought briefly. The name was very familiar. "It's an island somewhere off the coast near Tijuana, isn't it?"

Charity nodded. "It's been billed as the perfect paradise. It's become quite a jet-set hangout. Tropical weather, gambling casinos, great beaches. A combination of Monte Carlo and Acapulco."

"The Director's going to knock over a casino?"

"You're thinking too small," Charity said, shaking her head. "He's planning to knock over *the whole island*."

"Impossible!" Joe answered.

"Hardly," she continued, undaunted. "It's high season for the resort, but the nights are cooling off, so almost everyone stays inside then. The place has a token force of security guards, but there aren't any other real police on the island."

"And with that gas we stole from the navy tonight, the Director can knock the whole place out," Joe said, beginning to put it all together.

"You've got it," Charity said. "Cash, jewels, gold, all kinds of riches. They'll be just lying there for the taking."

Joe heard the engine of another boat and saw a dark mass ahead of them. "There's the cabin cruiser. Let's get them."

"That might be a little hard," Charity said. "They're turning."

It was true. The larger craft was circling around, until it was aimed back at them.

"It's going to ram us!" Charity warned. She spun the steering wheel and shifted gears.

The speedboat sputtered and came to a dead stop.

"What's the matter?" Joe said urgently. The cruiser bore down on them.

Charity turned the ignition, which made a sickly grinding noise. "It's stalled," she said. "But I think I can get it started."

Before Joe or Charity could move, the cabin cruiser plowed into the side of the speedboat. When the larger craft resumed its course to Puerto de Oro, it left nothing but scrap metal and driftwood in its trail.

Chapter

10

"GET OUT OF the car," Chavo said.

Frank Hardy, fueled by a thirst for revenge against his brother's killers, shook off his exhaustion. He was seated in the new car that Chavo had rented. They were stopped dead in traffic, with a long line of cars in front of them. In the distance Frank could see the bright lights of the Tijuana border station. "What's going on?"

"There's usually no trouble getting from the United States to Mexico," said Chavo. "Something's up. They're checking cars."

"Maybe they're looking for someone."

"Like us," Chavo agreed. "Time for another plan."

As car horns behind them began to honk,

Chavo pulled the car to the curb and parked it. Quietly he and Frank left the car and under cover of darkness stole toward the footbridge that ran across the border. There was little traffic on the footbridge, and Frank could see most of the customs officers over at the auto entrance. There was only one guard on the footbridge.

"Be nonchalant," Chavo warned him. "If you're not nervous as you walk past the officer, he'll pay no attention to you."

Frank nodded and walked ahead by a few feet. The officer was standing, reading a magazine. Apparently he wasn't noticing anything at all. As Frank passed him, he glanced up and smiled as if by rote. "Welcome to Mexico, senor," the officer said. "Have a good time."

"Thank you," Frank said, and walked on.

Chavo came up behind, and again the officer smiled. But now there was a cleverness in the grin. Chavo returned the grin, but as he passed the officer, he heard, *"Buenas noches,* Senor Chavo."

Chavo spun to swing at the officer, but the officer grabbed his wrist and twisted it behind his back. "How is the most famous criminal in all of Mexico tonight? We have heard much of you from our neighbors to the north."

"Frank!" Chavo called.

Frank had no choice. He whipped around,

catching the officer in the ribs with a karate kick. Frank felt as uncomfortable about attacking a policeman as he had about fighting the MPs, but Chavo was his only connection to the Director. As the officer staggered, Chavo turned and drove a fist into his stomach.

The officer flew back and landed, stunned, in the dust.

By now other officers had noticed the scuffling on the footbridge, and Frank saw them running toward them through the darkness. "Come on," Chavo yelled. "It's only a short way to the city."

Together they ran into the night, leaving the policemen behind.

Frank wasn't prepared for Tijuana. It was a thriving city with modern buildings and shops. As they walked down wide, newly paved streets, they passed manufacturing plants, shopping centers, and racetracks.

There was the Avenida Revolución, a bustling avenue of restaurants, nightclubs, and small shops where, even at that time of night, tourists wandered, snapping photographs. But Frank didn't have time to be a tourist. Everywhere he looked, he saw his brother's face, and the only thing on his mind was how to nail the Director.

He also remembered Charity. It was her fault they'd gotten involved in this. Frank promised himself that she, too, should finally pay for her crimes.

"In here," Chavo said as they came to the door of a bar. It was a dingy place. The bar was long, lined with rickety stools, and the rest of the place was a dance floor, where only a few couples moved lazily to Spanish guitar music played by a decades-old jukebox. At the far end of the bar a curtain of beads covered the entrance to another room. Perhaps two dozen men were on the barstools.

"What are we doing here?" Frank asked.

"Trust me," Chavo said. As they walked in, he called out, "Hey! Amigos!"

As one, the men on the stools turned around and stared balefully at Chavo. Silently they fingered their drinks, and several of them pulled large knives from their belts and set them on the bar.

"*El jefe!*" Chavo demanded in a loud voice.

"Do you want us to die?" Frank whispered to Chavo with some exasperation.

The scarred man called out something in Spanish, and the bead curtain swirled aside. A slender man stood there, and as he neared, Frank could see he had a carefully trimmed beard and mustache, and wore a white suit. There was a red handkerchief in the pocket.

At the sight of Chavo, he raised his arms and spread them wide, with a big smile. "Chavo!

Amigo!'' he shouted. Throughout the bar the frowns relaxed and men went back to their drinking. The slender man put an arm around Chavo and hugged him like a long-lost relative.

"Who is this?" Frank said.

Chavo looked at Frank as if he had forgotten he was there. "Where are my manners? Frank, this is Benito. Benito, Frank."

The man called Benito extended a hand and said, "Put 'er there, fellow American."

Frank blinked in surprise and shook his hand. "You're American?"

"Sure am," Benito said, winking at him. "Name's Benny. A Coney Island boy."

"We have no time for this," Chavo said. "Benito, we must get to the waterfront at Las Playas de Tijuana."

"See, Chavo and me, we pulled quite a few jobs together in the old days," Benito continued. "As a matter of fact, I seem to remember you owing me some money, Chavo."

"Not now, Benito—"

Benito snapped his fingers, and five men at the bar stood up. Four brought their knives, and the fifth smashed a bottle to a jagged edge against the bar. Slowly they moved toward Chavo.

"Now," Benito said, "about my money . . ."

Frank jumped Benito and got behind him, wrapping an arm around the slender man's neck. "Put them down," he said to the men with the weapons. He tightened his grip on Benito. "Put them down or I'll break his neck."

Hastily Benito spoke a phrase in Spanish, and the men, their eyes dark and suspicious, turned away and returned to the bar. Chavo laughed.

"Very good, Frank," he said. "As I was saying, Benito, we need transportation."

"Give him all the money in your wallet, Chavo," Frank said.

Chavo blinked as if he didn't understand the words. Then he laughed again. "Good joke, Frank."

But Frank wasn't smiling. "Shut up, Chavo. I've just about had it with you. Now, give him all your money, or whatever you owe him, or we won't get anywhere tonight."

Chavo stared at Frank for almost a minute. Finally he sighed and took from his wallet five one-hundred-dollar bills. "We'll forget the interest?" he said to Benito with a wink.

"Sounds good to me," Benito said, and Frank released his grip on him. "What kind of transportation were you looking for?"

Ten minutes later Frank was sitting in a sidecar on a motorcyle that Chavo steered down the Las Playas road. The motorcycle was a leftover from the Second World War, but

Frank found the sidecar quite comfortable. Chavo hadn't spoken to him since they left the bar. Now the scarred undercover man said, "Never do that to me again."

Frank lolled back in the sidecar, his eyes closed and his arms wrapped around himself to keep out the cool night air. "I'd like to know why everyone down here thinks you're a criminal. Sure you were telling me straight about being a Federale?"

Coldly, Chavo replied, "I built a good cover. The local police and the border guards have no need to know what I really am. Why would I lie to you?"

"I don't know," Frank said. "Maybe you're planning to rip off the Director and keep all the loot for yourself. Maybe you're setting me up to help you."

Moodily Chavo said, "Believe what you will," and didn't speak the rest of the trip.

Las Playas de Tijuana was a seaside community, less built-up and also less congested than Tijuana. It had a tranquility that masked what was happening on the fishing barge moored in the harbor. The motorcyle roared up to the gangplank, and Frank and Chavo got off.

"Who's the kid?" Brady asked Chavo as they walked out to the barge on the plank.

Brady sat at the ship end of the gangplank and greeted them with a pistol on his lap.

"Replacement," Chavo replied. "We lost some men on the navy raid. The Director had me sign this one up."

"I don't like it when plans get changed at the last minute," Brady replied as the barge got under way. "By the way, someone's waiting for you in the hold."

"I'll go down in a minute." Chavo and Frank caught their breath and watched the shore lights wink out as the barge moved away from land.

Finally they left Brady and climbed down the ladder into the ship's hold. Frank followed after Chavo and noticed that as soon as he had passed, Brady flashed a signal to Chrome Lasker, who was standing in the control tower. The barge lurched forward and began chugging out of the harbor. Brady followed Frank into the hold.

As Frank's feet hit the floor, a pair of hands grabbed him, yanking him off his feet. Everest had hold of him, and then red-haired Brady reached the floor and helped. The two of them pinned Frank against a wall.

Catching his breath, Frank saw that Chavo was similarly held. There were several crates in the hold, and two of them were pushed together at the center of the room to form a makeshift table.

At the table was Jolly.

Jolly sat next to a radio that was glowing softly and ran the blade of a knife through a candle flame. "Welcome," came the Director's voice from the radio. "Chavo, you are a disappointment to me. I trusted you.

"My friends inside the government have informed me that you are a Federale. Tell me what you've told them about my plans."

"No," Chavo said.

"We could torture you," the voice from the radio continued. "But you might not crack. Instead, let's torture your young friend. Perhaps you'll talk to spare him pain."

"Only one way to find out," Jolly suggested. He stood up, holding out a red-hot blade. Brady tore Frank's shirt open.

As Frank struggled uselessly, Jolly moved the blade closer and closer to his chest.

Chapter

11

How LONG had he paddled? Joe wondered. It seemed to him that he had been floating for hours. He could no longer tell time. His watch had been smashed in the wreck, and overhead the timeless moon just hung there, not moving. He was far from land now, and the ocean, dark and unchanging, spread out in all directions.

With nothing else to do, Joe thought back to the collision. He remembered grabbing Charity as the impact hurled him from the boat. The next thing he knew, he was struggling against the cold, churning waters of San Diego Bay. With a burst of energy he had sputtered to the surface, gasping for air.

Pulling himself onto a large piece of floating

fiberglass, he looked for Charity. But she was nowhere to be seen.

In the distance Joe spotted the cabin cruiser, speeding southwest across the Pacific. Even with the mist on the ocean, the moon was bright enough to show Joe the men on the cruiser's deck, laughing and pointing back at the wreckage. But before he could wonder if the men had spotted him, something else caught his eye. It was dragging behind the cruiser, hanging off one of the ropes that had once towed a rubber raft. It was flat and shiny, like a piece of glass, and in its center was a dark woman-shaped mass.

Charity!

After his strength had finally returned, he flattened himself on the fiberglass and started to paddle with his hands and feet, like a surfer swimming out to meet a wave. He was going to Puerto de Oro, the Port of Gold, no matter how long it took.

He had a brother to avenge.

Joe didn't know where he was. All around him was nothing but empty ocean. He felt sure that somewhere ahead must be the island of Puerto de Oro, but there were no lights, no sounds, only the silent darkness of the ocean on a moonlit night.

Then small waves beat against the fiberglass,

moving against the waves of the ocean. Joe looked around.

A boat was moving toward him, pushing the water before it. A fishing barge.

"Hey!" Joe yelled as the barge neared. Forgetting how tired he was, he paddled toward the boat. "Hey!"

His voice was lost under the sound of the engine. The barge plunged on with no sign of stopping. He waved, trying to get the attention of the two men who had wandered onto the deck. No one noticed him.

He pressed on, pushed back by a wake that grew stronger the nearer he got to the barge. The boat was so close he could smell the stench of fish that it gave off. There was no longer anyone on the deck, but he kept moving.

Water splashed into his face, almost knocking him off the fiberglass hunk, and he flailed to get a grip on it. His hands caught it, and he pulled himself back up.

The barge was right in front of him, moving in a straight line for him.

On the side of the barge, sticking out at right angles to it, was a series of iron bars leading down to the propeller that drove the boat. They were there so fishermen could climb down to the propeller for repairs, Joe realized. But he had another use for them. As another wave rushed at him, he leapt off the fiberglass and dived over the wave, splashing into the water behind it. For a second he was in still water, and he swam as hard as he could for the barge.

Another wave hit him, and he rolled to his side to slice through it with his body. He was almost to the barge. He reached out, fingers grasping for the lowest rung on the ladder of iron bars. They struck air, and he fell back.

If I can't go this way, Joe decided, there's only one thing I can do.

Taking a big gulp of air, he forced himself up as high as he could go, until he was straight up in the water. Then he plunged down, dropping like a stone into the inky depths of the ocean. There, he knew, there were no waves. It was his only chance to get near the barge.

Joe's mouth filled with water, but he forced himself not to breathe or swallow. The barge blotted out a lot of the moonlight, and he couldn't see what he was doing very well, but he managed to stay under the side of the barge, feeling along the edge with his hands.

But then something grabbed his legs and quickly pulled him toward the back of the barge. There the moonlight glistened, and he could see the flash of the propeller blade as it whirled. Joe realized suddenly he was caught in the undertow. It was steadily pulling him straight into the propeller.

Panicked, he swam, but the undertow had him. It came to him in a flash that he wanted to be back by the propeller. Joe stopped struggling and let the undertow pull him back.

As his feet inched closer and closer to the whirling blade, he reached around the side of the barge. His fingers finally locked around an iron bar.

Slowly Joe pulled himself free of the undertow. His head broke the surface of the water, and he took a deep, cool breath of air. As it hit his throat, he choked and coughed up seawater, but the next breath brought clear, sweet air.

Joe climbed the bars and rolled into the barge, landing in a pile of nets that had been stored there. He lay there laughing quietly to himself and staring up at the stars.

"I made it," he announced triumphantly.

Finally he sat up and looked around. The deck was empty. He recognized the kind of boat he was on. It wasn't the type of fishing craft that gets taken out by sportsmen for a long weekend. Professional fishermen who used barges like these usually went out early in the morning and were back at sundown.

What, he wondered, was this barge doing out in the middle of the night with no crew?

Just then, from below, he heard the muffled sound of a radio. It sounded like a man's voice coming from it, but Joe couldn't be sure. He wanted no one to know he was on board until he could check it out.

Crouching, he peered into the captain's tower. It was more of a little room set on top of the deck than a tower. A man stood there, steering the boat, and slowly Joe crept around the edge of the deck for a better look at him.

"Oh, no," Joe gasped as he saw the man's face.

Chrome Lasker stood behind the wheel in the captain's tower.

Joe scrambled out of sight. He had to think. If Lasker was steering the boat, then the boat was being used by the Director, probably on its way to Puerto de Oro.

Anyone else who was on the boat must be in the hold, Joe concluded. If he could capture the boat, he could bring the Director's schemes to a halt.

He crawled on his stomach across the deck, moving toward the hole cut into the deck that led down to the hold. Now he could hear more voices, and these not from a radio. But he couldn't make out what they were saying. He raised himself into a low crouch, checking to see that Lasker hadn't spotted him. Then he reached out for the hold cover.

Joe slammed it shut as muffled cries erupted from below. He grabbed a nearby fishing rod that had been carelessly abandoned on the deck and jammed the handle into the latch, locking the latch in place. No matter how hard they pounded, he knew pounding wouldn't get them out.

Joe sprang to his feet and raced for the door of the captain's tower. He sprinted up the two stairs and hurled himself against the door, hoping to take Lasker by surprise.

But the door was unlatched, and Joe tumbled in, his feet slipping out from under him. Before he could get up, Lasker had pressed a heel against Joe's Adam's apple, pinning him down. The bald-headed villain had drawn and was aiming a gun right between Joe's eyes.

"Well, well. The Kid," Lasker said in surprise. "Good to see you again."

He gave Joe a lopsided smirk. "Too bad you had to come this far to die."

Chapter

12

"WAIT," said the voice from the radio.

Jolly lowered the knife, frowning as he glanced at the radio.

When he finally answered the voice, he meekly said, "Yes, sir?"

But Frank saw contempt in Jolly's eyes as he looked at the radio and his fellow crooks. Scanning the room, Frank saw the contempt on every face there. It occurred to him that, given half a chance, each of them would turn on the others and walk off with all the loot. He filed the insight away, in the hope that he would have a chance to use it.

The radio came alive again. "Let's give Chavo one last chance to come clean, now that he understands the gravity of the situation."

One of the men holding Chavo landed a fist in Chavo's stomach, and the Mexican dropped to his knees, gasping. Another man lifted up Chavo's head.

"Talk," the man said.

Chavo curled his lip into a sneer.

"No go," Jolly told the radio. "Now can I cut?"

"By all means," the radio said. "Be my guest."

Jolly lifted the candle and ran the knife blade up and down the flame. "You know," he told Frank as he approached, "if a knife is hot enough, any wound that it opens will burn shut." Jolly spat on the end of the blade, and Frank heard a quick sizzle. "Unfortunately for you, my young friend, a mere candle will never make a blade that hot."

He stabbed the knife at Frank's bare chest.

As the blade moved, Brady and Everest flinched, and for just an instant Frank felt their grips loosen. Before they could react, he kicked out, catching Jolly in the elbow.

Jolly howled, and the knife flew out of his hand. At the same time, Frank threw his arms straight up in the air, and dropped, using his weight to pull himself out of the grip of Brady and Everest. As he dropped, he grabbed their collars, and they jerked forward. Their heads smacked together with a loud thud.

Frank let go and rolled, knocking Jolly's feet out from under him. The heavyset man, still smarting from the kick in the elbow, collapsed to the floor of the hold.

Then Chavo hurled himself backward, dragging his captors off balance. He rolled into a backward somersault and was free. He sprang to his feet, driving an uppercut into the jaw of the man closest to him.

Frank drove a right hook into the other—and both men fell.

Brady and Everest were already scrambling to their feet, murder in their eyes. Jolly crawled along the floor, frantically trying to find his blade.

Frank rushed forward, head down, and caught Brady in a football tackle, shoving him back against the wall. As they broke apart, Frank clamped his hands together and drove a two-fisted smash into Brady's jaw. The criminal sagged and slid down the wall. He was too dazed to react to anything.

In the meantime Chavo had grabbed Everest around the leg and shoulder and, as the man sputtered in disbelief, lifted him up in the air. Then Chavo lurched forward, body-slamming Everest to the floor. Everest flattened out.

"Pretty impressive," Frank said.

"I watch a lot of wrestling on television," Chavo replied.

Jolly shook the fog from his eyes and lurched to his feet. He waved his knife in front of him as he faced Chavo and Frank. But the heavyset man's confidence was gone.

"Should we flip a coin to see who gets to take the knife away from him?" Frank asked.

With a feeble grin, Jolly flipped the knife around and handed it to Frank hilt-first. "I believe I'm outnumbered."

Chavo tapped his knuckles against Jolly's jaw, and the heavyset man gave out a soft cry, more of surprise than of pain, before he fainted. Frank folded the knife and put it in his pocket.

From above there was a sudden banging sound, as the hold hatch was slammed down.

"They're locking us in," Frank said. He raced up the ladder and started pounding on the hatch cover, but it was no use. Someone had bolted it in place.

"Who?" Chavo asked. "Everyone's down here except Chrome, and he's steering the ship. Who could have put that hatch cover in place?"

"Beats me," Frank said. He eyed the men sprawled unconscious throughout the hold. "I'm more worried about them. When they wake up, they're going to want our hides. We sort of took them by surprise, and I don't think that's going to happen again.

"*Sí,*" Chavo agreed. He began to tear open crates. "We must get that hatch open or find something to tie them with. Help me."

Feverishly Frank and Chavo pulled open crates. There was nothing in them that would help their situation. "What'd you find?" Frank asked.

"One of the crates is filled with guns, another with gas masks." Chavo paused, stroking his chin and staring thoughtfully at nothing. "Gas masks. I begin to understand."

As Chavo grabbed two masks from the crate, Frank pulled out a pouch-size plastic wad. "Look at this. Inflatable life raft." He lifted two small plastic oars from the same crate. "If we ever get out of here, we can use this to get off the boat."

"We will not get out," Chavo said. Already, Brady was beginning to stir. "We need a lever to pry the hatch open."

"Why didn't I think of that?" Frank asked, and leaned back against a crate. It slid away from him, and he turned to see why. The box had been resting on something, and when he pushed against it, it rolled off. The metal something was a crowbar—probably there to pry open the crates.

"Will this do?"

Chavo grinned and dashed up the ladder. He jammed the bar into the small space between the hatch cover and the deck, and with all his strength, using his weight for leverage, Chavo strained at it.

"Hurry!" Frank shouted, picking up the life raft. Brady was on his feet, and the others were moving and groaning. Chavo also groaned as he strained, but the hatch cover stayed in place.

Brady staggered forward, almost blindly, and grabbed at Frank. Frank kicked him away, and the man staggered back to sit again.

"Almost!" Chavo said. He squinted and strained with the effort. The hatch budged.

It flew open all of a sudden, almost knocking Chavo off the ladder.

They emerged onto the deck, tensed and ready for action. There was no one there. Where was the person who had locked them in? Frank's eyes drifted toward the captain's tower, where Chrome Lasker was standing, talking with someone.

Frank shook his head and rubbed his eyes. He was imagining things. The man in the captain's tower with Lasker looked like Joe.

"Jump," Chavo ordered. They could hear the others stirring down below. Chavo leapt over the railing, and Frank followed, pulling the inflation cord on the life raft. It expanded as he fell.

They splashed into the water, and he and

Chavo pulled themselves into the life raft and began paddling away from the barge.

To the west, Frank could see the lights of the island of Puerto de Oro. It shimmered on the sea like a giant jewel, a fantasyland unaware of what was coming to it. All the lights reminded him of Fourth of July fireworks, and he imagined that he could hear the loud popping.

They're shooting at us, he realized.

He crouched down, making himself less of a target, and paddled harder until they were out of sight. The moon had cooperated and was now hidden behind a heavy cloud cover.

"It's good to see you, too, Lasker," Joe said.

Lasker laughed at his joke and tossed the gun on the control panel. Then he took his foot away from Joe's throat, and offered him a hand to help Joe to his feet. "Why are you crashing into my control room, Kid? I thought you were on the other end of the mission."

"I was," Joe explained, half-telling the truth. "In all the action on the other ship, I got thrown overboard. I drifted for a long time, until I spotted this ship, and I climbed aboard. I figured I'd capture it and get to Puerto de Oro that way. How did I know it belonged to the Director?"

"Well, you know now," Lasker said. "Some people are just born lucky, Kid."

As Joe stood, movement outside the window caught his eye. Someone had leapt over the side of the railing. "There's something going on down there." Then in a minute he saw the others, gathered at the railing, shooting into the ocean. Almost as one, they turned and raced to the captain's tower.

"Trouble," Jolly began to tell Lasker. He spotted Joe, and a pleased smile crossed his face. "Kid! Where did you come from?"

"What's the problem?" Lasker asked.

"Chavo has escaped." To Joe he explained, "He double-crossed us. And now he's escaping. We can't see his raft anymore, and our guns won't shoot far enough."

Lasker gave a big belly laugh and reached under the control panel. He pulled out a pair of night binoculars and a flare gun. "Let him escape this. This baby's got a range on it you wouldn't believe, and the flare on it'll burn that raft right off the sea."

"Chavo," Joe muttered, and again he pictured his brother being shot by the Mexican. He grabbed the flare gun.

"That direction, Kid," Jolly said, and he raised the special binoculars to Joe's eyes. Joe could make out a life raft, barely visible against the ocean. A man was in it. Yes, it was Chavo, all right.

Chavo, the man who had killed his brother. Joe knew this might be his only chance to make his brother's murderer pay for that crime.

Carefully he took aim at the raft.

Chapter

13

WHAT AM I DOING? Joe thought with a jolt just before he pulled the trigger. He was about to kill a man, and killing wasn't his style. He wanted to bring Chavo to justice, *real* justice.

That's what Frank would have wanted, he told himself.

He lowered the nose of the flare gun as he fired. An arc of flame shot across the night and exploded in fire and smoke on the ocean. In the blaze, he could no longer see the tiny life raft.

Jolly raised the binoculars to his eyes. "As near as I can tell, a perfect hit." He set them down and patted Joe's shoulder while the others cheered. "Welcome back, Kid. Now we've got to prepare for the main event. The world, as they say, is ours."

Something burst on the ocean.

Frank raised his head in alarm, to see that the sea was on fire just behind the raft. "What was that?" he asked.

Chavo ignored it. "Flare. We were the target. Let's use it to our advantage, as cover for an escape." He took one of the oars from Frank and began paddling. "So that's how he's going to do it."

"You mean the Director? You've figured out the caper?"

"*Sí,*" said Chavo. "Puerto de Oro is a self-contained island. It has few police and few buildings. If one were to take, say, the gas stolen from the naval base, and flood the buildings with it, then—"

"Then once you've knocked everyone out, you could wander through the buildings at will and take whatever you wanted," Frank continued. "Everyone would be dead. No witnesses."

"And they'll have plenty of time to leave the island without anyone contacting the mainland police. It's the perfect crime."

"Good thing you waited to figure this out until there's no possibility we can get help," Frank said with more than a hint of sarcasm.

"I'd hate to think we might need some backup to invade an island that's entirely cut off from the outside world and might be controlled by criminals."

"When we reach Puerto de Oro," said Chavo, "there I will get help."

"Chavo," Frank asked, "can I ask you a question?"

"Go ahead."

"Are you really a cop, or what?"

A burst of laughter erupted from the Mexican, and he said nothing else the rest of the way.

"Welcome to Puerto de Oro," Chavo said as they stepped onto the land ahead of the group on the barge. They had left the life raft in a massive harbor filled with private yachts and walked the rest of the way to the beach. Frank marveled at the sight of casinos and hotels styled like medieval castles, yet gleaming white, even at night. Electric lights made the streets of Puerto de Oro almost as bright as day.

But there was no one on the streets.

"This way," Chavo said, motioning down a street. "We must reach the police station and warn them. There's a radio, too. Men are waiting on the mainland for my orders."

As he ran, Frank's feet slid and skidded

across cobblestones moistened by the sea air. Which men did Chavo mean? Was he really going to call the Federales, or did he have some gang of his own stashed in Tijuana, waiting to come and horn in on the Director's master plan?

Frank resolved he would not turn his back on Chavo until he had the answer.

The police station was plainer than the other buildings, a simple box of stucco and stone. There were bars on all the windows. From inside came the tinny sounds of a mariachi band, played either on an old record player or a cheap radio. It seemed as peaceful and quaint as the rest of the island.

Chavo knocked on the door, yelling something in Spanish. From inside, a voice yelled, *"Qué desea usted?"* Chavo shook his head.

"He asked us what we want," Chavo said.

Frank pushed past him. "Your problem is that this is a resort that caters to rich Americans. Let me give it a try." He pounded on the door, shouting, "Help! Robbery!" Frank looked at Chavo. "How do you say 'I want to report a theft'?"

"Quiero denunciar un robo," Chavo replied.

"Quiero denunciar un robo," Frank repeated, pounding again at the door.

Finally the door opened a crack and a single brown eye peered out. "Come back tomorrow," a Hispanic voice called. "We cannot help you now."

Chavo hurled himself into the door, shoving it open. The figure at the door fell backward, and Frank and Chavo pushed their way in.

Frank helped the man on the floor to his feet. He was in his twenties, scrawny, and dressed in the uniform of a Mexican police deputy. Quickly he pulled his hand away from Frank and nervously brushed some dust off his khakis. In the meantime Chavo began to rummage frantically through the office. It was as small as it looked from outside, but it was packed with file cabinets. Next to the main desk was a teletypewriter. Chavo ripped pages from the teletypewriter, scanned them, and scowled.

"The radio," he insisted. "Where is your radio?" When the deputy refused to answer, Chavo stormed into the next room, toward the jail.

Frank expected the deputy to be angry about the break-in, but instead there was nothing but fear in his eyes. Those eyes weren't focused on Frank, but on the room that Chavo had just entered. He wondered why the deputy was so uneasy. There could be only one reason.

"Chavo!" Frank yelled as he flung the deputy aside. "It's a trap." He sprinted toward the door, but a man appeared in his way. The man was dressed in a white suit. A thick mustache adorned his upper lip, and grim mirth danced in the man's black, ratlike eyes.

It was Cat Willeford.

"Come in," he said, waving a gun at Frank. He motioned to the deputy. "You too."

"You won't shoot us," Frank said. "You'd bring the whole island down on you."

Willeford raised the pistol and fired at the ceiling. Powdered plaster rained down like a dust storm as the deafening roar echoed through the police station.

"Coming?" Willeford asked, and Frank and the deputy filed past him to the jail area.

Two others of the gang were also in there, tossing an unconscious Chavo into a cell. "Too bad," said Willeford. "I had to quiet him down." He flagged Frank and the deputy into the cell and slammed the door.

In the next cell Frank saw the chief of police and another deputy. He assumed that was all the law on the island.

"You're going to leave us here?" he asked Willeford.

"Not quite," the rat-eyed man answered before he vanished with his cronies into the outer office. Willeford returned a moment later, wearing a gas mask and holding a canister. He lifted up the mask. "Pleasant dreams." It sounded like a farewell.

Then he slipped the mask back on and crouched down. With a flip of his thumb he knocked open the valve on the canister. A white gas began spraying into the police station.

With a cheerful motion, Willeford dropped the cell-door keys on the floor outside Frank's cell, and then left.

As soon as the door closed, Frank was on his stomach, reaching through the bars. He stretched to grab the keys, but Willeford had dropped them just outside his reach. They lay there, tantalizing him, as the white cloud filled the room.

Coughing, his eyes stinging from the gas, Frank slapped Chavo. He wouldn't wake up. Frank slapped him again. Finally, the cell blurring before his eyes as the gas threatened to overcome him, Frank clamped a hand over Chavo's mouth and pinched his nose shut.

Chavo gasped awake, choking from the lack of air to his lungs. Before Frank could explain, he sized up the situation. The police chief and the deputies were flat on the floor, trying to reach the keys.

Chavo gave it a try and failed. He started to stand up, and then he sniffed at the gas. His eyes widened in terror, and he dropped back to his knees. Frank thought he looked sick.

"Knockout gas?" Frank asked, but he saw by the look in Chavo's eyes it wasn't so.

"Poison gas," Chavo replied weakly. "To kill us."

He threw himself against the bars, straining for the keys just out of reach as the cloud of death descended. Chavo slumped and shook his head. "It's no use."

They were trapped.

Chapter

14

FRANK PEELED OFF his shirt, holding it over his nose and mouth. Chavo ordered the others to stay down, breathing the air that remained under the thickening cloud. But Frank knew the dense gas would eventually force all the air out of the building. He had to reach the keys.

He got on his stomach again and stretched for the keys. Three inches, he thought. If only his arm would stretch three more inches!

He rolled onto his back, gasping for air. The gas stung his nostrils, choking him. He flattened against the floor, trying to stay beneath the cloud.

Something hit against his leg. Frank patted the floor with his hand, but there was nothing under his leg. He reached into his pocket.

There, forgotten, was the knife he had taken from Jolly on the barge.

Quickly he flicked the knife blade and stretched out again. The tip of the knife touched the edge of the key ring. He pulled it toward him. The knife blade slipped away. He tried again, slipping the blade under the ring this time. Slowly, so slowly Frank felt as if he wasn't moving at all, he lifted the knife, catching the ring.

The key ring slid down the length of the knife until it was in Frank's hand.

He pressed his face to the floor as far as he could, took one last breath, and stood up. As long as I don't breathe in, Frank thought, it won't get me. The thing that worried him was how long he would be able to hold his breath.

Frank worked the keys in the lock until the jail door swung open. He could see nothing but the white cloud. His ears and eyes stung as he staggered to the canister, but he held his breath as he tried to close the valve.

Willeford had broken it.

He lifted the canister, and the effort made him exhale, then inhale, without meaning to. Gas rushed into his lungs, and he felt himself weakening. With a loud cry, he lunged forward, into the front office, and smashed the canister through a window.

The bars stopped the canister, bouncing it

back into Frank's arms, but the window shattered. The rush of cool air cleared his head. Frank opened the front door to let in more air.

Standing outside on the steps was one of the men who had been with Willeford in the jail. Like Willeford, he now wore a gas mask. The gun he held was aimed at Frank.

Frank swung the canister like a baseball bat. It slammed into the side of the man's head, knocking him flat. Frank let go of the canister and fell to his knees next to the gunman, ripping at the thug's mask.

In seconds Frank had it on his own face. Then he rushed back into the deadly cloud in the jailhouse and, one by one, dragged the others to safety.

He sat on the ground in front of the police station, catching his breath as the others recovered. Finally he had the energy to remove the gas mask. He decided not to let it out of his sight. It might come in handy, now that the Director's scheme was in motion. Chavo entered a heated conversation in Spanish with the police chief, and when it was over he grabbed Frank by the arm and pulled him to his feet.

"The first thing Willeford did was smash the chief's radio," Chavo said. "We have one other chance." He jerked his head in the direction of the main hotel. "Brendan Buchanan, who owns the big casino on the island, has a two-way radio in his office."

Frank flashed Chavo a cocky grin. "Then we'd better get there before someone destroys that one too."

They moved stealthily and kept low. Frank noticed activity down by the docks. They crept closer for a better look, staying in the shadows.

The fishing barge was in, and the Director's gang was marching away from it. Each of them carried a large bag, and each wore a gas mask. The seven men marched toward the hotel.

"Seven?" Frank whispered to Chavo. "Where did they get a seventh from? There were only six on the boat."

"Don't forget the one who closed the hatch." Chavo watched grimly as the men blocked their path to the hotel. "We are beaten. There are too many of them, and we cannot get past them without them seeing us."

"Stay here," Frank said. "I've got an idea."

He slipped on the gas mask to conceal his identity and ran up to the line of criminals, trying not to make any noise. Without a sound, he slipped an arm around the neck of the last man in line, dragging him back. The man struggled, but the mask muffled his cry.

Chavo jumped up, ripped the man's gas mask off, and knocked him out. He slipped the mask on as Frank took the man's belt off and bound him with it.

"Perfect," Frank said, eyeing the masked Chavo. "You look like a master criminal again."

The hotel was filled with a bright pink gas that wafted in streams around Frank and Chavo as they entered. Elegantly dressed people littered the hotel lobby and stairs, an eerie stillness clutching their fallen bodies. Men in gas masks moved, taking watches, jewelry, and wallets from them and dropping the items in their bags.

They're breathing, Frank realized, relieved that here, at least, the thieves had not used poison gas.

They started up the stairs, and for a moment Chavo paused, looking back. Frank saw his eyes narrow. "What's the matter?"

"The seventh man from the dock," Chavo said. "The one we couldn't identify. I thought I saw him in the corner of my eye. I was mistaken."

They continued up. More bodies were on the stairs, lying where they'd fallen when the gas hit. From above them came the cry, "It's about time you got here. Let's go. The top floor hasn't been touched."

It was Everest. For a moment Frank froze,

sure they'd been spotted. Then he remembered the masks. Everest couldn't see who they were.

Chavo nodded, and Everest vanished back up the stairs.

"Let's go," Frank said. "According to the guide we passed on our way in, the manager's office is on the top floor."

They stopped on a balcony and looked at the activity below. The balcony opened out over a large casino, and masked figures scurried from table to table, robbing the gamblers and looting the money on the tables. For the first time, Frank fully understood just how big this crime really was.

He and Chavo continued up the stairs. Here and there men in gas masks popped in and out of hotel rooms. "There are more here than I recruited," Chavo said. "The Director must have had other scouts over here already in place."

"For a job like this, I can understand that," Frank replied. They reached the top of the stairs. On this floor there were no guest rooms, only offices. Frank went from door to door, until he found a plaque that read Manager.

"Here it is," he called to Chavo.

Gingerly he turned the knob. The unlocked door swung open.

The room was dark, and they dared not turn

on a light. Wisps of pink gas hung in the air, but it smelled sweeter than the air downstairs. Against the back window, which overlooked the harbor, was an antique desk.

A man sprawled with his face on the desk. Frank raised the man's hand, and it dropped back to the desk without pause. "Unconscious," Frank said. "I assume this is the manager."

"Never mind him," Chavo said. "Find the radio." He pulled books off the shelves and knocked open file drawers.

There was no sign of a radio.

"It's got to be here somewhere," Chavo insisted. He scratched his head. "Maybe it's one of those new miniaturized jobs. He could have it in his desk."

Frank stepped behind the desk and gently moved the unconscious manager to one side. He pulled open the desk drawers and rifled though them. Only papers. Exasperated, he slammed the top drawer shut.

His knuckle brushed against a button underneath the lip of the desktop. Curious, he pressed it.

A bookcase swung away from the wall, revealing a small room inside.

"The radio!" Chavo exclaimed, and rushed into the room. In seconds he was working the controls of the shortwave, repeating into the microphone, "Mayday! Mayday! Please acknowledge."

Frank stepped in, studying the hidden room. Why would a hotel manager install one? he wondered. He pressed his hand against the smooth white wall, and it gave way. As he heard Chavo speaking to the mainland police, he said, "I think we have a problem."

Behind the second wall was a small television studio.

"You do have a problem," the hotel manager agreed. He stood outside the door, very much awake, a pistol in his hand. "Yes," he said in answer to the shocked looks on their faces, "I am the hotel manager and owner."

Frank studied the man's face. There was something strangely familiar about him, though Frank was certain he hadn't seen him before. Under the man's nose, almost invisible, were nose filters. That, Frank realized, was how the manager had kept himself safe from the gas.

The manager gave them a tight smile. "Of course, you may call me the Director."

Chapter

15

WEARING HIS GAS MASK, Joe Hardy strolled through the casino. He had walked off the barge with the others, but since then had not joined them in their activities. He only watched as the criminals stripped Puerto de Oro of its wealth. Across the casino, at the roulette tables, two men were cleaning out the cash.

One crook picked up a diamond necklace and held it up to the light, checking its quality. The thief wiped the lenses on his gas mask with a sleeve, and when he still couldn't see well enough, he slipped the mask off and held the diamonds to the light again.

A satisfied smile crossed the man's lips. On the other side of the room, Joe's blood began to boil.

The man with the diamonds was Cat Wille-ford.

A thick hand clapped down on Joe's shoulder, startling him. He was at the point when he wanted to hit someone who deserved hitting, and his first thought was to spin around and start swinging. He held himself back. Like the others, this guy's face was masked, but Joe couldn't mistake the voice or the shape.

"You'd better do your share, Kid," Jolly said. "We wouldn't want you to miss out on your cut of the take, now, would we?"

"Someone would have to turn me in," Joe replied. "You wouldn't do that."

Jolly sighed. "I might hate to, that's true. But if the money was right . . ."

"What do we do with all this stuff once we get it?"

"Didn't they tell you, Kid? There's a central collection point, a truck out in the town square. We take everything there."

"And?" Joe asked.

"I don't get you."

"How do we get paid? And how's a truck going to help us? This is an island."

"You worry too much," Jolly replied. "The Director wouldn't be dumb enough to run out on us. There are enough guys here who'd be glad to track him to the ends of the earth to make him pay.

"On the other hand . . ." Jolly rubbed the back of his neck, still thinking about Joe's question. "That point about the truck is well-taken. I hope nothing is wrong. I get most unpleasant when someone betrays me."

"Sorry to hear about that," Joe said. Whipping around, he swung up, knocking the gas mask from Jolly's face. His fist landed in the heavyset man's stomach, and Jolly sucked in a lungful of pink gas.

"Kid," Jolly said softly, sadness in his voice. He opened his mouth again, as if to shout, and then dropped to the floor. The gas had taken effect.

Joe glanced around the room. No one had noticed his scene with Jolly. He stashed Jolly under a blackjack table, then picked up the bag of loot Jolly had been carrying. The heavyset man had been right about one thing. Joe would be a lot less conspicuous if he were carrying a bag.

He wanted to stay inconspicuous—he had a lot of scores to settle, starting with Cat Willeford.

A big bag tossed over his shoulder, Willeford left the casino and headed into the dining room next door. Joe followed. None of the others paid any attention to them. And if they found Jolly lying there? Would they raise the alarm?

No, Joe decided. They'd probably rob him of any valuables he had left.

Willeford was in the kitchen when Joe caught up with him. Joe called his name, and the rat-eyed man looked up.

"I've been looking forward to this," Joe said.

"Who are you?" asked Willeford.

Joe lifted his gas mask for a moment, and Willeford smiled. "Kid, you've got almost as many lives as I do."

"The name's not Kid. It's Joe Hardy. You should never have tried to kill me." Joe clenched his fists and took a step toward Wille-ford. "You're out of lives now, Cat."

Willeford ran. He and Joe left their bags sitting in the kitchen, and Joe chased him into the main hallway. Other criminals watched them as they ran, and Joe could hear them laughing. He knew none of them would lift a hand to help Willeford. They were too inter-ested in their loot.

Joe stopped dead in his tracks as he reached the hallway. Two masked figures were starting up the stairs, and one of them turned his face just enough for Joe to recognize the eyes. He'd never forget those eyes.

That was Chavo, the guy who'd killed his brother. Joe started after Chavo.

Willeford took advantage of Joe's shift of

attention, catching Joe under the chin with his forearm. The blow knocked Joe off his feet and sent him crashing on his back on the floor. Willeford dropped down like a piledriver, smashing both fists into Joe's chest.

Joe tried to shake off the haze that was swallowing him. Somewhere he was dimly aware that Willeford was clawing at his face, trying to slip his mask off. Struggling to keep the mask on, Joe tried to stand. Willeford went for a new hold, wrapping an arm around Joe's head while Joe was still bent over.

Joe stood suddenly, locking one hand under Willeford's shoulder and the other in the man's belt. He kicked backward, and Willeford was in the air as Joe tucked himself into a roll. They both crashed to the floor on their backs.

Willeford hit first, and he hit hard. While the crook thrashed around, trying to pull himself together, Joe punched him again. Willeford stopped moving and lay still.

Joe turned his eyes to the stairs. Now it was Chavo's turn.

"You're robbing your own resort?" Frank said in disbelief.

"Certain financial setbacks make it necessary," the Director said. "Everything was planned, except for the interference from you and your brother."

As the Director spoke to Frank, Chavo inched toward him. The Director calmly turned and pointed the gun at Chavo's heart. "Uh-uh," he said. "Please don't interrupt."

Frank and Chavo stood back as the Director continued.

"Take Mr. Chavo here, a Federale operating undercover as a criminal. He was the perfect tool. I could use him to recruit the people I needed and set up the operation. And he fell right in line, eager to arrest large numbers of crooks in the commission of a crime."

"You knew about Chavo all along?" Frank asked.

"My boy, he's the most important part of my plan. When the Mexican authorities raid this island and capture the army of criminals I've assembled, I won't have to pay any of them. I, and the millions of dollars collected here tonight, will simply disappear."

"That's why you relayed everything through radio or television," Frank said, "and why you appeared fully masked. Why would anyone associate a hotel manager with the mastermind who robbed the place? You're in the clear."

"Except for us," Chavo said tensely. "We know who you are."

The Director picked up a shoebox, pressed a button on it, and slid it across the floor of the secret room. "I was coming to that. The final part of my plan is for my office to be bombed. It's the perfect way to cover my tracks. Of course, it would appear to all as if I'd been killed in the blast—"

"Of course," Frank said.

"Now it seems your bodies will be found in the wreckage. The thief who planted the bomb"— the Director gestured to Frank, then to Chavo—"and the brave policeman who tried to stop him. How tragic."

The Director checked his watch. "Five minutes. I really must be going." He stepped back, and the secret door began to close.

Frank leapt for the Director, but he was too slow. The man swung his gun, cracking Frank on the skull. He fell back, unconscious, but Chavo moved, knocking the Director back before he could pull the trigger. They tumbled together out of the radio room, and the pistol slipped from the Director's grip, skittering across the floor. When they stopped rolling, Chavo was on top of the Director, pinning his arms down.

"It's all over," Chavo said.

But another masked figure appeared from nowhere and slammed the back of Chavo's head. He slumped weakly to the floor. The Director scrambled to his feet, racing out the door as Chavo, clutching his head, looked up.

Joe Hardy stood over him, ready for business. "You killed my brother, you slime."

Beneath the gas mask, Chavo's eyes widened at the sound of Joe's voice. He tried to get to his feet, but Joe held him down. Then Joe grabbed him by the collar and lifted him up, knocking the gas mask from Chavo's face.

Joe planted a punch on Chavo's jaw, and Chavo staggered back but remained on his feet.

"Your brother's alive."

Joe could barely hear Chavo's voice.

"What?" Joe said. He couldn't believe his ears. "You're just saying that to save your skin."

"No. Please. You must listen if you want to save him." Chavo half-raised a hand and pointed to the secret room. "Behind that wall—I was just with him." He took a faltering step forward, dread written all over his face. "He's in there with a bomb."

He's lying, Joe told himself. But there was a look of true panic on Chavo's face, and Joe knew he couldn't pass up even the slightest chance that Frank still lived. He lunged for the secret door.

It was too late. The wall disintegrated from the force of the blast.

He flew back into darkness, hoping against hope that Chavo had been lying about Frank.

Chapter

16

SOMETHING STUNG JOE'S CHEEK. He tried to wave it away, but it stung him again. Finally he opened his eyes a crack—then he parted them wide.

Frank was kneeling over him, gently bringing him around. He saw dark smudges on Frank's face, and his clothes were tattered, but he was alive!

"You're still breathing, brother," Frank said, smiling. "We both made it."

Joe sat up and saw Chavo standing impatiently behind Frank. Frank turned to the Mexican and said, "Go ahead. We'll catch up in a few minutes." As Chavo left, Frank helped Joe to his feet.

"What happened?" Joe asked. "That bomb

knocked me clear across the room. You couldn't have survived if you'd been right on top of it."

"You should have seen all the great electronic equipment in there." Frank laughed. Then his face turned serious. "A fan's dream, all this radio and TV stuff—very bulky. When I realized I couldn't get out of the room, I put the bomb in one end and pushed the equipment to the other."

Joe began to grin. "And you hid behind the equipment when the bomb went off." He shook his head. "It's just like you to leave me to take the worst of it."

"The equipment took the worst. There's not much of it left," Frank said. His face grew grim. "I'm really glad to see you, Joe. I thought you were dead."

"I thought *you* were, too." Joe gave his brother a big hug. "Let's try never to go through that again, okay?"

"Deal," Frank said. "Now let's find Chavo."

When the Hardys caught up to him, Frank asked, "Do you trust us to get the Director while you try to reach the police?"

"I suppose I do not have a choice," Chavo replied with a grin. "I will have to find another working radio at another hotel."

"Good." Frank cocked his head toward the

door and glanced at Joe. "Now, why don't we go round up the Director."

The hotel was empty, except for the still-unconscious guests and staff. Every room had been stripped, every safe-deposit box looted. The Director's plan had worked almost flawlessly.

"Get back," Frank said. They both jumped for the shadows as two criminals, loaded down with bags, walked by. "They'll probably lead us to the Director as well as anyone." Staying out of sight, they followed the two thieves to the town square, where everyone had lined up to pour jewelry and money into an old dump truck.

"A truck?" said Frank.

"Jolly said something about this," Joe explained. "It's supposed to get all this stuff off the island."

"How can a truck get out?" Frank said in disbelief. "It doesn't look very seaworthy."

"That's what we were told," Joe said. "I guess we'll find out soon enough."

"Come on." Frank glanced around. "I've got an idea." Quickly he led Joe to the nearest building. Frank jumped up, catching the fire escape. They climbed up three sets of metal stairs, until they were on a roof overlooking the bizarre scene.

They watched for a while.

"Look," Joe said, breaking the silence.

Out on the ocean, a fleet of lights grew brighter and brighter as they approached the island. A high-pitched whine became louder, then softer, then louder still.

"It's the police," Joe said.

"Then Chavo did find another radio." Frank nodded. "But the Director planned on this. Hang on, little brother. I think we're about to catch the ride of our lives."

On the ground, the criminals were reacting to the oncoming sirens. Joe watched in amusement as they frantically pointed out to sea. Several rushed the truck and tried to get into the driver's cabin, but the doors were locked.

"That's not the Director driving," Joe said.

"No, but I bet he'll be where the truck's going," Frank said, watching it careen down the street. "Get ready."

"What are we supposed to do from up here?"

"Jump," said Frank.

"Jump?"

"Jump!"

Together, they leapt.

The Hardys fell three stories, to smash into a lumpy pile of loot. They were in the back of the old dump truck, speeding through Puerto de Oro at a breakneck pace.

As he bounced around on the jewelry and cash, Frank imagined the look on the Director's face when he got to his destination and found them waiting for him.

The truck turned off the street and onto a dirt road, heading for the heart of the island. Far behind were the casinos, criminals, and police. Now the scenery was tropical forest so thick that it was almost jungle, and the road turned to a trail barely wide enough for the vehicle. It looked as if no one had ever lived on this part of the island. It was almost wilderness.

The police would never look for the Director here.

They rode up a mountain, then down the other side. Joe stood and looked out over the hood of the dump truck. The truck was heading toward a small inlet, lit orange and purple by the rising sun. There was a long stretch of beach beside the water, and on the sand, a dark winged object.

"You're not going to believe this," Joe said. "I guess you can get anything from government surplus if you try hard enough."

Frank took a look. "I believe it. It's the only way his plan could work."

The truck rolled onto the beach and into the fuselage of the cargo plane waiting there.

The Hardys lay flat on the loot as the aircraft's engines started one by one. The truck door slammed, and Frank could hear the Director barking orders. The ramp up to the airplane was pulled in, and the entrance bay closed. Then the plane started to move. Frank and Joe began to slide over the loot as the plane rose into the air.

"Frank," Joe began as the plane leveled off, but Frank clapped a hand over Joe's mouth, silencing him. The Director's triumphant laughter echoed in the belly of the plane.

Then came a grinding noise. "Oh, no!" Frank yelled, no longer caring if he were heard or not.

The front of the dump truck began to tip up.

Frank and Joe crawled through the loot, trying to reach what was now becoming the top of the mound, but the farther they crawled forward, the more the slipping pile of riches carried them back. The back gate of the truck opened, the loot spilling onto the floor of the airplane. The Director danced around the pile with joy.

Then he saw the Hardys, and his face changed. "Nick! Charlie!" he called, going for the pistol stuck inside his belt.

Joe dived, tackling him. A shot rang out, ricocheting off the wall of the plane. Then Joe reached the Director, grabbed his gun hand, and tore the pistol from his grip.

"Drop it," a voice snarled. "Hands where we can see them." Joe spun, pistol ready, to find himself facing two unshaven men with automatic rifles. The one who spoke wore a T-shirt, and his black hair was cut close to his head, almost like a skullcap. His gun was aimed straight at Joe. The second gunman trained a rifle on Frank.

Sagging, Joe dropped the pistol and raised his hands.

"This one's no problem, Nick," the other man said as he shoved Frank to Joe's side. The Director picked up his fallen pistol.

"The Hardys," the Director said. "Is there no getting rid of you?"

"Smarter guys than you have tried," Joe answered defiantly.

A slow smile spread over the Director's face. "That may be true. But I'll be the one to succeed." He signaled the two other men, who nudged Frank and Joe toward the bay door.

"Let me introduce Nick and Charlie," the Director went on. "They've had quite a bit of experience with smuggling by air. For instance, do you know what they do with contraband when the police are closing in?"

He hit a switch, and the bay doors opened. Frank and Joe looked out over the dark Pacific, half a mile below.

"We dump it," Nick said with a grin.

The Director grinned back. He pointed to the bay door, then turned to the Hardys. "To have gotten into the truck, you must be good at jumping."

The smugglers cocked their automatic rifles and pressed them in the Hardys' ribs.

"I'd like to see a demonstration," the Director said. "So jump."

Chapter

17

"A HIGH-DIVE COMPETITION is no fun with just two people, Director," a woman's voice said. "Maybe you should join them."

The Director and the Hardys all turned at once, shock on their faces.

"Charity!" Joe yelled.

"Get her!" the Director shouted to the smugglers. Nick just turned where he was, training his rifle on his supposed boss.

Charity stepped from the cockpit. "I don't think your men will follow your orders anymore, Director. I've bought them off."

"Imp-p-ossible." The Director stuttered over the word. "I offered them a cut of the loot! How could you top that?"

Charity shrugged. "I offered them *half* the

loot. Once we take it from you, of course. Now, if you'd be so kind—'' She waved them toward the open bay door.

"You can't!" Joe said.

She laughed. "True enough." To the Director she said, "Close that door. I've never killed anybody, and I don't want to pick up bad habits."

"Any *more* bad habits?" Joe sneered.

Charity feigned a brokenhearted look. "Why, Joe. And after I just saved your life. How ungentlemanly." She signaled, and the two smugglers shoved the Hardys and the Director into the plane's interior. Charity reached into her pocket, pulling out two pairs of handcuffs.

"Souvenirs from police I've run into," she explained.

The smuggler named Nick opened the driver's door of the dump truck, lowering the window. He stuck Joe on one side of the open door and Frank on the other, holding their hands up. Then Charity snapped the cuffs over their wrists. They were stuck, trapped by the door. The smuggler named Charlie handcuffed the Director to the truck's rear bumper, just out of reach of the loot.

"You lied to me," Joe accused Charity. "You're no government agent."

She began to laugh. "Of course I lied. I'm a thief. It worked out so much better this way."

"I can understand why you wanted to rip off the Director," Frank said, looking back at the loot. "But why bring us into it?"

"The oldest reason in the world, Frank," Charity said. "Misdirection—keeping the enemy off guard. You were the wild cards. While the Director was busy watching you, he couldn't keep an eye on me."

"So you pulled that heist in Bayport just to lure us in." Frank was talking out loud to explain it to himself.

"I think you'll agree it worked out well." She studied Joe's angry scowl. "Or maybe not. We don't have to agree on everything."

The Director sat on the floor, his tear-filled eyes fixed and staring. "How did you know? How did you know?"

"You're going to think this is funny," Charity explained. "I was in Puerto de Oro six months ago, when you were planning this caper. You write everything down, did you know that? It's the sort of thing that will get you in trouble one of these days."

"I destroyed all those notes!" the Director burst out. "No one ever saw them except me."

"And the woman who robbed your safe," Charity added, to the man's surprise. "Me. It was a good plan, but I think mine was better."

The Director sank into silence, his face gray with shame.

"What are you going to do with us?" Frank asked. "You can't let us go. We know too much."

"*What* do you know?" Charity countered. "You don't know who I am or where I'm going. No, you really can't do me much harm at all." She looked wistfully out the window. "We'll be in Guatemala before too long. The plane will land there, we'll take the loot out, and leave you with the plane. How's that?"

"Just great," Joe said sourly.

She patted him gently on the cheek, trying to raise his spirits. "Don't take it like that, Joe. You'll get free pretty quickly. I'll see to that. Then all you have to do is find the Guatemalan police and explain everything to them, and by the time you do that, I'll be long gone.

"It's a shame, really," Charity said, looking at the Hardys. "We made such a good team. Maybe we can work together again someday."

"Over my dead body," Joe muttered.

"Don't say things like that," Charity scolded him. "Someday you'll run into someone who'll take that suggestion seriously."

Like the Director, Joe sank into silence and fumed. He couldn't believe it. Charity had outwitted them again.

The plane dipped, and Frank saw light com-

ing from around the front end of the plane,
streaks of bright red. The sun was almost up,
but it had risen to the right of them.

She's lying again, he thought to himself. If
the sun is to the right, we're flying northeast.
That means we're over the United States.

"This is where I get out," Charity said. The
plane landed, skidding along a landing strip
crudely scratched out of the desert. When the
plane came to a halt, Nick opened the bay
doors.

A man stood at the bottom of the ramp, half-
hidden in the morning grayness. He was short
and thin, with thinning dark hair that formed a
widow's peak. His thick glasses reflected the
lights from inside the plane. Behind him was a
rent-a-van, the kind used by millions of people
throughout the country. Once they got on the
highway with that, Frank knew, the thieves
would vanish without a trace.

The man walked up the ramp, into the lit
area.

"Renner!" Joe shouted. Forgetting the handcuffs, he lunged for the insurance investigator
but jerked back abruptly, stopped by the end
of his chain.

Renner frowned. "What are they doing
here? This ruins everything. They'll destroy
my career."

"You'll be rich, remember?" Charity reminded him. "You won't need a career. Let them be."

Nick went outside and backed the rent-a-van to the cargo-bay doors. A third smuggler, the pilot, came out of the cockpit and, with Renner, Charity, and the others, shoveled the loot into boxes, piling them in the back of the van.

Frank and Joe watched this without comment. The Director, on his knees with one hand cuffed to the truck, desperately scratched and clawed at any loose baubles or money that fell as they were loaded. Laughing, the smugglers let him keep whatever he could grab.

Renner, though, snatched the loot away from the Director and stuffed it into the last box.

When the final box was in the van, Charity blew goodbye kisses to the Hardys. "Thank you, boys," she said. "I couldn't have done it without you." She walked down the ramp out the bay door to the van.

Renner called the smugglers into the cockpit of the plane. There were three dull thuds, and moments later, Renner reappeared alone.

In his hands were two containers of gasoline.

"Charity!" he called pleasantly. "Could you come back here a moment?"

Joe could see her against the spreading morning light. Now that Charity's schemes were finished, it seemed to Joe that all the energy had gone out of her. She yawned with disinterest and started up the ramp again.

Renner pressed his back against the wall next to the bay door and pulled a revolver from under his coat. He cocked the hammer.

"Run!" Joe yelled. "It's a double cross!"

Angrily Renner spun and snapped off a shot at Joe. It hit the driver's mirror on the dump truck and shattered it. Renner leapt onto the ramp. Charity had just reached the van when Renner fired a shot over her head.

"The next one goes in your back, Charity," he said.

Charity stopped. Putting her hands behind her head, she walked back into the plane. Keeping his gun at her back, Renner cuffed her to the Director, wrapping the handcuff chain around the dump truck's back bumper.

"Congratulations," she said to Renner. "You win."

Renner sneered. "But I'm not safe. I won't be, until none of you can threaten me." He went back to the gasoline containers, uncapped them, and splashed gas throughout the plane.

With a theatrical bow, Renner faced the Hardys and Charity. "I want to thank everyone for making me very, very wealthy. I'll never forget you." He hit the bay-door switch and ran outside.

Just before the bay door closed, Renner lit a

match and tossed it back into the plane. The match landed in a pool of gasoline, and in a flash the plane was in flames.

Frank and Joe struggled against the handcuffs as the fire raced toward them, but the chain held. There was nothing they could do.

The plane was going up in smoke, and it would take them with it.

Chapter

18

"JOE, PULL DOWN on your end of the chain," Frank ordered.

Joe dropped to his knees. On the other side of the door, Frank pushed himself through the truck window and somersaulted to his feet on Joe's side of the door.

"Very good. And here I thought I'd have to do *all* your thinking for you," Charity said.

"I supposed you had this planned all along," Joe chided. Charity flashed him a sly grin.

"We haven't got time for clever chatter, Joe," Frank said as the flames grew near. With his free hand he pulled on the bumper holding Charity and the Director down. "We've got to get them out of here. Where's the handcuff key, Charity?"

"Save me," pleaded the Director.

"I'm afraid Renner has the key," Charity said coolly. "But if you'd take that pin off my lapel . . ." Frank undid the gold lapel pin and handed it to her. With her free hand she inserted the sharp point of the pin into the handcuff lock—freeing both herself and the Director.

"Where do you think you're going?" Joe said as Charity bolted for the bay-door control. He grabbed her wrist and pulled her back.

"Nowhere, from the looks of that," she said, pointing out the fire that blocked the exit.

"Get into the back of the truck," Frank ordered Charity and the Director. "Come on, Joe."

The Hardys dashed to the cockpit. The three smugglers sprawled in the pilot seats, unconscious. Joe slapped Nick awake, and as the smuggler woke, the smoke filling the cabin told him the situation. "Help us get your friends out of here," Frank told Nick. "Or you won't get out either."

They dragged the other two to the back of the truck. Fire devoured the cargo bay. Still handcuffed together, Frank and Joe climbed into the driver's cab. Frank started up the engine.

Seconds later, the burning truck smashed through the side of the plane. The truck tumbled to the ground and rolled, spilling its passengers. It took one more tumble, then came to a stop on its side.

Frank and Joe, bruised, crawled out together. They ran across the sand and fell in the flash of heat as fire roared over the truck and plane. Exhausted, Frank sprawled out on the ground.

Joe raised his head. For the first time he realized they were in a desert, and as he watched, Charity and the others spread out and ran off. Joe tried to spring to his feet, but the handcuff pulled him down again. "They're getting away!" Joe said insistently. "We've got to stop them!"

"We don't need to," Frank said, his eyes closed. "Listen."

Overhead there was the familiar *thwipping* of helicopter blades. Three choppers descended in a triangular pattern, and armed police officers leapt out. In seconds the police led Charity, the Director, and the smugglers back to Frank and Joe. The Hardys stood up to face a scarred Mexican agent who was with the police.

"Chavo," Frank said in surprise. "Glad you could make it."

"*Sí,*" replied Chavo. "As you can see, I really am a policeman. We caught all the others on Puerto de Oro, all except these." He swept his arm at Charity and the Director. "Once we find the stolen jewels and cash, the case is, as you say, all wrapped up."

"Mind if we borrow a helicopter and some cops?" Joe said. He held up their cuffed wrists. "And could we get out of these things? There's no key, but the cops have experience with this sort of thing, don't they?"

Chavo went to speak to the police, and a second later came back with an officer, who had Charity in tow. She poked her pin into the locks, and in seconds the handcuffs popped open.

"This lady has something to say to you," Chavo said.

The smile on Charity's face was warm and sincere, without a hint of deceit. "Looks like you won this one, Joe. Maybe next time it'll be my turn again."

"There's not going to be a next time," Joe said. He put the handcuffs on her and handed her over to the policeman. "Don't let her out of your sight, officer. She's tricky."

Dust and sand were whipped around by the wind from the blades of a helicopter as it set down a dozen yards from Chavo and the Hardys. On the helicopter were the markings of the U.S. Border Patrol. "Come," Chavo said. Sprinting, he led the Hardys to the chopper. A door flew open, and a border patrolman reached out to help them inside. There were two other patrolmen on board, as well as the pilot. As the door clicked shut behind them, the helicopter rose twirling into the sky, to fly in ever-widening circles over the desert.

"There's San Diego," Joe exclaimed, spotting the downtown area off in the distance.

"Is that what we're looking for?" Chavo asked.

"No," Frank replied. They sped across the sky, and Frank scoured the roads that led across the desert. One led north and petered out after a mile. Most of the others ran toward San Diego, but there was no sign of a van on any of them. "Head east," he said to the pilot over the pounding of the blades.

On the road to the east, a plume of dust rose. At the tip of the plume was the rent-a-van.

"That's him," Joe said. As the helicopter flew over the van, Chavo opened a footlocker inside the police helicopter and took out several shotguns. He handed one to Frank.

Frank shook his head. "I'd rather not use a gun if I can avoid it."

"Renner won't give us any more trouble," Joe said as he settled in the seat next to the pilot. He snatched a microphone from the dashboard and asked the pilot, "Is there an external loudspeaker on this thing?" The pilot nodded and switched it on.

"You might as well give up, Renner," Joe said into the microphone, and he was thrilled to hear his voice boom back at him from the outside. "You can't get away."

"Good job, Joe," Frank said, his eyes on the road. "He's speeding up."

"Take it down," Chavo ordered with a sigh. He cocked the shotgun. "Get ready."

The chopper set down on the road, blocking it. As the van began backing up, the three border guards charged out of the chopper, firing warning shots into the air.

The van came to a dead stop. Renner stepped out, gun in hand. Spreading his arms wide, he crouched down and dropped the gun to the sand, then stood with his hands up. The border patrolmen rushed him.

"What's the matter?" Joe asked Renner as the police pushed the insurance man to the helicopter. "How come you're not throwing your weight around now?"

Feebly Renner looked at the patrolmen and said, "My name is Elroy Renner. I'm an insurance investigator, and you're interfering with a case. You'll all be in big trouble."

"Save it," Frank said. One by one, he emptied Renner's pockets.

A large sapphire fell from his pants pocket to the sand. Joe crouched to pick it up.

"Well, well," Joe said, holding the Star of

Ishtar up for examination. "I guess this gets Chief Collig off the hook. You stole it all along."

"Get him out of here," Chavo told the patrolmen, and they loaded Renner into the chopper. They watched as it took off.

Turning to the van, Joe said, "I guess we'd better take it back."

"Perhaps . . ." Chavo said in a dreamy voice. His eyes glazed over, and a hungry smile came to his lips. "So much wealth in this van. Split three ways, it could make some people very rich."

"Are you *sure* you're a cop?" Frank asked.

Laughing, Chavo gave a happy-go-lucky shrug. "A man can dream, my friend." He climbed behind the steering wheel of the van. "Do you need a lift anywhere?"

Frank and Joe got in. "How about back to what's left of the plane?"

Chavo shrugged again, and in silence they drove to the west.

The van pulled up beside the charred remains of the plane, near a cluster of policemen who had gathered around the criminals. Joe noticed their agitation. He hopped out of the cab and ran to them, scanning for a face that was missing, feeling his own face flushing with anger.

"Where's the woman?" he shouted. "Where's Charity?"

The police officer Joe had left Charity with turned red with embarrassment, and Joe felt his temper rising. "I can't explain it," the officer said. "I was handcuffed to her one minute, then there was this commotion and I turned away, and the next minute the handcuff was open and she was gone." Seeing Joe's growing rage, he hastily added, "But she can't have gotten far in this desert. As soon as we're in the air, we'll spot her."

"You won't," Joe assured the policeman. He realized Frank was now standing beside him, and exclaimed, "I don't believe it! She got away again." He shook his head, the anger flooding out of him. Somehow there seemed no point in staying mad.

"Look on the bright side," Frank said. "At least this time she went away empty-handed. We'll get her in the next round."

"Oh, no," Joe said as they walked back to Chavo, ready to begin the trip home. "We are never having anything to do with that woman ever again."

Frank nodded his agreement. But deep down, both of them knew that Joe was wrong.

THE DEADLIEST DARE

Chapter

1

"AH-AH-CHOO!"

That's how it started—with a sneeze.

Quite a few sneezes, actually.

But Frank Hardy didn't hear them over the loud music he was dancing to. The Cellar was Bayport's newest rock club—somebody had redone the cellar of an abandoned mill on the outskirts of town. The dark brick walls and pillared arches were right out of an old monster movie, but the lights and special effects were strictly science fiction.

Frank just let his tall, lean body go with the pulsing beat, but his girlfriend, Callie Shaw, tried out some serious moves. Frank's dark eyes gleamed as he watched her blond hair fly wildly in the multicolored glare of pulsating strobe lights.

"So what do you think?" Callie yelled over the blast of the hugely amplified live music.

"Eh?" he inquired, cupping his ear. "Can't hear you over all this noise."

"Yes, you can," she accused, poking him in the ribs with her forefinger. "I was asking you how you liked the group. That's why we're here, remember, to hear this group?"

"Our buddy Biff Hooper seems to be enjoying them," Frank said, leaning in toward Callie. "I noticed Biff and his date dancing really close to a slow song a while ago. Any group that can make Biff feel romantic must be okay."

"But what do *you* think? Come on, Frank."

With a laugh, he danced closer and took Callie in his arms. "Me? I always feel romantic." He looked across the crowded dance floor to the bandstand, where laser lights flashed overhead in time to the music. They glowed eerily as fog was blown across the dancers. "Which one is your friend again?"

"Mandy, the bass player. She's—"

The rest of Callie's reply was cut off when somebody sneezed nearby.

"Oh, the one with the purple hair. Very nice." Frank looked up. The sneezing seemed to be coming nearer.

2

"It's only a wig. Don't judge her musical ability by—excuse me—" Callie's nose wrinkled, and she brushed at its tip. Then she tilted her head back, leaned over, and sneezed. She sneezed again, then twice more.

At the same instant the thickset young man dancing beside them began wheezing, then let off a thunderous sneeze. The single gold ring in his ear jingled as he put his hand to his chest, then sneezed again.

Frank stopped dancing and started staring. He wasn't alone. Out on the foggy floor, dancing couples were halting and stumbling. Most of them were sneezing now and coughing, wiping at their watery eyes.

Frank took a moment to glance around and see how Biff and his dark-haired date were doing. But he couldn't spot them in the crowd.

As Callie tugged a tissue out of the pocket of her jeans, she asked him, "Wha-wha-CHOO! What's going on?"

Frank was busy staring over her head. "There it is—see up there?"

Drifting out of the vents near the arched ceiling of the club was some kind of silvery powder. Frank watched it flicker and glisten in the colored lights until it mingled with the fog down closer to the floor.

Frank put his arm protectively around Callie's slim shoulders. "Somebody's managed to slip a little whoopee powder into the air system," he said, guiding her through the wheezing crowd. "We have to get some fresh air, Callie. I'm going to sneeze, too." And he did.

Callie took a deep breath through her half-open mouth. "I sure do need—" She sneezed again. "Excuse me. I can use some fresh air, yes."

Frank tapped a few shoulders and made follow-me gestures. When they reached the rainy parking lot at the side of the club, they were leading a good-size group—with more people joining them every minute.

"Well, at least there's not a wild rush for the doors," Frank said. "Maybe I should go back in there to warn the management."

"Don't, Frank." Callie caught his arm and took off for her car to get out of the rain. "They must be getting the message by now."

Still more couples were coming out of the place, most of them sneezing and crying, searching for clean air.

"You know, there've been quite a few dumb practical jokes like this around town lately," said Frank, jogging beside her. "I'd like to find out just what—"

"Frank, I know you're a great detective, but do me a favor and cool it for now." Callie put the speed on and ran full-out to the far end of the parking lot. "I happen to have met the folks who run the Cellar. They're not really nice guys—and they might think you're the prankster if you go poking around."

Frank had to grin at the way Callie had pegged him so quickly. Frank and Joe Hardy were brothers and known for solving mysteries. Their last case, *Thick As Thieves,* had sent Frank and Joe on a wild cross-country chase to stop the heist of the century. But his smile softened as he looked into his girlfriend's tearing eyes.

"Okay—I guess I can pass up getting to the bottom of the case of the Perilous Prankster. Maybe the guy was just a music critic."

"Ha, ha," Callie told him, wiping a finger under her eye. "I don't think I can drive in this downpour. And I would like to go home."

Frank opened the door on the passenger side of the car, and Callie gratefully ducked inside. "Give me the keys and I'll play chauffeur."

She started to smile appreciatively, but was cut short by two new sneezes. "Anyway, did you like Mandy's group or not?"

"I don't think tonight's show—or at least the way it ended—helped them any. It pretty much cleaned out the place."

Frank climbed in and headed out of the parking lot. The rain was coming down heavily now, and Frank slowed the car on the winding hillside road that cut through forest on both sides. "There's a pattern all right," he was saying, "but I'm just not sure what it is."

Callie touched at her nose with a fresh tissue. "It does seem like we're in the middle of an epidemic of pranks and practical jokes, doesn't it?"

"It started about three weeks ago, right after the start of school vacation," he said. "A little grafitti on the school gym, then came the box of frogs that mysteriously opened in the middle of the library. There've been others as well. Joe already thought all the pranks were tied together somehow."

"Why didn't he come to the Cellar tonight, by the way?"

"He said he'd heard your friend Mandy's band already." Frank gracefully guided the car around another curve of the woodland road.

"You and your brother have absolutely no musical taste."

Frank said, "This powder thing tonight at the club—in a way it's more than a simple joke."

"Because it hurt Mandy and her group?"

"More than that—it could have caused panic. People could have gotten hurt."

"Well, a lot of practical jokes have a nasty side," Callie said. "They're not always good, clean fun."

"That's one of the things that worries me."

Frank stared out the rain-whipped windshield. "Maybe what we've got out there is someone or a group that gets its fun by hurting people. What scares me is that they're eventually going to get bored with just jokes."

Callie leaned back in her seat. "Well, it still could be nothing more than some goons who don't realize they've gone too far with their idea of humor."

"I hope so. But I have a hunch it's—"

He cut off his speech just then as the car hopped, then whipped in zigzags back and forth across the dark, slippery road. It wobbled, rattled, bumped, and slid.

"Rear tire," Frank muttered, his grip tightening on the wheel. "It's flat."

He didn't hit the brakes but struggled to control the fishtailing vehicle, steering with the skid as much as possible.

"Those trees, Frank!" warned Callie in a high, choked voice.

The car's course was going to take it smack into a stand of heavy, dark oak trees close to the edge of the road. Frank desperately fought the steering wheel, but the car wouldn't respond.

It hurtled off the slippery road, and for several awful seconds it seemed to float in air.

Then the car smashed head-on into one of the big, old trees.

Chapter

2

JOE HARDY SAT at the desk usually occupied by his father. Before leaving with Mrs. Hardy for a brief vacation in Florida, Fenton Hardy had asked his sons to update some of his reference files.

While that kind of organizational job was more up Frank's alley, Joe had decided to take it on that night. He'd had a few run-ins with Callie's friend Mandy and didn't want to hear her band again.

As he worked, Joe grew more and more fascinated. Fenton Hardy was a first-rate private investigator, and his files were full of valuable reports on crime syndicates, felons, pending court cases, and state statutes. Joe knew that such information could make—or break—a serious investigation.

Joe had both elbows resting on the desktop and was just finishing sorting through a stack of memos sent on by some of his father's government agency contacts. After pausing to take a sip from his mug of cocoa, Joe started on another stack of the memos.

The rain was hitting hard at the windows of the house—Joe could hear it even in the basement office. Every once in a while, the night wind rattled tree branches, which caught and scratched against the walls.

Hanging around this basement is more interesting, Joe told himself, than a trip to the Cellar.

One of the many confidential memos in this stack caught his attention. It was from the Federal Crime Bureau and concerned a man named Curt Branders. He was alleged to be an international hit man, specializing in assassinations of high-level government and industrial figures around the world. One of the sentences on his background form caught Joe's eye. It was a town name—Kirkland, which was only ten miles from Bayport. Kirkland was Branders's hometown. He still had a younger brother, Kevin Branders, living there.

Kevin Branders? Joe leaned back in his father's swivel chair, ignoring the squeaking sound it made. I met him at a party once, I think. He frowned at the memory. Yeah, a thin, blond guy—nasty, not very likable.

Then he shrugged. Having an older brother who was a fugitive international killer would make anybody nasty.

Even having an easygoing older brother like Frank could be a pain sometimes.

Joe hunched his shoulders slightly, rereading the memo about Curt Branders. Nodding to himself, he slipped it into the proper manila folder and continued on with the stack.

The phone rang.

Joe grabbed the receiver. "Hello?"

"Joe Hardy?"

"Speaking."

"This is Officer Hunsberger of the Highway Patrol. I'm at the emergency room of the Bayport Hospital—"

"What's wrong?" asked Joe, swallowing hard.

"I didn't mean to upset you, Joe. I don't think it's anything serious," said the patrolman. "But your brother and Callie Shaw had a slight . . . um . . . accident."

"But they're okay?"

"Frank is fine, but Callie has a mild concussion. Your brother's in the emergency room with her now, so he asked me to call you."

"I remember you now. You're a friend of

11

his, right?" Joe said. "Did I hear you wrong or do you suspect this wasn't really an accident?"

"If it had been only Frank and Callie's car, we'd probably have written it off as an accident," answered Hunsberger. "But there were a lot of others. Frank will explain."

"I'm on my way." Joe charged out into the slashing rain, hopped into the boys' van, and headed for the hospital.

After a short drive he was rushing through the emergency room entrance.

"Hey, kid," warned the hospital security guard, "slow down. We've got enough banged-up kids around here tonight."

"Sorry." Joe slowed his pace slightly as he headed for the reception desk.

There were three kids that he knew sitting on uncomfortable red molded-plastic chairs. One girl had a large bandage across half her pale forehead. There were lots of other kids he didn't know—an overflow crowd, it looked like.

The white door to the emergency room swung open and Frank stepped through it. "I'm not hurt, Joe," he said, coming up to his brother.

Joe eyed him up and down. "You sure? You're pretty muddy."

"Haven't had time to clean up."

"What about Callie—how serious is it?"

"Her seat belt came loose, and she hit her

head against the dashboard." Frank put his hand on Joe's shoulder, led him over to a quiet corner. "The doctor—a Dr. Emerson, a resident—wants to keep her overnight. Her folks are on their way over. They want to see how she is and talk to the doc."

"Who was driving?"

"I was, but it wasn't an accident."

"Yeah, that's what your friend Patrolman Hunsberger told me. But he didn't go into details."

Frank made a sweeping gesture with his hand. "There have been seven other car accidents tonight so far."

"Too many to be a coincidence."

"Exactly," Frank said in a level, angry voice. "And when I looked at Callie's tire that had gone flat, I found a small piece of plywood with nails hammered into it caught in the treads. Ride on that long enough, and any tire will go. I'm betting all the other cars had these little presents, too."

Snapping his fingers, Joe said, "The pranksters. What do you think?"

"It's got to be."

"Where do you figure the setup was done? At the Cellar?"

"Looks like it," Frank replied. "And that isn't the only practical joke that was played tonight."

"They've sure been busy for a rainy night. You do think it's more than one person, don't you?"

Frank nodded and paused to look at the door to the street before filling his brother in about the sneezing powder at the club. "But that stuff," he concluded, "was mild compared to the tire business. Sabotaged tires and slippery roads—it's just lucky nobody got seriously hurt so far."

"Are you expecting Callie's folks right away? You keep eyeing the door."

"I know." Frank shrugged. "Yes, I am expecting them, but I was also wondering if Biff Hooper and his date had any trouble tonight."

"Was Biff at the Cellar?"

"Yeah. He was with a nice-looking girl. I didn't know her. I think they left before we did."

"Maybe they left the parking lot before this tire prank went down."

"Could be. I didn't see them go."

Joe looked at his brother, and a muscle twitched in his jaw. "We'll have to take a serious look into these pranks now, Frank. They're not funny anymore. You could have gotten killed—and so could Callie."

Frank Hardy nodded grimly. "We've got to find the sickos behind this and really nail them."

Chapter

3

THE RAIN WAS even heavier the next day. Thunder rumbled and crashed in the hills above Bayport, making it impossible to sleep late. So Frank and Joe were up early—if not bright—to check out the Cellar's parking lot.

Seen in the wan daylight, without the sparkle of the Cellar's lights, the old mill building looked as if it had been lifted out of a black-and-white horror movie. It was a narrow brick building, covered with soot, most of its windows covered over with metal shutters. Only on the ground floor had anything been done to spiff the place up.

"I've heard that if the club really makes it, they'll be turning the rest of the building into

15

condominiums." Joe stifled a yawn as he stared up at the mill. "So tell me, what are we supposed to be looking for?"

Frank shrugged, halting their van in the middle of the parking area. The lot had been bulldozed flat and covered with gravel by the club owners. Weeds and scraggly prickle-bushes still clung tenaciously to the edges of the lot. And where car wheels had scuffed away the gravel, huge puddles had formed from the rain.

"I hope they've got valet parking," Joe said.

Frank didn't answer. He just pulled up the hood on his windbreaker, stepped out of the van, and started searching the ground for any bit of evidence.

He looked for about an hour, until his jacket was soaked and his jeans were heavy with rain. Joe had quickly decided it was hopeless—the gravel wouldn't hold any tire- or footprints, and anyway, it was all torn up by the departing cars. He'd checked in the quieter corners, the ones shaded by the bushes, but hadn't found anything remotely resembling a clue.

"No rare European cigarette butts—not even a gum wrapper," he'd reported to Frank. "I'm getting back in the van before I'm washed away."

But Frank had stubbornly gone on searching, and Joe let him. He could remember lots of times that Frank had backed him up, even when he'd tried some pretty stupid stunts. Sometimes they paid off.

At last, though, Frank had shrugged his shoulders and slid back into the van. "I had hopes of finding another of those little boards with nails the pranksters used last night. The police have the one from Callie's car. I thought maybe if we had one, we could find something."

"Well, either they all stuck to the tires, or the cops searched last night—" Joe began.

"Or whoever left the blasted things cleaned up after themselves before the cops arrived."

Frank was about to say more when a bright red four-wheel-drive truck came roaring into the lot. When the driver saw them, he moved his truck so it blocked the exit to the parking lot.

The man who leaned out the window of the truck was big and beefy—with "bouncer" written all over him.

"Hey, champ," he yelled, "this is private property. We had enough trouble last night without jerks coming around to gawk." His face hardened with suspicion. "Or maybe you're the jokers who *caused* the trouble."

"If you want to check us out, come over and check us out," Frank said.

The bouncer glared at Frank, then glanced up at the rain. At last he let the truck coast

17

away from the exit. "Nah. Just get out of here."

They did.

The early visiting hours had started at Bayport Hospital, and when they arrived there, the Hardys got good news—Callie's folks would be taking her home that afternoon. The Hardys headed for the mall—and Mr. Pizza. Their pal Tony Prito was the manager there and an excellent source of information.

As they came in, he was standing behind the counter, demonstrating his famous "toss the dough in the air" technique.

"Tony, any hot gossip gets discussed among the kids here—and you hear it," Frank said.

Tony shrugged, still deftly twirling the pizza dough. "I suppose so," he admitted.

"So what's the scoop on this gang of jokers?" Joe asked.

"Everybody has been talking about them," Tony said. "You wouldn't believe some of the stories I've been hearing."

"Try us," Frank said.

"I'll just give you the best—I caught a couple of kids saying it's some kind of cult. They have secret meetings around bonfires in the woods, with everyone wearing robes."

"That sounds real secret," Joe said sarcastically, shaking his head. "I mean, who'd notice a bunch of people in robes dancing around a fire?"

Frank grinned. "I think somebody's been renting too many scary movies from the video store. Isn't there one about a cult that wears hoods?"

Joe and Tony both broke into laughter. "I'll have to remember that, the next time I hear the kids talking," Tony said.

"But has anybody linked the pranks with any of the usual gangs, or any one group of kids?" Frank asked.

Tony shook his head. "Nobody from around town is bragging," he said.

"How about kids from outside of town?" Joe asked.

"No. I'd remember that. Sorry, guys."

"Well, you can make up for it," Joe said. "Sell us a couple of slices."

They spent the rest of the afternoon talking to friends, trying to get some kind of handle on the prank gang. They got nowhere. Phil Cohen hadn't heard a word, while Chet Morton told them Tony's cult story all over again.

When evening came, it was still raining, and they hadn't really gotten anywhere.

Joe walked into the living room with a jacket in one hand and a folder from the basement tucked under his arm. He tossed the file on the coffee table next to a bowl of fresh flowers.

Frank, dressed to go out, was carrying an extension phone and talking into it as he paced a small circle near the fireplace. "Well, if the doctor doesn't think you ought to go out," he was saying, "then you'd better not."

Joe dropped onto the sofa, tapping his leg with impatience.

"Well, naturally we could use your help on this investigation, Callie," continued Frank.

Joe poked his tongue into his cheek, gazed up at the ceiling as though he were seeing it for the first time.

"Trust me," Frank said into the phone while scowling at his brother. "I'll fill you in on anything we dig up. Sure, of course, I'm sorry you have to stay home and rest up tonight. But, Callie, that's better than staying in the hospital another day, isn't it?"

Joe discovered a fleck of apple skin caught between two of his front teeth and began digging for it with the nail of his little finger.

"I miss you, of course. Right. Me, too. Yes, he is. Uh-huh, sitting right here and gawking at me in his usual dimwit way. I'll tell him. Good night, Callie." Frank hung up and gave his brother a look. "Remind me to explain 'invasion of privacy' to you someday, Joe."

"How's she doing?"

"Better. But her doctor wants her to take it easy for a couple more days."

"What'd she tell you to tell me?"

"It's best you don't know," Frank assured him. "You ready to go?"

Nodding, Joe tapped the folder. "I went over all the newspaper clippings we've compiled on these pranks one more time," he told his brother. "Each time one is pulled off, it gets a little more serious."

"Right. The first one was just somebody spray-painting some dumb, smutty grafitti on the side of the school gym. Now, though, they've worked up to causing car crashes."

"Some of the pranks obviously took a few people to pull off. Last Thursday night there were two separate pranks—the smashed shop windows on Marcus Street and the eggs thrown at the Grange Hall across town. They took place at about the same time."

Frank said, "Maybe we can find out something by talking to the people out at the Cellar," he said. "It gives us a place to start. If one of the staff or customers noticed anyone or anything in the parking lot, we'd finally have a lead."

Joe stared at his brother. "So you want to go back to the place where you have friendly chats with big, husky bouncers?"

Frank held up his forefinger. "Merely one,"

he answered. "And you're obviously forgetting how diplomatic and persuasive I can be."

"Right, I was forgetting." Joe stood up. "Okay, let's get going—"

"Don't tell me you two boys are actually thinking of going out in this storm?" Their aunt Gertrude was frowning at them from the doorway as she took off her apron.

"It's just a light drizzle, Aunt Gertrude," said Joe, smiling.

Lightning crackled just then and thunder rattled the windows. Joe sighed.

"No, it's a bad storm. You'll have another accident, for certain."

"That wasn't an accident, Aunt Gertrude," Frank reminded her. "Somebody deliberately fouled up Callie's tire."

"And look where the poor girl ended up—in the hospital."

"She's home now, and fine," he said.

"And didn't I hear both you boys sneezing just before dinner?"

Joe laughed. "We were trying out some different kinds of sneezing powder, Aunt Gertrude."

"It sounded like colds coming on to me. Of all the colds you can suffer from, there's none worse than a summer cold. So my advice would be to forget—"

The phone began ringing. "Maybe it's Biff,"

said Frank, picking up the receiver. "I've been trying to get in touch with him all day. Hello?"

The caller spoke in a muffled, anxious whisper. "Get over to the old Hickerson Mansion. Right now!"

"Who is this?" Frank said.

The voice cut him off. "Just show up there. The prank tonight is going to be worse—much worse!"

Chapter
4

JOE DROVE THE VAN up the road along the cliffs over Barmet Bay. "We took a field trip to the Hickerson Mansion years ago," he said, watching the headlights cut two short swatches in the rain and fog. "But I don't remember much about the place."

"Elias Hickerson was a big wheel around Bayport about a hundred and fifty years ago," Frank said. "He was a rich merchant. They say he built his mansion up here so he'd be the first to see his ships come into the harbor. Anyway, his family left the house to the town. It's full of Victorian furniture and is being kept in trust as sort of a museum."

Joe rolled his eyes. "Sounds real exciting."

"It's history," Frank said. "I just hope I don't mean that literally."

Lightning suddenly lit up the whole road, turning the cliffsides a brief, intense electric blue. Thunder slammed and rumbled, the few stunted trees shook.

"You know," Frank went on, "there was something familiar about that voice. I have this feeling I heard it recently."

"It was a girl, you thought, trying to disguise her voice."

Frank nodded. "I'm pretty sure it was."

"The voice may have belonged to someone I met last night even," Frank said, thinking about it. "All I know is that I can't seem to identify it. I hope it'll come to me."

"The man with the computer brain," Joe murmured mockingly.

They drove higher, onto the top of the cliffs. The rain kept hitting hard at the van, and the wind gave it a powerful shove every now and then.

"Whoever she was," said Frank, "she warned that the prank was going to be rough tonight."

"They've gone beyond pranks and into vandalism."

Frank shook his head. "I've got a very bad feeling about this whole business."

After a moment Joe said, "You know, being

summoned to this old mansion by a mystery woman might be a prank itself. I mean, what if these jokers want to lure us out here to put something over on us—or worse?"

"That's a possibility." Frank nodded grimly. "But we have to check it out. We'll just have to be very careful."

"There's the mansion, coming up on that knoll to our right."

"We'll drive on by, then park in that patch of trees up ahead."

"Good idea. I—Frank, look!"

"What?"

"Didn't you see it? The beam of a flashlight inside the place as we drove by."

Carefully Frank and Joe worked their way down along the slippery cliff walk that led to the rear of the three-story wooden mansion.

Frank held an unlit flashlight in his right hand, swinging it at his side. He suddenly stopped, wrestling with a thornbush beside the path to get his jacket sleeve loose.

Coming up from behind, Joe touched his brother's shoulder. "There's definitely somebody in there," he whispered.

"Right—I saw the flashlight shining around in there, too. It seems to be near the front rooms of the place."

"This doesn't look like a trap then, does it?

I mean, they wouldn't be this obvious if they were all in there waiting to jump us with baseball bats.''

"We'll be careful, anyway.''

There was a narrow white gravel parking lot at the rear of the Hickerson Mansion. The Hardys stopped beside the safety fence and watched the big white house.

The wind spun the rusted weathervane up on its cupola perch. The faded brown shutters creaked, the back door was open and flapping.

"Now we know how they got in,'' said Frank. "Shall we follow?'' After tapping Joe on the arm, he wiped the rain from his face and started running for the wooden steps to the historic mansion.

Joe trailed just behind him.

They went up the stairs single file, Frank first. He pointed up at the cut wires above the doorway. "That's where they took care of the alarm.''

Frank stepped across the threshold, then stopped dead.

Lightning flashed, and for a few seconds he could see a length of carpeted corridor in the crackling light. The hallway was empty, but there were two sets of muddy footprints on the faded carpeting and running through the doorway at the far end.

Clicking on his flash, Frank said, "Come on,

28

they must be somewhere up at the front of the house."

On both sides of the hallway stood a row of shoulder-high pedestals. Each of them held a marble bust of one of the Hickerson clan.

Making his way along the shadowy corridor in the wake of his brother, Joe chanced to bump against one of the wooden pedestals. The heavy bust of a gentleman with substantial whiskers began to teeter.

"Oops," said Joe quietly, making a grab for the swaying pedestal.

He caught it, but the marble bust went sliding off the top. It did a wobbly somersault, then fell to the floor to crash into three pieces.

Frank swung his flashlight back at Joe. "Want to bet they heard that?" he whispered, but his tone of voice showed that he didn't think there was any need for secrecy—now.

"Sorry. I didn't see him."

From the front of the mansion came the sounds of feet running and then of a door slamming.

"They're taking off." Frank charged for the doorway that led to the front.

"Catch you later, sir," Joe told the fallen bust and took off after Frank.

Frank reached the heavy oak sliding doors, slid them open, and dived into the next room.

Joe followed him but stopped short just inside the room, next to his brother.

The room they'd burst into was on fire.

The crackling flames were a glaring orange. They were climbing up the brittle old curtains that were hanging at the windows across the front of the parlor.

Paintings had been removed from walls and dumped on top of the sofa. Then the whole pile had been doused with gasoline—the dirt-smeared red can still lay on the floor—and set on fire. Over near the small fireplace, three cane-bottomed chairs had been smashed up and were blazing away, too.

Joe spotted a fire extinguisher, sprinted across the room and grabbed it off its peg. He turned the thing upside-down and started spraying chemicals on the blazing curtains. "If these walls catch fire, the whole place will go up."

"I saw another extinguisher back in the hall." Frank went running back for it.

The flames leapt from the burning sofa and started eating at the dry, dusty drapes. Smoke spiraled up until the air of the room was visible as black soot.

Frank put the second fire extinguisher to work on the pile of smashed chairs.

In the distance outside, they could hear sirens steadily growing louder.

Joe had succeeded in pulling the curtains down and dousing them. Wiping the perspiration from his forehead, he started on the burning sofa. The only sound in the room was the rasp of harsh breathing, cut by hacking coughs as the smoke did its best to choke the two brothers.

"How're you doing?" Frank called hoarsely after a moment. He had the pile of broken furniture under control, and the last of the flames had just been smothered.

"I got this mess put out. You?"

"This one's out, too."

"Good thing we got here in time," said Joe, setting the extinguisher on the floor.

Frank picked up the flashlight he'd put aside. He surveyed the room. The walls around the windows were black, and much of the paint and wallpaper had burned away. There were black gouges in the hardwood floors, a large charred hole in the rug, and splotches of soot everywhere. A bitter, acrid smell hung over all the room.

The shrieking of the sirens flared up once right outside the house, then died.

"If we hadn't gotten that phone call, this whole place would've been just so much charcoal," said Joe, still wiping his face.

"Let's take a look around," suggested

Frank, "and see if our phantom arsonists left any other clues besides that gas can."

"If I were you, boys," said a deep, unfriendly voice from the dark doorway, "I wouldn't move so much as an inch."

They turned to see the gleam of a pistol barrel pointed at them.

"Nope," the voice went on. "What I'd do is just raise my hands, real slow and easy."

Chapter

5

JOE RAISED HIS HANDS, but he laughed while he did it. "You've got the wrong firebugs, Officer Riley."

"Joe Hardy?" A large flashlight clicked on.

"And me, Con," said Frank.

The heavyset policeman entered the room, putting away his gun. "Okay, you don't have to keep your hands up, boys," Officer Con Riley said. "But I would like to know what you're doing here."

Three uniformed firefighters came trudging into the parlor.

"We've already put the fire out," said Joe hopefully.

"Let us decide that, kid."

Con Riley gestured toward a door that led to the front porch. "We'll talk out there," he said.

There was a broad wooden roof over the wide porch, and the rain was drumming down on it relentlessly.

Riley took his cap off, running thick fingers through his hair. "This was obviously arson," he said. "So you can start off by telling me just what you know about it."

"Not as much as we'd like." Joe glanced over at the fire engines and police car.

Frank said, "We got a phone call, Con."

"Who from?"

"I'm not sure. The person didn't identify— herself."

"But it was a girl."

"I'd guess it was," said Frank. "All she said was that there was going to be trouble here at the Hickerson Mansion. She wanted Joe and me to get over here right away."

"Why did she call you?"

Joe said, "Well, people—some people anyway—think of us as being able to handle trouble of this sort."

"Yeah? Me, if I was expecting a fire—I'd phone the fire department."

"I have a theory as to why she couldn't do that," offered Frank.

"Theories I don't need just now," said

Riley. "What I'd like is the names of the people who tried to burn this place down."

"I'm afraid we can't help you much," said Frank. "We don't even know who telephoned us."

Joe added, "And we didn't get a look at them after we got here."

"But somebody was in the house when you two arrived?"

"We heard noises from the front," replied Frank. "See, we'd come in the back way, where they'd disabled the alarm. You might mention to whoever takes care of this place that they'll need a much more sophisticated security system than the one they've got. Otherwise—"

"Yeah, I'll whip off a memo to them first thing in the morning," the impatient policeman cut him off. "So, you didn't see anyone. Did you hear anything?"

"Running feet," said Joe, shaking his head. "That's all."

"How many kids would you say?"

"Two," said Frank. "But we can't be sure they were kids, Con. Every case of vandalism that happens around here isn't necessarily pulled by some kid."

Riley scowled at each of them in turn. "In the past month we've had more vandalism in Bayport than we get in a whole year," he told them. "Now, maybe a little old lady sprayed that obscene graffiti on the side of the school, and it's possible a middle-aged banker dumped powder in the Cellar's air conditioners. But somehow, I'm betting it was kids. And when we finally nab them, don't be surprised if the perpetrators turn out to be some kids you know."

"Did you investigate what happened at the Cellar last night?"

"That I did, Frank."

"And?"

"We' haven't tied it on anyone yet," Con said. "Do you figure this fire was set by the same bunch?"

"Seems like a good possibility," said Joe.

Frank asked, "Would you mind, Con, if we took a look around inside—after the fire department is through?"

"As a matter of fact, I would. What I want you boys to do now is go home," he said, nodding toward the street. "Have some cookies and hot cocoa and go to bed."

"But if we could—"

"Nope, I'm handling this investigation."

Frank gave a resigned shrug. "It might be better if we cooperated."

"That's just what I'm saying—so why don't you guys cooperate with me?" he said. "If you get any more loony phone calls, get in touch with me."

"But—" Joe tried again.

"Look, the chief is biting our heads off because a bunch of kids is making the force look stupid." Con Riley's face showed annoyance. "I'll try to make it really simple for you." Con jerked his thumb, pointing off the porch and into the darkness outside. "Do you understand?"

Joe said, "Sure, we get you, Con." He started down the steps.

"Listen," said the police officer, "I do appreciate the way you put out the fire. Okay?"

"Sure, okay." Frank headed off into the rain.

Hands deep in his pants pockets, shoulders hunched, Joe trudged along the rocky pathway back toward their car. "Unsung," he muttered.

"What?" asked his brother.

"I feel like an unsung hero," complained Joe. "A prophet without honor."

"Con Riley is a pal, but he's also a police officer," Frank pointed out. "He takes a very traditional approach to detective work—especially when Chief Collig is breathing down his neck. You can't let it get you down."

Joe said, "But even he suspects that all those pranks are the work of the same bunch."

"He asked what we thought, he didn't say he accepted our theory."

"Were you serious when you suggested this might not be the work of kids?"

"We really don't know who's doing any of it. I suppose when you look at the kinds of pranks and the places they've happened, it does look like younger people are behind it all." Frank frowned. "But I get pretty tired of hearing adults automatically assume that kids are always responsible for certain kinds of trouble."

The rain was slipping down Joe's neck in spite of his turned-up collar. "I'll tell you something that annoyed me."

"Go ahead."

"I had been thinking how good a cup of hot chocolate and some of Aunt Gertrude's cookies would be," said Joe. "But no way can I have them now—*after* Con told me to."

Frank laughed, then said, "We can probably take a look around the Hickerson place at some time tomorrow."

"The same way we saw the parking lot—after it had been gone over. It may be too late."

"Well, it's the best we can do."

They finally reached the scraggly woods, and the road where their van was parked.

"If I hadn't been so clumsy and knocked

over that statue, we might—hey, look!'' Joe reached out, snatching something off a thorny bush at the side of the road.

"It's somebody's scarf." He spread out the square of expensive-looking paisley silk. Something fluttered from the folds.

Frank caught a cream-colored envelope in midair before it touched the ground. "This stuff wasn't here when we went in."

"You sure, Frank?"

"I am, yeah. I caught my sleeve on this same bush on the way in."

Tucking the envelope inside his jacket, Frank said, "Let's get in the van and take a look at it."

"So we found a couple of clues after all," said Joe, opening the door on his side, "in spite of Con Riley."

"We found *something*," said Frank, getting in, "that somebody wanted us to find."

Back home, Frank leaned over his work-table, using a pair of tweezers to slip a sheet of typed paper out of the envelope they'd found. "No fingerprints," he said, checking out both the paper and envelope with a high-powered magnifying glass. "Except for mine."

Joe sat straddling a straight chair, the pale green-and-gold scarf dangling from his left hand. "Okay, that means the people who tried to torch the mansion were wearing gloves," he said. "Since it's obvious that this scarf and the envelope were tossed near our van while they were making their getaway."

Nodding, Frank perched on a stool. "I'd say it's a good chance that the girl who phoned the warning is the one who left this for us."

"She probably left it on the sly, since she didn't want whoever she was with to know about it." Joe shook his head. "What bugs me is why she's doing this—does she want to get caught?"

"She wants to put a stop to this group." Frank picked up the typed message again, "This gang of vandals who call themselves the Circle."

Joe stood up, dropping the scarf on the chair, and went around to his brother's side of the table. "This must be their insignia," he said, picking up the envelope and examining its face. "A circle with a twelve in the middle, printed in waterproof crimson marker."

"That must have something to do with these guys—the Circle of twelve, Ring of twelve, or some such nonsense." Frank read the message aloud again. " 'Team: Your challenge is to enter the Hickerson Mansion unseen no later than ten tonight. You will then set a fire in the front parlor. If you fail to meet the challenge, you shall be expelled from the Circle.' "

"These people in the Circle must really want to be members," said Joe. "Even our mystery girl didn't want to go, but she went out and helped set that fire."

"Groups can be like that. People will do nasty things rather than go against the crowd."

Joe tapped the tabletop with the envelope. "Okay, we can assume the girl who phoned us is in this Circle," he said. "But she doesn't like what they've been doing lately."

"I guess she sees how the pranks are getting more and more serious. So she wants to do something."

"For some reason, though, she just can't quit."

Folding up the note, Frank set it aside. "So that's where we come in," he said. "She wants us to discover what this Circle is and where it's located. Then we bust it up and save her from harming anyone without any of her Circle members blaming her."

"I don't know," said Joe. "It seems like she's taking the long way around. She could just call the police."

"Maybe she feels she'll be arrested if she does. Right now, Joe, all we can do is speculate as to what her motives are."

"Right, what we need are facts." He tossed the envelope on the table, walked back to his chair. "This scarf has a label from a boutique

41

over in Kirkland. It's a place called Chez Maurice—very exclusive and expensive, I hear. I'll go over tomorrow and see if I can find out who bought it."

Frank said, "This paper is expensive—it even has a watermark in it. That's what I'll track down."

"My job sounds like more fun."

"Depends on your outlook."

Joe wound the paisley scarf around his fist and stared at the phone. "Of course, if we're lucky, she may phone us again with more information."

"You didn't hear her over the phone," Frank said. "She sounded scared. And the more I think about it, the less I believe she was worried about the Hickerson Mansion."

Frank's face was grim as he shook his head. "I wish we knew more about this Circle—and what they do to people who talk."

42

Chapter

6

JOE'S HOPE TURNED OUT to be premature. They weren't lucky—the phone didn't ring all night.

However, the rain had finally ended early the next morning. By midday the sky was a clear pale blue over the water at the town of Kirkland. Joe was sitting on a white bench in the small park by the river, eating a hot dog he'd bought from a shop called Best Wurst.

Three ducks came waddling up from the river and immediately fell to squabbling over the remains of somebody's hot-dog roll.

Grinning, Joe wiped his hands on his paper napkin, stood up, tossed the napkin in a bright green trash barrel, and crossed to the main street of the town.

Halfway down the block, he stopped in front of the store he was looking for. The clothing boutique was in an old, narrow building. Its front window was large enough for only a single female mannequin, headless and painted stark white, wearing a candy-striped dress.

After studying his reflection, Joe decided he looked right for the part he was going to play. Taking a deep breath, he went on inside.

At the other end of the shop a plump woman of about forty stood behind a small glass counter. Since Joe didn't resemble the usual customer of Chez Maurice, she started to frown.

"Excuse me, ma'am," he said, smiling at the woman in a hopeful manner, "I sure hope you can help me."

"That depends, young man, on what you have in mind." Her frown deepened as he approached her.

Joe's smile got a little shy now. "Well, I think I've fallen in love."

She took a sudden step back. "And what can that possibly have to do with Chez Maurice?"

Resting one elbow on the counter, Joe said, "You look like the sort of person who's—well, romantic at heart."

"And if I am?"

"You see, I want to buy the girl I love an expensive present from your store," he began timidly. "My father gives me an allowance of considerable size."

The frown began to fade. "Ah, yes, I see, young man. You wish some advice in selecting the proper gift, is that it?"

"That's exactly right," Joe admitted. "But first, ma'am, I'm going to have to find out the girl's name."

"Beg pardon?"

Very carefully, Joe drew the paisley scarf out of his trouser pocket. "I guess maybe you'll think I'm sort of crazy," he began. "And, believe me, I don't often do things like this. Anyway, I was at a dance last night, at the Bayport Country Club."

"A very—nice—place. Many of our customers belong."

Joe spread out the scarf he'd found near the Hickerson Mansion the night before. "At the dance I saw this absolutely terrific girl. It took me quite a while to work up the nerve, but I finally asked her to dance."

"You don't strike me as someone who's especially shy."

"Not usually, perhaps," Joe said. "But when I met this girl—well, I don't know. I could hardly say two words to her. Then things became a bit complicated. I don't know how to explain—she left before I could get her name. All that she left behind was—well, it was this scarf."

"That's a charming story," said the clerk, smiling. "And I don't know if it's struck you, but your story is quite close to that of Cinderella."

"Why, no," said Joe, blinking, "that hadn't occurred to me, ma'am. Now that you mention it, though, I do see some similarities." He held up the scarf. "I noticed the label here—since she bought this at Chez Maurice, I'm really hoping you'll have some record of who she is."

The woman took the scarf from him, then examined the distinctive Chez Maurice label. "Yes, it is one of ours," she said, spreading the silken square out on the counter. "Ordinarily, we don't give out the names of our customers, but . . ."

"It would mean so much to me."

"Very well, let me find our record books from about three months ago. We sold out our supply of these rather quickly and weren't able to order more." Crossing to a small antique desk, she slid open a drawer and lifted out a thick leather-bound volume. "There are some shops that use computers, but Chez Maurice's doesn't believe in them."

46

Joe came over to the desk. "I hope you can help me find her."

"Well, let's see now." She started flipping through the pages. "Here's one—and another—two more." She began writing names in pencil on a sheet of lavender paper. "Here's one—and another. That's the lot, I believe." She closed the record book, returned it to the drawer. Then she brought the list up close to her face. "How old is she?"

"Um?"

"The young lady—how old is she?"

"Oh, she's—about my age."

The plump clerk crossed off two of the names. "I assumed as much," she told him. "That leaves four. I happen to know two of these young girls personally. What color hair does your girl have?"

"Color hair?"

"Yes."

Joe looked up at the pale green ceiling. "Well, actually, ma'am, it's a shade I find difficult to describe," he said finally. "The truth is, last night at the club almost feels like a dream. I—I can't exactly recall every detail. All I remember is gazing into her sparkling eyes. . . ."

The saleswoman sighed and handed Joe the list. "You'll no doubt find she's one of these four. But, whatever you do, young man, don't mention that Chez Maurice helped your little romantic quest in any way."

"No, certainly not. I—Aha!"

"How's that?"

"Nothing." He folded the slip and dropped it in his shirt pocket. "As soon as I locate her, I'll be rushing right back here to buy her a present."

Joe hurried out of the shop, went back across the street, and sat on the white bench. He'd just recognized the third name on the list—Jeanne Sinclair. She lived here in Kirkland, had very wealthy parents, and went to an exclusive private school. Over the last couple of months, Joe had met her several times. And each time he'd met her, she'd been with Biff Hooper.

Joe was betting Jeanne was the one who'd left the scarf and envelope for them to find. And that meant she was the girl who'd phoned the warning last night.

He walked over to an outdoor phone stand, took out the local directory, and looked up the Sinclair address.

"Now to drop in on Jeanne," he said to himself as he started for his van, "and ask her if she's lost a scarf recently."

* * *

A high stone wall surrounded the huge Sinclair estate. But as Joe drove up, he saw that the wrought-iron gate was open.

Joe slowed as he turned onto the curving driveway that circled through what had to be an acre of perfectly manicured lawn.

The house was a white colonial mansion with a five-car garage next to it. A small gray van with *Goodhill Antiques* lettered on its side was parked in front of the row of garages. All the doors were closed, but the front door of the house was wide open.

Something isn't right here, Joe thought. He parked his car in the drive, jumped out, and ran to the red-brick front steps.

Very slowly and quietly he climbed the steps to the gaping doorway. He halted for a second at the threshold, straining his ears.

Not a sound came from inside the big house.

Joe stepped into a long hallway that stretched the length of the house. At the far end, a high, wide window threw a long rectangle of bright afternoon sunlight onto the floor.

The edge of it just touched the body on the floral carpet.

It was a bald man dressed in black, probably the Sinclair butler. He lay facedown thirty feet from Joe and the doorway. His left arm was twisted under him, and there was a smear of blood across the hairless top of his head.

Joe thought he saw the man stir, moving his head slightly. So, he's not dead, Joe thought. But he sure needs help.

He rushed inside to aid the injured man— and that was his mistake.

Before he'd taken five steps, someone stepped out from behind the door. Joe's only hint of danger was a slight creak in the floorboards behind him. Then came a blinding clout to the back of his head. A second blow, even harder than the first, spread fire across his temple.

Joe managed to turn on wobbly legs. The whole world became gray, then went dazzlingly bright. He only saw his attacker in silhouette, a dark shadow raising an object to strike again.

Joe had to stop this guy, fight back, beat him off. But his arms and legs would only move in slow motion. Either that, or this guy moved incredibly fast. Before Joe could even raise his fists, he was blackjacked once again.

That was it. His arms dropped, and his legs lost it altogether. Joe fell to his knees. He swayed there, trying to get up again, but his body betrayed him. His muscles wouldn't obey, and his head pounded.

He managed one wild lurch, but it didn't bring him to his feet. Instead, thrown off balance, his dazed body merely toppled to the floor.

Strangely enough, as he fell, his vision became clear for a moment. He saw the broad floral pattern of the carpet clearly as it came rushing up at him.

Joe hit the floor with a thump—and then there weren't any flowers, there wasn't any floor.

There was absolutely nothing.

THE HARDY BOYS CASEFILES

Chapter
7

FRANK SAT, STARING down at the faded Persian carpet. Or rather, he kept a wary eye on the calico cat stalking across it.

The problem was, this cat wasn't built for stalking. Her well-padded stomach brushed the floor as she moved forward, and she waddled rather than slunk toward his ankle. The cat darted forward—to rub against his leg, making a rattling, wheezing noise.

"Mehitabel," said the heavyset, gray-bearded man across the study, glancing up from his cluttered desk. "Don't go annoying Frank."

The cat ignored him.

"She's not annoying me, Professor Marschall," Frank assured him, trying to shift his leg away from the huge cat. Wherever he moved it, the cat followed with its rattling purr.

The professor was holding the sheet of cream-colored paper up to the light from a narrow, leaded, stained-glass window. "This is a fascinating watermark," he said.

"Can you identify it, sir?"

Marschall chuckled, causing his whiskers to waggle. "My job at the university is authenticating old manuscripts. Certainly, this paper is less than three hundred years old. But did you doubt I could identify it, Frank?"

"No, sir, that's why I brought it to you."

Professor Marschall smoothed the sheet out on a clear patch of desktop. Then he stared at it through a large magnifying glass. "Quite interesting, yes." Leaning back in his chair, he shut his eyes.

The elderly professor was a friend of Fenton Hardy's and had known Frank and Joe since they were small. When he was a little kid, Frank had thought the professor knew everything. Even today, he was sure of one thing— Professor Marschall knew more about paper than anyone else.

The big cat climbed up Frank's leg, jumped briefly into his lap, climbed across his chest, and sat on his shoulder.

Professor Marschall opened his eyes. "You

shouldn't let Mehitabel take advantage of you, Frank," he advised. "Next thing you know, she'll be trying to sit on your head—and she's too old for that."

"Too heavy, too," Frank muttered under his breath.

The professor returned his attention to the sheet of paper that Frank and Joe had found near the Hickerson Mansion the night before.

Frank gave the cat a couple of pushes. She dug her claws into his shoulder. He pushed a bit harder.

Suddenly the fat cat fell off him, plummeting down to hit the rug with a furry thump.

"Oh, no! I didn't mean to—"

"She's not hurt. It's merely one of her stunts."

The cat rolled over on its back, thrust all four paws upward, and began snoring.

Professor Marschall grunted once, pushed away from the desk, and rolled back in his chair to a bookshelf. He tugged out a fat volume, brought the title up close to his face, shook his head, and jabbed the book back in place.

Then he selected another book, grunted in triumph as he looked at the title, and brought it back to his desk. Brushing a stack of notes to the floor, he set the book down and opened it. "This is perhaps the most exhaustive book on paper samples," he said, leafing through pages. "It ought to be. I assembled it myself."

Professor Marschall sucked his breath in through his teeth. "Yes, of course. I thought as much."

Frank got up, avoided stepping on the sleeping cat, and went over to the desk. "Will this really tell you where this paper comes from?"

The professor pointed to a sample of paper in the book. "You'll notice that this has the same exact watermark. Fortunately for you, it's a unique one—the letters *E* and *B* entwined with a leaping stag."

Frank attempted to read the notes scrawled under the sample—not easy, given the professor's spidery, sloppy handwriting. "Buchwilder?"

"Bushmiller." He returned Frank's sheet of paper to him. "This stationery was made exclusively for the Bushmiller Academy here in Bayport."

"You mean that old ruin up on Woodland Lane?"

"It was not, much like myself, always a ruin, Frank, my boy. Bushmiller Academy was once a very fine private school—a sort of junior military academy." He grinned. "I believe it made most of its money handling young men who were a bit too devilish for a regular school situation."

"But Bushmiller Academy hasn't been in operation for years."

"Thirty-five years, to be exact," answered the professor. "A long and tangled family feud has kept the place empty all this time, and for at least the past ten there hasn't even been a watchman."

"But there could still be a supply of this particular paper there?"

Professor Marschall ran a thoughtful hand over his gray beard. "Perhaps," he finally said. "This is an excellent grade of paper. It could last that long, especially if it was in a protected environment—say, locked in a desk."

Frank stared down at the paper sample on the desk. "Interesting. But it doesn't look like it's locked in a desk anymore. I wonder what else is going on up there?"

Frank left the professor's house and headed down the rickety front steps and across the weedy, overgrown lawn. The house was on a steep hill on a quiet, side street. A low, lop-sided picket fence encircled it.

Stepping through the creaking white gate, Frank followed the road down to where he'd parked. He'd done Callie a favor that day and picked up her car from the body shop. The

Hardys were good customers there—somehow, every one of their cases wound up with a car needing repair work. Frank had decided to use the extra set of wheels to get to Professor Marschall while Joe took the van to Kirkland.

Frank slowed as he got close to the little green Nova. Something was bothering him.

Frank's glance took in a wide circle.

There were only two other cars parked on the block, both of them empty. An old man was slowly pushing a nearly empty shopping cart uphill across the street, a collie dog was drowsing on the front lawn of the neat shingle cottage across the way. There were no other people or animals around.

The breeze picked up a little, and Frank saw something move by the driver's door of Callie's car. The door was not quite shut. In fact, it couldn't close. The safety belt was dangling out, holding it slightly ajar. The silver buckle glinted.

Frank's frown deepened. He hadn't locked the car, but he knew he'd shut the door tightly.

Walking up to the car, he yanked on the door and saw immediately that the glove compartment had been ransacked. Papers, garage receipts, the driver's manual, and a brush and comb belonging to Callie were spilled out on the passenger seat and the floor.

After scanning the afternoon street again,

Frank slid into the driver's seat. He gathered up the scattered stuff, put it back in order, and returned everything to the glove compartment.

Doesn't seem like they took anything, Frank said to himself.

He went to thrust the key into the ignition, then hesitated. Instead, he pulled the hood release and got out to check the engine. After a long, slow look, he slammed the hood down.

"No sign of tampering," he told himself out loud, "and nobody's planted anything."

Frank got back inside the car and drove off. He turned right at the corner and before too long was on a winding road that cut through a stretch of wooded hills.

I'm probably getting too suspicious, he thought. Frank shook his head as he drove. Somebody did search the car, sure. But I don't think we're actually involved with anybody who'd put a bomb under my hood.

The roar of a powerful car engine cut through his thoughts.

Then came the unmistakable sound of a gunshot.

Frank stomped on the gas pedal and slid a little lower in his seat. Maybe I wasn't as paranoid as I thought, he decided as the car screeched along the road.

The other car came roaring up behind him.

Again, the throbbing of its engine was drowned out—this time, by two shots.

Frank glanced into the outside side-view mirror as a bullet tore into it.

He wouldn't see where the next shot was coming from.

Chapter

8

THE ROOM WAS SMALL, shadowy, and window-less. It went in and out of focus, as if someone were using a zoom lens—and not doing a very good job with it.

Joe Hardy wondered what the movie was. Then he realized it wasn't a movie. It was real—painfully real—life.

He groaned, managed to open his eyes fully, and ran his tongue over his teeth. He discovered, at just about the same time, that he had a horrendous headache and that he was tied to a straight-back wooden chair.

There was old furniture piled everywhere. Joe saw nests of wooden chairs, a gilded love-seat, rolled-up carpets, huge vases, marble Venuses—one of them had a gold clock built into her stomach—and a lot of dust.

Nobody else seemed to be in the storeroom, as far as he could tell, but the shadows in the corners could have hidden an army. And the entire supply of light came from a bare forty-watt bulb dangling from a twist of black cord just over his head.

Since his hands were tied behind him, there was no way to get a look at his wristwatch to find out what time it was. The clock in the Venus's stomach wasn't running. The clock in Joe's stomach told him it had been a long time since he'd had that hot dog in beautiful downtown Kirkland.

Exactly how long have I been unconscious? Joe wondered, then shrugged. I guess there's no way to tell.

He gave a tug at his bonds—there was no give at all. Someone had lashed him to the chair with plastic line, and the knots felt strong and tight.

I wonder if this is the Goodhill Antiques shop, he thought, remembering the truck that had been parked outside the Sinclair place.

Whoever had knocked out the Sinclair butler had probably done the job on Joe. There was no trace of the butler—apparently he'd been left in the Sinclair estate.

Joe blinked, his head still throbbing. That

made sense. But why had the kidnappers taken Joe along? Why not leave him at the scene of the crime, too?

And what about Jeanne Sinclair?

She was probably a member of a group of pranksters calling themselves the Circle. She'd gotten scared and alerted Joe and Frank—in a sort of roundabout way.

Joe had a strong suspicion that the slugger with the blackjack had been at the house either to scare Jeanne Sinclair—or to kidnap her. Either way, he'd walked in at the wrong moment and now he was tangled up in the whole mess, too.

Okay, so far everything fits together pretty well, Joe told himself. At least as well as my broken head can put it all together.

But then he stopped and thought. Practical jokers, even slightly dangerous ones, didn't usually go around with blackjacks in their pockets. They didn't knock people out, and they probably wouldn't go in for kidnapping because there wouldn't be much joke in that.

So who had bopped Joe on the head? Why had he been snatched? Joe knew he'd never find out if he didn't get away.

Although his head hurt when he turned, Joe looked around, trying to spot something he could use to cut the ropes.

A fragment of a vase might do, but the vases

were across the room and out of reach. If he'd been closer, he could have knocked one over.

He glanced to the left, then to the right.

Sure, he had enough room on each side of him. Joe shifted his weight, first one way, then the other. With luck, and patience, he could tip this chair over. It was an antique and didn't look all that sturdy. The fall ought to break it, and then he could slip free of the bonds.

Every time he rocked, the throbbing in his head got worse. He kept at it, anyway.

Finally, after what felt like half an hour, Joe succeeded in getting the old wooden chair to fall to the right. It hit the cement floor hard. Joe winced at the jolt, jagged little lightning bolts of pain shooting around behind his tight-shut eyes.

But he also heard the satisfying sound of wood cracking and splintering.

Joe strained against his bonds. Yes, one arm of the chair was shattered. He could move his right hand. He wiggled, twisted, and succeeded in working free of the twists of plastic line. He stood at last, shedding rope and fragments of chair.

Glancing at the closed door, Joe grabbed a chair leg and hid in the shadows. He'd made a lot of noise getting free. It was possible somebody would burst in on him.

But no one appeared.

Very carefully and quietly Joe picked his way across the room. Finally he reached the single entrance, a blank wooden door.

Dropping to one knee, he risked a peek through the rusty keyhole. All he could tell about the next room was that it was also a storeroom, just about as cluttered and poorly lit as the one he was in.

No reason to stay here, he decided.

To his surprise, the door wasn't locked. Joe turned the knob very slowly, pushed the door open, and crossed into the next room.

"Hello, Joe," said a vaguely familiar voice.

He spun, giving himself a new pain in his skull. "Jeanne Sinclair," he said.

A pretty, dark-haired young woman was sitting on an old-fashioned striped sofa. Joe noticed she wasn't tied.

"So what's the story?" he asked. "Are you really into old-fashioned furniture, or were you just waiting for me to wake up and lead the way out?"

Jeanne shrugged, staring down at her hands clasped tight in her lap. "I—I'm sorry," she said. "I didn't know what to do."

"Well, we'd better start deciding." Still rubbing his aching head, Joe looked around the tiny room. At the far side was still another wooden door. Joe pointed, asking, "Is that door locked?"

"That one isn't, no," Jeanne answered. She stayed huddled on the old sofa, her voice low.

"But the door on the other side of that one is made out of solid steel—and it's locked and bolted."

A slug screamed past the driver's-side window of Callie's car. Sliding down low in the driver's seat, Frank stomped the gas pedal.

This is all I need, he thought as the tops of the trees lining the road blurred into what seemed like a continuous wall. I pick up Callie's car and bring it back full of bullet holes. She'll kill me.

Another shot rang out as he zigzagged down the road. "What am I thinking?" Frank said out loud. "These guys may kill me!"

The little Nova shimmied through a tight turn, and squealed as Frank swung it off the road and into a grassy field.

The car slammed to a stop near a wooded area. Frank grabbed the passenger door, shouldered it open, and bailed out. He hit the ground hard, rolling through the high grass until he got his feet under him and ran for a stand of trees. An old oak's thick trunk provided him with some cover.

The car that had been chasing him came roaring around the corner. Frank peered from behind a low branch to see a sleek silver sports car with dark-tinted windows screech to a halt. A gloved hand holding a gun thrust through a slit in the passenger window. The unseen gunman fired twice at Frank's abandoned car.

Frank winced as he saw one of the tires go flat. But he stayed where he was until the pursuit car accelerated and sped away.

At last he returned to his car and got out the jack and spare tire.

Either those guys were the world's worst shots, or they just wanted to scare me, he said to himself as he changed the flat. And they did a pretty good job.

Frank turned away from the living room window at home, shaking his head. Darkness was closing in.

His aunt Gertrude came into the room, carrying a ham sandwich on a plate. "You really ought to eat something, Frank," she suggested. "You haven't had any supper—nothing at all since you got home hours ago."

"It's okay, Aunt Gertrude. I'll wait until Joe shows up."

"Standing there staring out the window isn't going to bring Joe home any faster." She set the plate on the coffee table.

"Joe didn't phone while I was out, didn't leave any message?"

"Honestly, Frank," said his aunt, shaking

her head. "You ought to know by now that I'm perfectly capable of remembering messages and conveying them to the various harebrained members of this family."

She shook her head. "Having spent as many years as I have around Fenton and you two, I'm used to getting cryptic phone calls and strange notes and making sure you get them. Joe didn't phone." She frowned. "The poor boy is on the verge of a serious cold, too. He really ought to be home in bed."

"Joe doesn't have a cold."

"He will have one. He was out stomping around in the mud last night until all hours, getting soaked to the skin." She sat on the sofa and watched Frank as he started to pace. "And what were you two up to this afternoon, Frank?"

"Nothing special," he said. "Although it looks as though someone wants to scare Joe and me off this case."

"Well, if you're worried that Joe's in danger, shouldn't you call the police?" She picked up his sandwich and took a bite.

"Aunt Gertrude, I'm not sure this is a police matter. Joe just got delayed—we'll be hearing—"

The phone rang, and Frank pounced on it before his aunt could reach for it.

"Hello?"

"Frank?"

"Oh, hi, Callie," he said. "How are you feeling?"

"Okay."

"Listen, I'll call you back later. Right now I want to keep the line open for a while."

"What's wrong?"

"Nothing, it's just that I'm waiting to hear from Joe."

"Is he in trouble?"

"I don't think so."

"But you aren't certain?"

"Well, no."

"All right, I understand. If you need my help, call. And thanks for returning my car." She hung up.

Aunt Gertrude picked up the second half of Frank's sandwich. "This could have used a bit more mustard," she said. "Was that Callie thanking you for picking up her car?"

"Yes."

"She's a nice girl. It's a wonder, though, that she puts up with you."

The phone rang again. Frank caught it on the second ring. "Yes?"

"Is that you, Frank?"

"Yes, who—"

"Con Riley. I don't imagine your brother is home."

"He isn't, no. But how did you know that?"

"Do either of you boys know a girl named Jeanne Sinclair?"

"That's it. *She's* the one."

"Huh?"

"I mean, yes, I know her." That was the voice Frank had been trying to remember, the one he'd thought he recognized when he'd picked up the warning phone call. "Why are you asking about her, Con?"

"It looks like maybe she's been kidnapped. Unless it's another of those little jokes."

"How does Joe tie in with this?"

"The police in Kirkland found your van parked in her driveway. They asked me to check up on him."

Frank's mind raced as he listened. Joe must have traced the scarf to Jeanne and gone out to her house.

"There's no sign of the Sinclair girl," Con went on. "Her folks are in Morocco on a vacation, and besides Jeanne, the butler was the only one home this afternoon. He went to answer the door and got rapped on the head. When he came to, he was sprawled on the floor—alone. So he phoned the police."

"This doesn't sound like a practical joke."

"I think," said Con, "you'd better come to the station and have a chat with me, Frank."

"Soon as I can get there," he promised, and hung up.

70

His aunt was staring at him. "What is it? Has Joe been hurt?"

"I don't think so," he told her. "But I have to go out and take a look at something. If Joe phones, tell him to come home." He started for the door. "And if Con Riley calls, tell him I got delayed a little, but I'll get to him eventually."

"Are you in trouble with the police, Frank?"

"No, Aunt Gertrude," Frank said as he ran from the room. "At least, not yet," he added under his breath.

The night was foggy, and Frank, driving his dad's car, almost missed the turnoff.

The kidnapping of Jeanne Sinclair had to be connected with the activities of this Circle bunch. And if they were using the old abandoned Bushmiller Academy buildings as a headquarters, then Frank figured he'd be able to find out something there, and with luck, Jeanne and Joe.

As he drove, Frank fit the little he knew into a theory on his brother's disappearance.

Joe must have walked in on the kidnapping when he went to the Sinclair home in Kirkland to talk to Jeanne about her scarf and the club.

But why *take* Joe? They just knocked the butler out.

"Riley didn't say anything about a ransom,"

Frank said to himself, turning the van onto an even narrower hillside road.

Frank's frown deepened as two new ideas struck him. Maybe, if the Circle guys had kidnapped Jeanne, they knew she was giving away information about them. And if they'd taken Joe Hardy, they knew who was getting the information, as well.

Frank's lips straightened into a thin, grim line as he continued to mull over the situation. Yes, that was certainly a theory that covered all the available facts.

He saw the spires of the gray brick buildings of the academy to his right, looming dark in the mist beyond a partially tumbled down stone wall. He drove on by.

Jeanne had tried to warn them about the Circle—but before they could talk to her, she was kidnapped.

Frank shrugged. I suppose that's one way to keep us from getting any information from her, he thought.

But what could she know that was so important? Sure, she could get the other members of this prank club in trouble if she talked, but the trouble they could get into for kidnapping her was a lot worse.

A quarter of a mile beyond the academy Frank parked the car.

"No, there's something else going on here,"

Frank told himself, opening his door. "It's linked with the Circle, but it's a lot more serious."

And if it was serious enough, that meant Joe and Jeanne must be in danger—life-and-death danger.

Chapter

9

AN OWL HOOTED mournfully up in the tangled branches of a tree. The night fog swirling around him, Frank stood near the back of a high stone wall that had once completely surrounded the three buildings that made up the Bushmiller Academy. He held his unlit flashlight in his right hand.

A large section of the wall had fallen away, and through the gap Frank could see the vacant buildings. The fog partially masked them, but any light in them would have been visible. And there was only darkness.

Frank moved forward to step through the jagged opening in the high wall. The grass was waist-high, some of the weeds even higher. Still not using his light, he headed for the largest of the three buildings.

It stood three stories high and had a spired tower at each of its four corners. It must have been pretty impressive once upon a time, but now one of the spires had begun to list. Mist tangled around the sagging structure like phantom flags.

Slowly and carefully Frank circled the dark building. When he was nearing the large arched front entrance, he spotted what he was looking for.

A recent path had been worn in the wild grass. It came from the direction of the front wall and led straight up to the cracked stone front steps of the academy's main building.

"So somebody has been using the place," he muttered, climbing the steps.

There was a large metal door, but it wasn't quite shut. He gripped its edge and tugged it open. The door made no noise, didn't creak at all. Someone had recently oiled its hinges. Taking a deep breath, Frank stepped into the darkness inside.

A mixture of smells hit him. Mildew, dampness, mice, decay, and—a newer smell—cigarette smoke.

He halted in the tall, cavernous foyer, listening. Far off something was dripping, but there was no sound or sign of life.

Frank clicked on his flashlight.

On the hardwood floor he saw tracks in the thick dust. Following the beam of his light, Frank made his way down a long hollow corridor. Hanging on the dank walls were cobweb-shrouded oil paintings.

The dusty trail stopped at a double door with peeling gilt letters that said Gymnasium. Taking hold of the brass handle, Frank slowly pulled the right-hand door open. Again, there was no creaking.

The gym was two stories high, with long dark brown marks tracing water damage along its walls. In the center of the cavernous space were a dozen folding chairs, arranged in a circle around a small table. On top of the table sat an empty goldfish bowl.

This is the place, Frank thought.

As if he needed any more proof, the group had left its own calling card. Spray-painted on the wall, in bright crimson, was a large circle with a 12 inside it.

Frank was starting for the table when he heard voices echoing in the hallway. People were heading his way.

Frank took a rapid look around the gym. At the back of the big room, near a place where more folding chairs had been piled, was a wooden door. He darted for it as the voices out in the hall came nearer.

He took hold of the doorknob, turned it. The door opened, making a thin squeak. Frank flashed his light around and discovered it was a small storeroom. Shelves ran up one wall, holding just one battered old cardboard carton and a great deal of dust. There was a frosted-glass window at the rear.

Frank entered the room, turning off his light. He left the door open about two inches. Through the slit he could see the meeting table and the chairs surrounding it.

The doorway from the hall opened and three dark figures entered. Two were carrying lighted candles, and each wore a black robe with a black hood.

Frank blinked in disbelief. So, Tony Prito's story was correct. But even seeing it, Frank had a hard time believing this kind of mumbo jumbo was going on in everyday Bayport.

"We need some more candles, Biff," said one of the hooded figures, placing his candle on the table.

"So get some, Kevin."

"Hey, don't forget who you're talking to."

The biggest of the three figures was wearing a robe that was tight on him. Frank figured he had to be his football-playing friend, Biff Hooper.

Biff said, "Yeah, I know you call yourself number one in the Crimson Ring of Twelve.

78

But I'm getting tired of your ordering me around."

"Perhaps we better discuss that at tonight's meeting." Anger showed in Kevin's voice.

The third figure placed his candle on the table, saying, "Look, I'll get the candles. Where are they?"

Kevin answered, "Back in the storeroom."

"Okay." The hooded figure, whose voice Frank didn't recognize, started walking right toward the room he was hiding in.

"They're not back there," called Biff, his voice muffled by his dark hood. "I stored them over there under the stage."

"You weren't supposed to do that," said Kevin.

"So?"

"You sound like you've got an attitude problem."

"Yeah, and I'll tell you why. I don't like what you did to Jeanne."

"I didn't do anything to her."

"But you know who did, Kevin," accused the hooded Biff. "When I went by to pick her up tonight, their butler told me Jeanne had been kidnapped. Why? Where is she?"

"She's perfectly safe, Biff."

"Whose word do I have for that—just yours?"

"Just mine, yes. And I suggest you don't push this any further just now."

Biff took a step toward Kevin. "I haven't even begun to push yet. Where is she?"

"In a safe place. That's all I can tell you."

"That's all you can tell me, huh? How about telling me what any of this has to do with the Circle."

"A decision was made," answered Kevin. "For the good of all concerned, Jeanne Sinclair has to be kept out of the way for two days."

"Two days? What has this got to do with this club or with any of us? How can you just decide that my girlfriend is going to be—"

"The decision wasn't made by the club."

"Who made it then?" Lunging, Biff caught hold of the other guy's robe. "I thought *we* ran the Circle and made all the decisions."

"You misunderstood."

"Then you'd better start explaining things to me."

Kevin pulled free of Biff's grasp. "Chill out, Biff," he said evenly. "When the time is right, you'll be told all you need to know."

"That's great. That's just great. Maybe one fine day you'll get around to explaining just what—"

"Take it easy for now," advised Kevin, smoothing the front of his black robe. "But keep this in mind—if you don't make any trouble, Jeanne will be just fine.''

Biff stood silently for a moment. "And if I *do* make trouble?''

"Trust me, it wouldn't be a good idea. Not at all.''

The third young man said, "I don't like any of this. And I don't like the way the Circle has been going lately. Kevin, things are getting completely out of hand. I think I'd like to quit.''

"Nobody is going to quit. Not yet, anyway,'' said Kevin. "Anybody who tries—well, just keep in mind what happened to Jeanne.'' He nodded at the doorway to the corridor. "Now, calm down, both of you. I hear some of the others coming.''

The door opened and five more robed and hooded figures came in—three young men, two young women.

Frank moved back from the open door. He worked his way, slowly and silently, to the single window.

What he had to do was slip outside and wait. When the Crimson Circle of Twelve meeting broke up, he'd tail the one called Kevin. He had a good idea he'd turn out to be Kevin Branders, someone Frank knew casually and didn't like. Kevin would more than likely lead him to where Joe and Jeanne were being held.

Frank inched the window open, so slowly that it made no noise. Then, tucking his flashlight into his belt, he climbed out over the ledge.

There was a ten-foot drop to the ground.

He lowered himself until he was hanging from the window ledge by his finger tips.

That was when a gruff voice from below said, "Hold it right there, son. Unless you want to get shot."

Chapter

10

JOE RAMMED HIS SHOULDER into the thick metal door, straining against the handle at the same time. Nothing budged.

"Pretty solid," he finally admitted, leaning back against the immovable barrier. "You were right about it, Jeanne."

"I'm really very sorry about all this." Jeanne Sinclair had gotten up from the antique sofa she'd been sitting on. Now the dark-haired young woman stood in the doorway of their storeroom prison, staring down the short hall that led to the metal door. "If I'd used my head a little earlier, we wouldn't be in this mess now."

Joe came back into the storeroom. "Suppose

you tell me exactly what *is* going on, Jeanne—and why you tried contacting us."

She sighed and perched again on the sofa. "How much do you know about the Circle?"

"Just about nothing. You mentioned it in that note you left for us to find."

She nodded. "Yes, I was able to toss that—along with my scarf—out of the car window. I was hoping that you and your brother would be able to figure out the clues."

Grinning ruefully, Joe said, "I did follow your trail. The problem is, it ended up here."

Jeanne didn't share his smile. She flopped back on the couch, shivering. "I didn't think they'd get this violent, trying something as serious as kidnapping me."

"Who are *they?*"

Jeanne shrugged sort of helplessly. "Well, Joe, first off there's the Circle. That's twelve of us who got together to . . ." She paused, looking down at her twined fingers. "At first, really, it was just going to be a sort of dare thing. Almost like a party game, a scavenger hunt."

She looked up, half smiling. "We'd put challenges in this bowl and then draw one out. At first the dares were simple, just fun. Well, I guess some of them were mean—like spraying paint on the school. Still, they were meant to be just pranks—honest."

"But why start the Circle at all?"

Jeanne looked embarrassed. "I don't know. I was bored a lot of the time, my folks were off traveling—which they almost always are," she said. "There I was all alone in that big dumb house with nobody but Rollison. He's our butler, Rollison. Have you met him?"

"Not exactly. He was out cold the only time I saw him."

Jeanne gasped. "They knocked him out, too?"

"They did." Joe stood up. "Jeanne, are you telling me that you and your pals were so bored and restless that you actually went around smashing windows and setting fires?"

She looked down again. "When you put it that way, it does sound stupid. I don't know—Kevin was so persuasive, and, well, it was sort of exciting at first. We all felt like secret agents or private eyes or something."

"Would Kevin be Kevin Branders?"

"Yes. Do you know him?"

"Slightly. And I know something about his brother."

"Brother?" Jeanne frowned. "I didn't even know he had a brother."

Joe asked, "Was this Red Circle bunch or whatever you call it Kevin's idea?"

"The Crimson Circle of Twelve," she said. "Yes, it was more or less Kevin's idea. He talked the rest of us into it, came up with the costumes and the secret headquarters. And it was Kevin who suggested we increase the difficulty of the dares."

"Costumes?" Joe said.

"We wear robes with hoods to hide our identities. I knew most of the kids in the Circle by their voices. But there were a few I was never sure of." She shook her head. "It sounds crazy, doesn't it? But somehow Kevin made it all work. I guess he's had practice. He's always had to try twice as hard, since his family lost its money. In a town like Kirkland that's worse than death."

Joe couldn't believe what he was hearing. "You mean, you actually went around in hoods? We heard stories about that but figured it couldn't be."

Jeanne nodded. "One of the guys talked a little after Kevin made a guy go on a really dangerous dare—smashing the window of Fowler's Jewelers. I got scared," Jeanne shuddered. "I didn't like what was happening—all of a sudden, everything was too heavy-duty."

"So you decided to quit."

She nodded her head vigorously. "Yes, but when I told Kevin, he said I'd already done things that were against the law. And if I left the Circle, I'd get in a lot of trouble," she said.

"He hinted that if I quit, he'd see to it that the cops found out I'd been one of the vandals."

"He couldn't very well turn you in without implicating himself."

"That's exactly what I told Biff, but he said Kevin had a lot of ways to hurt us and that we just better go along with him—for a while, anyway."

"Biff Hooper belongs to this Circle, too?"

"Don't blame Biff. *I* was the one who kept at him to join with me," Jeanne said. "He wasn't very happy about it. But then I pretty much told him if he didn't join, I'd quit dating him." She shook her head again. "He told me a lot about the famous Hardy brothers."

"So when you got scared," said Joe, "you decided to see if you could get Frank and me to expose the group."

"I was hoping you'd find me—and, well, maybe we could work out a way for everybody to put a stop to the Circle without any of us getting hurt."

"Sure, let the Hardys work out a way for everybody to avoid the consequences of what they'd done." He shook his head, frowning at her.

Very quietly the girl began to cry. "I guess I'm not exactly a perfect person," she said, sniffling. "My mother says I'm spoiled rotten, but then she doesn't like me much."

Joe went over and patted her on the shoulder. "Okay, Jeanne, okay," he said. "Now, why did they kidnap you?"

She rubbed tears from her cheek with the heel of her hand. "Somebody must have found out I'd contacted you."

"How'd they find out?"

"I don't know, but for the dare at the Hickerson Mansion last night, I was teamed up with Kevin," she said. "He probably suspected I'd called you when you and Frank showed up there."

"Yeah, but kidnapping is serious. It's risking a long prison sentence—just because you *may* have talked to us."

Jeanne was silent for a while, thinking. "One of the guys who grabbed me said something about my having to be away for just two days or so."

"You mean they didn't kidnap you for ransom?"

She shook her head. "He said they'd let me go in a couple of days—if I behaved myself and didn't make trouble."

Joe said, "Is the Circle planning something important during the next two days?"

"Not that I know of."

"Yet they want you out of the way, where you can't tell anybody about them." Joe rubbed a thumb knuckle across his chin. "The people who brought you here—were they members of the Circle?''

"I don't think so. They were older, bigger men. They had to be at least thirty," she answered. "I'm not sure what they looked like, since they were wearing ski masks."

"Something's going to go down, something important." Joe frowned in thought. "It feels like the Circle is just a cover for it." He looked at Jeanne. "Do the members of the Circle talk about future plans? Have you heard anything strange?"

Jeanne shrugged, then paused for a second. "Does the name Gramatkee mean anything to you?" she asked. "While they were driving us here, I was tied up and gagged in the truck. I heard one of the men say something like, 'Now let's hope we can just take care of the Gramatkee job.' " She looked hopefully over at Joe.

"I don't know the name," he said, "but I think I know who's behind all this. I suspect this whole business is tied in with Kevin's brother."

"I don't understand."

"I'll explain later," he promised. "But right now we have to concentrate on finding a way out of—"

The harsh click of the heavy bolt on the metal door cut him off. The lock rattled, then the door groaned outward.

A lean, tan man in his late twenties stepped into the room. He had short-cropped, sun-bleached blond hair and wore dark jeans and a dark pullover sweater. In his gloved left hand he held a 9-millimeter Beretta pistol.

"Curt Branders," said Joe, recognizing the man from photographs he'd seen in his father's files.

Branders smiled thinly. "I'm a bit disappointed in you, Joe," he said. "Didn't you suspect that I might have a bug in here to listen in on your conversation?"

"I didn't," admitted Joe. "I guess it took me too long to realize that this whole deal is a lot bigger than a bunch of dumb practical jokes."

Branders leaned in the doorway, letting the pistol dangle from his hand. "I'd like to suggest a deal," he said in a cool voice. "If you remain here quietly and don't make waves, you'll be released in two days."

"All we have is your word on that."

Branders gave Joe a thin smile. "That's about the best guarantee you can hope to get, right now. But I keep my word," he said. "So just relax, don't try to escape—and I won't have to kill you."

When Jeanne realized he was serious, she started crying again.

"By the way, Joe," Branders went on, "why

not keep your detective theories to yourself? There's no need to upset this innocent young lady. Talk about homework or music—something safe."

"You're going to be outside listening?"

"Someone will, around the clock."

Joe nodded, saying, "That's sure comforting."

Branders glanced over his shoulder and spoke to someone as yet unseen. "Get in here and tie these two up. The less they can move around, the better I'll feel."

Meanwhile Frank hung from the window, staring down at a thickset man of about thirty-five who stood in the high weeds directly under him. The guy was almost completely bald, his fringe of hair and droopy mustache almost the color of straw. In his right fist was a .45 automatic. It was pointed straight at Frank.

"Now, here's what I'd like you to do, kid," he said. "Just drop on down here. Then I'm going to turn you over to some friends of mine for a little chat."

"Hey, mister, don't turn me over to the cops," Frank pleaded, faking a shaky, scared voice. "I didn't mean any harm. And you can see, I didn't steal anything."

"It's not the cops I'm taking you to, punk."

"You're not going to tell my folks?" Frank

started to shake as he clung to the sill. "I've never done this before, honest."

"Are you going to get down here? Or do I have to shoot you off?"

"D-don't shoot! I mean, hey, I didn't swipe a single thing. I was just—"

"Look, kid, I'm getting awful tired of this. Just do like I tell you and drop down here." The man's gun wavered a little in annoyance, and Frank took his chance.

He came down, all right, but not in the way the gunman expected. Releasing his hold on the window ledge, Frank kicked hard against the wall with both feet.

That sent him out, as well as down. He landed right on top of the surprised thug.

Even as he was flying through the air, Frank was lining up his first blow. As they fell to the ground in a tangle, Frank's hand reached out for the gunman's wrist.

But the thug was strong. Before Frank knew what hit him, the blond guy had the gun muzzle pressed against Frank's forehead!

Chapter

11

JOE, TIED IN an antique wooden chair with more of the same plastic line, scanned the ceiling of the cluttered storeroom. He couldn't see anything that looked like a video camera. That meant Branders and his thugs could only *hear* what was going on, not see Joe or Jeanne.

"You go to Miss Sheridan's School, don't you?"

The dark-haired girl was still on the sofa. But now her hands were tied behind her and her ankles were bound. "Are you really going to carry on some dumb conversation like that guy suggested?"

Joe winked as broadly as he could. "Well,

we'll be stuck here for two days, Jeanne. Might as well pass the time as pleasantly as we can."

"I don't believe you, Joe Hardy. I thought at least—"

He shook his head and winked again. "Come on, I know when I'm beaten."

Jeanne stared at him for a long moment, then nodded back. "Well, maybe you're right."

"I hear it's a pretty good school."

"Not really. It's boring, very strict, and there are no boys. It was my mother's idea, sending me there."

"What are you taking?" After speaking aloud, Joe mouthed another sentence, "I'm going to tip this chair over—make it break." It was barely a whisper.

"Isn't that danger—I mean, I'm taking English. I hate it, though, because I have to read and write so much."

"What else do you take?" He mouthed, "Keep talking to cover the noise."

"Oh, political science. I really like that. I read the *Bayport Times* every morning."

"After I fall and get clear, start screaming," he whispered.

"Yes—uh, I think it's the duty of our generation to take an interest in the world situation. Otherwise the future's going to be as stupid as the present is."

"Yell that I'm hurt and bleeding. You're afraid I'm dying," he mouthed.

Nodding, Jeanne kept on talking, about school, her parents, dates, her favorite television shows.

Joe took just a few minutes to make the wooden chair tip over. It smashed quite satisfactorily on the hard floor.

Joe got clear, moving to a position at the side of the door, clutching a chair leg. He gave Jeanne a nod.

"Help!" she cried, sobbing. "Oh, please, can you hear me? He fell over, and he's hurt his head. There's blood all over!"

As the guard burst through the door, Joe circled down on him with his best roundhouse punch.

Frank took a big chance and threw himself forward, smashing the guy's gun hand down. He heard the big automatic thump to the ground.

Frank rose, kicked the gun into the shadows, and ran through the high, wild grass around the old academy.

He found another break in the stone wall, ducked through, and dashed for his car. The tires screeched as he took off, barely masking the sound of the gunshot not far behind.

He drove on, until he found a diner. The fat

man behind the counter looked up as Frank came through the door. "How about a dozen doughnuts?"

"Uh, actually, I just want some change for the phone," Frank told him.

"A half dozen, then," the man said. "A half-dozen doughnuts for fifty cents is a good deal, my boy."

"I'm not denying that. But I—"

"See, I'm planning to close this place in exactly one half hour. Usually I sell out the doughnuts, but tonight I'm stuck with a full dozen left over."

"Okay, give me a half dozen." Frank slapped a dollar bill on the counter. "I'll use the change for the phone."

"Why not go for the whole dozen, my boy? You can have them for seventy-five cents. That's an even more astonishing bargain."

"Fine, great. Just so I get change for the phone."

The counterman picked up the dollar bill, carried it to his ancient cash register. After whapping it a few times with his fist, nudging it with an elbow, and pushing several keys, he got it open. He returned with the change jingling in his palm. "Eighty, eighty-five— ninety—one buck it is."

Frank ran to the phone booth at the back of

the empty coffee shop. Dropping in his money, he punched in the Hardy home number.

His aunt Gertrude answered at once. "Hello?"

"It's Frank. Any news about—"

"Yes, Joe just called. He's on his way home."

"Is he okay?"

"Well, he claims to be, but he sounds as though he's coming down with something," his aunt answered. "He said to tell you he's found the owner of the scarf and is bringing her, too."

"I'm on my way now." Frank had been debating whether or not to track down Kevin Branders and make him lead the way to where Joe and Jeanne were being held. But he'd decided to check home first. Now he wouldn't have to visit Kevin. Not yet, anyway.

He was nearly out to the street when the counterman called out, "Hey, wait, you forgot your doughnuts."

Joe dug his hand into the paper bag, pulling out another doughnut. "Sure, I can eat at a time like this," he assured his brother. "Just watch me."

The Hardys and Jeanne, after Frank had persuaded their aunt Gertrude to withdraw, were meeting in the living room.

"Fine—enjoy them." Frank turned to face Jeanne on the sofa. "Now explain how you got clear of the kidnappers."

"He was very clever," said Jeanne, smiling at Joe.

"Well, actually the guy Curt Branders left to guard us was big, but he wasn't smart," Joe said modestly as he took a bite of his second cruller. "After I knocked him out, I figured it was a good idea for us to get clear of that furniture warehouse as soon as possible."

"You saw Branders? He's in Bayport?"

"And he's up to his neck in whatever's going on," answered Joe. "He's just using this Circle thing as a cover for something much more serious."

"But how does this Gramatkee fit in?" Jeanne asked.

"Willis Gramatkee?" Frank stood up. "The big industrialist? Dad did mention last week that Gramatkee's being pressured to sell out his empire to a big European group."

Joe frowned. "I knew the name was familiar. Sounds like Gramatkee doesn't want to sell."

Frank nodded grimly. "But Curt Branders will take care of that, so they can buy from whoever inherits after Gramatkee dies. It works perfectly. Gramatkee has a mansion somewhere between here and Kirkland."

"Right in Branders's old stamping

grounds," Joe pointed out. "So he gets his brother Kevin to start up the Circle as a distraction for the Kirkland and Bayport cops."

"Better than that," Frank said. "If Gramatkee got killed during, say, a burglary, it'd be blamed on the kids. Nobody would even know about Curt Branders. He'd be out of the country, with no one the wiser."

"I think that has to be what's going on," agreed Joe.

"Do you think he'll try to go through with it?" asked Jeanne. "I mean, his plans are falling apart. Thanks to Joe, I'm free and can talk."

"In the league Branders plays in, he doesn't have a choice—he'll have to go ahead." Frank started pacing. "What we have to do, Joe, is get in touch with the police. I think Con may listen to us."

Joe opened his mouth to protest, but Frank cut him off. "We may be talking about an assassination here, Joe. We need all the help we can get to prevent it."

"You're right," Joe agreed grudgingly.

Jeanne asked, "What about Biff?"

"That's right, he's tangled up in this mess, too," said Frank. "I saw him at the meeting place."

"If we're going to the police," said Jeanne, "Biff should have the chance to come along with us. It's my fault he's in this. I don't want them treating him as though he's some kind of criminal, taking part in Curt's plan."

"Okay, we'll call him." Joe picked up the telephone and dialed the Hooper home.

Biff's mother answered. "Yes, hello?"

"Hi, Mrs. Hooper, it's Joe Hardy. Could I speak to Biff, please?"

"I'm afraid he's not here." Mrs. Hooper sounded worried.

Joe checked his watch and noticed it was close to midnight. "Would you happen to know where he is?"

"I'm somewhat concerned about him myself, Joe," she answered. "He came home a little while ago, very upset, but he wouldn't tell me what was wrong. Then a few minutes ago somebody came by and he went out again."

"Who was it?"

"A boy I don't know very well, or care for. His name is Kevin."

"Kevin Branders?"

"Yes, that's who. He was even more upset than Biff, saying something important had come up—they had to have a special meeting—"

Mrs. Hooper suddenly cut off, then said, almost pleadingly, "Do you have any idea what Biff's got himself mixed up with, Joe? I can't help feeling that something is wrong. This isn't like the time he went off to that survival camp, is it?"

Joe hesitated for a second, remembering how Biff had gotten himself kidnapped by a bunch of mercenaries. Before it was over, Frank, Joe, and Biff had all nearly been killed. "I wouldn't worry, Mrs. Hooper," he finally said. "Would you have any idea where they were going?"

"I heard Biff say something about not being able to use the academy. And the other boy said they'd use the old barn."

"Okay, I'm sure you'll be hearing from him soon. Good night, ma'am." Hanging up, Joe turned to Jeanne, "The old barn—where is it?"

"It's the one at the deserted apple orchard about a mile above the academy," she said.

"Obviously they can't use Bushmiller Academy now," said Frank. "They know somebody's been checking the place out."

"Maybe they've been spooked into moving their schedule up," Joe said. "Maybe they'll try to do something tonight—and now it looks like they've dragged Biff into it!"

Chapter

12

JOE WAS IN LUCK—or so he thought.

The boys had split up. Frank's job was to find the industrialist Willis Gramatkee and warn him that Curt Branders was in town, ready to use him for target practice.

Joe, in the meantime, was to head to the old barn where the Circle was holding its emergency meeting and get Biff away. Jeanne, with Aunt Gertrude watching over her, was remaining at the Hardy home. Once Joe called in with the good news about Biff, they were supposed to alert the cops.

Leaving the van a safe distance from the abandoned apple orchard, Joe moved quietly through the night-darkened fields. Then he cut through the orchard itself.

Up ahead stood a big ramshackle barn. The light of several candles showed, flickering, inside the deep shadows of the old structure.

Then Joe had his lucky break.

Something—some*one* passed between him and the candles in the barn. Joe ducked behind a tree. Peering around it, he made out two robed figures.

"Come on, Chad, we're late."

"In a minute. I'm not going to break my neck because Kevin Branders says so."

"Kevin won't like that."

"Well, too bad. Who died and left him boss?"

The other figure sounded dubious. "I don't know, Chad. Look what happened to Jeanne Sinclair."

"Maybe Branders can get away with pushing girls around, but just let him try me. Everyone says I'm the best boxer at Chartwell."

Oh, *please,* Joe said to himself.

"Fine—but I'm going in. See you inside, Chad."

"Yeah, yeah, Willie."

Very carefully Joe moved closer, darting from apple tree to apple tree.

Chad was a lean, dark-haired young man of about eighteen. Joe didn't know him. He was standing at the edge of the orchard, about to slip his black hood on.

Joe made a quick decision.

Then he went walking right up to him. "Hey, Chad," he said.

"Huh?" Chad started to turn. "Who—"

Joe punched him twice, short jabs to the chin.

Chad wobbled, moaned once, and then his eyes rolled up and closed, and he fell to the weedy ground.

"Sorry about that, Chad," Joe said. "I guess the boxing class at Chartwell hasn't gotten up to that move yet."

Swiftly Joe tugged off the kid's robe. He used Chad's belt to tie his arms around a tree and improvised a gag out of his sweater.

A moment later Joe had on the robe and the hood and was walking into the meeting of the Circle.

There were only nine others standing in the ragged circle made by the candles planted on the rough stone floor of the beat-up old barn. Six of them were boys; three, girls. Joe scanned the circle. One guy was much taller and stockier than the others—something even the black robe couldn't disguise. That had to be Biff. Now to move over to him . . .

But just as Joe took a place at the edge of the group, one of the hooded figures moved to the center of the circle, where a glass bowl was resting on an overturned apple barrel.

The guy raised his right hand. "Brothers and sisters," he began, and Joe recognized the voice as that of Kevin Branders. "Brothers and sisters of the Crimson Circle of Twelve, we have been summoned here tonight because our group faces a grave and most serious challenge."

Joe shifted from one foot to the other, trying to see if he recognized any of the other masked figures.

"In order to grow and thrive," continued Kevin, "a group, like the trees in this orchard, must be pruned and cut from time to time. Better that one dies than have the group perish. So I suppose you should know that this very day we have had—a pruning."

Joe swallowed hard, looking around the circle of kids. He couldn't see their faces beneath the hoods. But just from the way most of them were standing, he could tell that they were scared out of their minds.

"We had traitors in our group," Kevin went on. "People who lost their nerve, who would have turned us over to the police. They left messages and even gave away the place of our headquarters."

Worried murmurs rose from the hooded kids.

"We've taken care of the problem," Kevin cut in, calming them down.

Hidden by his hood, Joe smiled. Let Kevin think that.

"But there's still more treachery to be punished." Joe's shoulders tightened as Kevin's voice rose. "Believe it or not, we have a spy right here in our midst."

He turned to point an accusing finger right at him. "Don't we, Joe Hardy?"

All the members of the Circle whirled toward Joe as he yanked off his hood. "You clowns may as well quit playing this game right now," he told them, deciding to bluff. "The police know all about you. They're—"

"Get him," Kevin ordered.

The two nearest figures grabbed for Joe's arms as he started to dart away. He wasn't used to the robe—it slowed him down for a crucial second. Then he was mobbed.

Joe struggled desperately, blocking punches, returning a few. But there were five guys beating on him—even Biff had joined in.

"Biff," shouted Joe. "You don't have to do what these bozos tell you anymore. They kidnapped Jeanne. But I got her out!"

The big figure he'd assumed was Biff didn't stop punching, but he did start laughing.

Joe managed to get one arm free and grabbed for Biff. His hand caught in the big guy's hood, tearing it away as someone yanked him off balance.

The hood came off—but Biff's face wasn't under it. With a sinking sensation, Joe recognized the face grinning at him. It was the guard Joe had slugged back at the warehouse.

"I don't think I'm going to like this," Joe muttered.

With the others holding his arms, Joe watched the guard wind up for a knockout punch.

"You got it, punk."

The last thing Joe saw was an enormous fist, blotting everything out as it came toward his face.

Frank screeched to a halt on the drive of the Gramatkee estate, jumped out, and slammed the door of the van. He ran along the flagstone path leading to the Gramatkee mansion, then flew up the steps two at a time.

He saw lights shining in most of the first-floor windows of the large modern glass-and-redwood home. Maybe his quest would end quickly. Frank jabbed the doorbell.

Chimes rang inside the big house, but nothing else happened.

Frank knocked on the door with his fist.

A minute more passed. Then the door

opened a couple of inches. "Yes? What do— Hey, Frank Hardy!"

He didn't recognize the slender red-haired girl who smiled out at him. She was pretty, about his age, and obviously knew him. Maybe that would help him.

"Is Mr. Gramatkee at home?" Frank asked.

"You don't recognize me, do you?"

"Not actually, no. Look, it's important that I—"

"Sandy Fuller. I met you last Christmas at that dance over in Kirkland."

"Sandy, I have to see Mr. Gramatkee."

"He isn't here. You were with Callie Shaw, and I had a date with this real nerd named—"

"Where is he?"

"That nerd? I haven't seen him since that party."

"No—where's Gramatkee?"

"I'm baby-sitting the two children. Mrs. Gramatkee is in Paris."

"Sandy, this is life and death—where's Gramatkee?"

"Down on his yacht. He goes there by himself once a week to be alone." The red-haired girl shrugged her shoulders. "The name of the boat is the *Golden Fleece,* and it's moored in Bayport Harbor. Are you serious about this life-and-death stuff?"

"I'll tell you later, Sandy. Thanks for your

help." Frank ran down the steps, hopped back into the van, and drove off.

He had a stiff drive ahead of him—the yacht harbor was over ten miles from there.

Frank didn't need to be a detective to tell that something was wrong at the yacht club.

The gate in the cyclone fence that cut off the yacht harbor from the rest of the waterfront hung open. In the guard shack just inside the gate a lean, weather-beaten man lay on the floor, tied, gagged, and out cold.

Frank picked up the lamp that had been knocked off the desk and knelt beside the guard. At least the man was breathing regularly.

"I'll have to cut you loose on the way back," he promised the unconscious man. "Right now I have to see about stopping a murder."

He ran along the planks of the dock. Various-size boats were moored along it, bobbing gently. None looked like a millionaire's yacht, but out in the dark waters of the harbor he saw three large boats anchored.

The roar of a motor launch coming to life brought Frank to the end of the dock, just in time to see a craft heading for the biggest of the yachts. He recognized the big guy at the wheel—Biff Hooper.

"Biff!" he called through cupped hands. "Wait!"

But Biff didn't hear him.

The launch circled the well-lit yacht and disappeared around its other side.

That ship must be Gramatkee's *Golden Fleece,* Frank concluded. Biff's going aboard right now. And unless I can do something, he may get tangled up in a murder.

Frank pivoted and ran for the other side of the marina. What I need now is a boat of my own, he thought.

Running along wooden catwalks that shifted with the tide, Frank worked his way toward a slip where a small white speedboat bobbed in the water. Blue letters across its stern read *Napoli.*

Lucky I remembered Tony Prito keeps a boat here, Frank thought as he hauled up one of the plastic bumpers that kept the boat from scraping against the dock. And even luckier that I know where he keeps the spare key. In moments Frank was heading out into the bay.

A few moments after that, Frank was climbing a rope ladder that hung down the side of the huge yacht. There was a strong brackish smell in the night air, and a faint, ghostly white mist was drifting in from the sea. Frank shivered as he climbed on deck.

He froze for a moment, standing still to

listen. His ears caught the creak of ropes and the lapping of the water but not a single human sound.

Carefully Frank started along the deck toward where he judged Gramatkee's cabin would be. Frank carried a flashlight in his right hand.

I wonder how Kevin talked Biff into this, Frank thought as he made his way forward. It must have something to do with Jeanne. Maybe Kevin promised Biff that if he came out to the yacht, he'd find Jeanne.

Obviously Biff would never let himself get involved in any kind of big crime. Kevin must have conned him to come out to the *Golden Fleece* so he could be the fall guy for Gramatkee's murder.

Dim light shone around the door of one of the cabins. Frank didn't knock. He simply turned the knob and pushed it open. "Mr. Gramatkee, I—"

The center of the cabin was taken up by a desk. Its small brass lamp provided the only light in the cabin. Slumped at the desk was a heavyset man of sixty.

Frank went over to him.

When he got close enough to the sprawled body, he discovered that Gramatkee was alive. The millionaire had obviously been slugged—there was a welt over his left ear.

Frank saw Biff Hooper now, too. The big blond guy had fallen unconscious behind the desk. One big arm was draped over the overturned wastebasket.

Frank dropped to one knee. "Biff—Biff, are you okay?"

"He's just fine, Frank. They both are."

Behind him in the shadows was Curt Branders. The hit man's Beretta automatic was pointed at Frank.

Branders smiled.

"No one is dead—yet."

Chapter

13

JOE WOKE UP to find himself lying on the cold floor of the old barn. His face was bruised, his sides ached, and his hands were tied behind his back. Two fat candles sputtered away on the stones near his feet.

"So you're not that smart after all, are you?" Kevin Branders was dressed in jeans and a dark sweater now, sitting on the apple barrel and smirking down at Joe.

"Still a bit smarter than you," answered Joe, finding it tough to talk clearly through his swollen upper lip.

"We suckered you in very nicely, I think," continued Kevin, looking at his wristwatch. "And—it was great—you fell for the whole scam. Clever Joe Hardy sneaks up on unsuspecting Chad, the dumb Circle member.

"He knocks Chad out and takes his place. I mean, who could outwit Joe Hardy, the smartest detective in Bayport." He laughed loudly. "We figured one of you, or maybe both, would come out here. So we had everyone planted and waiting. How'd you like my speech? I bet you thought you were eavesdropping on some real heavy mumbo jumbo, huh?"

"Okay, maybe I didn't show my usual brilliance," Joe admitted. "But that doesn't mean any of you guys are especially smart. Listen, the police know all about you. Any minute now, they'll—"

"I don't believe the great Hardys would call in the law," Kevin told him. "No, I think you wanted the chance to show off, to bust in here, and capture the fiendish gang on your own. Hey, I'm always reading about your cases in the papers. You like the glory. It makes you feel like you're really worth something."

"I came here, but my brother, Frank, drove straight to the Bayport police station."

"I doubt that, Joe." Kevin jumped down off the barrel. "I'd guess Frank is off hunting for my brother."

"Why did you ever get involved in all this?"

"Involved in what?"

"You must know what it is Curt does for a

living. Why did you let him use the Circle as a front for something like that?''

"What is it you think he is?"

"Curt Branders is an international killer for hire," answered Joe. "He's wanted by the authorities of at least a dozen countries for—"

"That's not true!" Angry, Kevin walked over and kicked Joe hard in the ribs. "Curt isn't the kind of nine-to-five jerk they admire so much around here. He's a thief, I admit that. An international thief, but he's never killed anyone."

"Is that what he's told you?"

"That's what I *know*." Kevin laughed. "See, Joe, once upon a time, our father was a very successful businessman around here. Then about eight years ago he went bankrupt—and not one of his old friends lifted a hand to help him."

"I guess I don't see why you're laughing about that."

"You will in a minute," promised Kevin. "After my father went bankrupt—well, he got sick. He died about a year later." Kevin checked his watch again, looking toward the door. "After that Curt and I made a couple of promises. One was that we'd make a lot of money in our lives—and the other was that we'd never let the system beat us the way it had killed our father."

117

"Look, I understand," conceded Joe. "But I wouldn't admire the way your brother is going about it. He really is a hit man, Kevin."

Ignoring Joe, Kevin said, "Most of the kids around here think I live on some little trust fund money somebody in my family left for me." He laughed again. "But everything—our big house, the servants—is paid for by Curt's activities."

"Some joke."

"That's not the best joke," he said. "The best one has to do with how I dreamed up the Circle and talked all those fools into joining it. It was beautiful the way the poor little rich kids went for it."

Kevin's face lit up with a bitter grin. "See, Joe, we've just about come to the payoff now. I'm going to go away soon and leave them here to face the consequences of all the fun they've been having."

Joe frowned up at him. "You really don't know, do you?"

"Know what?"

"Your brother is using the Circle as a cover for something else," Joe told him. "He's going to see they get blamed for a lot more than vandalism."

"I know all about it. Tonight he's going to pull a major burglary." Kevin nodded, smiling to himself. "Too bad I won't be around to see them trying to get out of that."

Outside in the night a horn honked.

Kevin said, "About time. We'll be going now, Joe."

"Where to?"

"Well, to play out the last hand in the game."

"Actually, Frank, I wish I had a bit more time," said Curt Branders, glancing at the clock on the wall behind the unconscious Gramatkee. The Beretta in his hand pointed unwaveringly at Frank. "You seem like a relatively intelligent guy. Maybe we could have had an interesting conversation."

Frank stared at the hit man. "What exactly are you planning to do, Branders?"

"Is that really how you want to spend your final minutes?" the killer asked impatiently. "Basically the setup is this. The police will believe that your pal Biff Hooper sneaked aboard the *Golden Fleece* to pull off a burglary. Poor Biff—goaded into that reckless sort of stunt by the thrill-seeking rich kids who belong to the Circle."

Frank nodded. "So you did set up that Crimson Circle stuff just as a cover."

"Of course," Curt Branders said. "Not that

my brother didn't enjoy making fools of those spoiled idiots with checkbooks for brains."

"And you're going to kill Gramatkee?"

"That's exactly what I was hired to do by some of his business rivals. In fact, I was just about to take care of that chore when you came stumbling aboard."

The hit man shook his head. "If you're going to play spy and secret agent, Frank, you'll really have to learn to move a good deal more quietly." Curt paused, laughing. "But none of that will make any difference after tonight, will it? I ought to apologize for criticizing you during your last minutes on this planet."

"You figure to kill Gramatkee and then rig it to look as though Biff did it while attempting to pull off this dare?"

"That's it, yes. Gramatkee has a gun in his desk there—I've already made sure of that." The assassin moved closer to the unconscious man's desk.

Curt pointed down at Biff. "The jock here is surprised by our business tycoon friend. The old boy has his gun in hand. Biff, noted for brawn rather than brains, panics and grabs for the weapon. It goes off and Gramatkee is fatally shot. But as he is breathing his last, he manages to shoot Biff. And then he shoots—"

"Me," supplied Frank. "Sure, that's the

only way it's going to work now. You have to silence me, too."

"I'm afraid so, Frank." Curt eased behind the unconscious man's desk, keeping his eyes and the barrel of the pistol aimed at Frank.

"What do the police think I was doing here," asked Frank, "according to your master plan?"

"You were helping your pal carry out his dare."

"That won't wash." Frank shook his head. "They know I'm not a member of the Circle."

Curt gave an indifferent shrug. "Then perhaps you trailed Biff aboard in hope of persuading him to give up his life of crime and pranks."

He slid open the desk drawer with his free hand. "It's an old, familiar story for the police. There was a struggle, a gun went off, and people got killed. There are any number of variations, but they've seen them all. Whichever one I end up arranging, Frank, you're going to be dead and done for."

"Eventually the authorities are going to pin this on you."

"Eventually I'll be safely out of the country and lying low at my villa in—" Branders grinned at Frank. "Let's just say in an out-of-the-way spot." Slipping a pencil through the trigger guard, Curt lifted a .32 caliber revolver out of the drawer of Gramatkee's desk.

While the gun was still in midair Frank said, "Only one major flaw, Branders."

Curt hesitated. "Oh? And what might that be?"

Frank knelt down beside Biff on the cabin floor. "You're never going to be able to convince anyone that Biff did any shooting. You hit him too hard on the head," said Frank. "He's dead!"

"He's what?" Involuntarily the assassin looked away from Frank and over at Biff.

Frank had been waiting for that. He scooped up the fallen wastebasket, hurling it right at the hand that held the 9-millimeter Beretta.

Curt's hand was knocked up and to the side. His finger squeezed the trigger, and the gun went off. The roar of the shot mixed with the smashing of the desk lamp.

The room went dark.

Two more shots rang out.

Chapter

14

THE HARDY BOYS CASEFILES

THE MOTOR LAUNCH cut across the dark waters of Barmet Bay, sending up chill foam and spray. Kevin Branders glanced back from his place at the steering wheel. "I love this sea air. Are you enjoying the ride, Joe?"

Joe Hardy, his hands still tied, was sprawled uncomfortably on one of the seats. Before taking him aboard, Kevin had also run a loop of rope around Joe's ankles. The younger Hardy could hardly move. He had to squint into the darkness, since the spray rolling back off the boat's bow kept splattering his face.

"Is your brother already on Gramatkee's yacht?" Joe asked.

"Sure. Why do you think we came over to

Bayport tonight from Kirkland? I'm bringing this boat to pick him up."

"And you still won't believe me, will you, Kevin? I'm telling you, Curt is on the *Golden Fleece* to kill Gramatkee."

Kevin laughed. "You'll have to try harder, Joe. No way am I going to fall for a desperate story like that. Curt's out there, all right. He's making sure your friend Biff gets framed with a burglary rap."

Joe kept his eyes on Kevin. "Why does he need you to meet him?"

"After I pick him up, we'll be going to—to a place where there'll be a plane waiting."

Was it only hope, or did Kevin sound a little less sure of his brother's story? Joe decided to press the issue.

"Why didn't he take his own motorboat out to the yacht?"

"He was waiting on the boat Biff picked up at the yacht club. It actually belongs to your new pal Chad," Kevin explained, his eyes on the course ahead. "I thought that was a nice touch."

"Great," Joe said.

"Of course, Biff didn't know Curt was hiding out on his boat. That way any witnesses who happened to be around will see only Biff heading for the yacht at the time of the burglary."

The launch hit a rough patch of water and

the gas can stored near Joe's bound feet rattled on the wooden boards of the boat's bottom.

"How about tomorrow?" asked Joe. "What will you be doing then?"

"I'll be going away with Curt for a while, until this whole Circle thing blows over." Kevin gave him a wolfish grin. "But I'll want to come back eventually, so I can laugh at all you jerks."

Joe shook his head. "You're never coming back, Kevin."

Kevin Branders gave him a quick angry glance over his shoulder. "I don't like that kind of stuff, Joe," he said angrily. "You go talking about things that are going to happen and—and it jinxes them."

"The police are going to find Gramatkee's body on that yacht tomorrow," Joe said. "I hope you'll be able to live with yourself when you find that out. Because part of the fault— the *guilt*—will be yours."

"Stop trying to twist things around," Kevin burst out furiously. "You don't know what you're talking about. Gramatkee isn't even on that stupid yacht."

"Did your brother tell you that?" Joe rocked back and forth in his seat as the boat hit choppy water. Kevin was more busy glaring at Joe than steering the launch.

"Yeah, and Curt never lies to me." The

conviction in Kevin's voice tore at Joe's heart. "I don't know how it is with you and your brother, Joe, but Curt and I never lie to each other. We decided that a long time ago."

"Well, maybe *you* never lie to *him*."

"Lay off me," shouted Kevin. "I don't need to hear any more of this garbage."

"Kevin, your brother is a hired killer," persisted Joe. "I've seen the files on him, trust me. The FBI knows about him, the Federal Crime Bureau—and so do the police in a dozen other countries. If he's told you he's nothing more than a sort of dashing gentleman thief, then he *has* been lying to you. And he's been lying to you for years."

"Shut up, Joe!" Kevin's voice was ragged. "Just shut up!"

"Right now he's planning to kill Gramatkee. And more than likely he'll kill Biff, too."

Kevin glared at him. "No, he'd never do anything like that."

Joe shrugged. "Okay, when you pick him up, ask him.

"I will. Then you'll see how wrong you are, jerk!"

Ahead in the darkness, the lights of the *Golden Fleece* drew nearer.

As Kevin swung the launch around to approach the yacht, they heard the rapid *crack* of a gunshot. The echo of the shot moved out across the dark water. Then came a second *crack*—followed rapidly by one more.

"I don't understand this," said Kevin, a nervous note entering his voice. "There wasn't supposed to be any shooting."

After the slug tore through the desk lamp and plunged the cabin into blackness, Frank made a grab for the .32 revolver that had dropped from Curt's hand to the desk.

His fingers closed on darkness. He'd missed the gun! Groping desperately, he managed to scoop it up on the second try. Frank dropped to the floor, rolling into the safety of a dark corner.

Curt blindly aimed his Beretta toward the sound of Frank's shuffling and fired twice. He missed, but the cabin was illuminated by the flash of the shots.

Frank crawled behind a chair. It was a fat armchair on wheels, and he rolled it quickly in front of himself to serve as a shield. Then he started backstepping, pulling the chair with him toward the partially open door of the cabin.

Curt sent a bullet into the chair.

The bullet dug into the padding but got lost there. Even so, the impact lifted all four legs of the chair off the floor, setting it to wobbling wildly.

Frank thrust the gun around the chair and pulled the trigger. The hammer clicked on an empty chamber.

He kicked the chair forward into the room. Again, Curt Branders fired blind. While he was murdering the armchair, Frank managed a shaky somersault that threw him out the doorway. Hitting the outside deck, Frank pushed to his feet and started running.

His feet thumped on the damp teak planks of the deck. The next door he came to, he grabbed hold of the handle and pushed.

Then he dived inside.

Frank found himself in a large room, illuminated by a single night-light. This was a library, with shelves of books covering three walls and a half-dozen armchairs circling a low oak coffee table.

Sprinting, Frank threw himself behind one of the heavy chairs and dropped to one knee to examine the gun he'd just gotten hold of. But when he flipped the chamber open, he only sighed. Great, he said to himself, the thing's not loaded.

He took a quick survey of the cabin to see if he could find anything to use as a weapon against Curt.

The floor lamp next to the chair he was using for a shelter might do. Frank yanked the lamp's plug out of the wall and grabbed the five-foot-long metal shaft.

He stood by the door, hefting the metal tube for what felt like forever. Where was Branders?

Then, out on the deck Frank heard angry shouting, followed by gunshots. He cautiously edged the door open.

"Try to shoot me, will you?" one voice shouted angrily.

"Idiot!"

It was Biff Hooper and Curt, wrestling around on the misty deck in the darkness. Biff must have recovered consciousness and gone for Curt just as Frank had headed out of Gramatkee's cabin.

He couldn't make out the two of them very clearly, but he could hear the grunts and punches. Apparently Biff was keeping Curt from using his gun again.

Finally, one of the figures staggered to its feet. It went lurching toward the rail, then seemed to be trying to climb over it.

The dark figure hesitated there for a moment, then dove overboard.

Chapter

15

KEVIN BRANDERS CUT the engine on the launch when he saw someone leaping from the *Golden Fleece*.

"Curt?" he called across the water. "Curt, is that you?"

The swimming figure raised an arm, waving it.

"Over here," cried Kevin. "Come on."

Joe Hardy squinted across the dark waters of the bay. So, it was Curt Branders who'd dived over the railing of the yacht. Now the hit man was floundering in the water near Kevin's idled launch.

"Give me a hand," Curt Branders gasped.

With a good deal of splashing, Kevin finally managed to haul Curt into the launch.

The older of the Branderses leaned against a seat, shedding water and coughing. "Quick, get us clear of here," he ordered. "Sooner or later one of those idiots will find my gun and start shooting."

"What happened?" Kevin wanted to know. "What went wrong?"

"That dumb jock was getting the best of me."

Kevin started the engine and guided the motor launch away from the *Golden Fleece*. "Where are we heading?"

"Straight out—away from the yacht and the town. Just head for the mouth of the bay, for a few minutes, then kill it." Curt Branders was staring down at the can of gasoline. Joe didn't like the look in his eyes.

"But I thought—"

Curt Branders cut his younger brother off. "Just do what I tell you, Kev."

"What was the shooting about on the yacht? Did Gramatkee show up or what?"

Curt turned away from Kevin for a moment. "Something like that," he finally admitted.

The boat chopped its way toward the far end of the harbor.

Joe finally spoke up. "Why don't you tell him that you shot Gramatkee?" he asked.

132

"What are *you* doing here?" Curt gave Joe a deadly scowl. "You know," he said, "there are too many Hardys in this world."

Kevin asked, "Did you have to shoot Gramatkee?"

"I was shooting at Frank Hardy and Biff Hooper," answered his brother angrily. "Your buddy Biff was trying to kill me."

"Not Biff," said Kevin, shaking his head. "He's not that kind of guy."

"Why don't you keep your mind on steering this thing?" Curt said. "And leave the thinking to me."

"Give him a break," Joe told the hit man. "Don't take it out on Kevin because your plans went wrong."

Grinning coldly, Curt said, "Oh, not everything's gone wrong. I've just suffered a temporary setback, Joe."

Kevin was still glancing nervously at his brother. "But, Curt, there wasn't supposed to be any shooting."

"Obviously there was, Kev," Curt said stonily.

"Getting Biff and the others into trouble with the cops is one thing," said Kevin as he killed the engine again. "But you promised me that nobody was going to get shot or seriously hurt."

"So things changed some." Curt lifted the

gas can. "Now quit whining and pay attention. We've got some serious business ahead of us."

Curt's left hand swung out with a jerk, pointing in the direction of the *Golden Fleece*. "Gramatkee's still aboard that thing," he said. "And thanks to Frank and Biff, he's still alive. I accepted money up-front on this hit. So I can't leave here until he's dead."

Kevin's hands dropped to his sides. He inhaled sharply through his mouth, and his voice trembled as if he were close to crying. "It's true," he said numbly. "It's all true."

He sounded like a little kid who's been told there's no Santa Claus. Joe realized that Kevin Branders was losing his childhood hero.

"We've got to douse this boat with gasoline, aim it at the yacht," Curt went on, not even noticing the look on his younger brother's face. "We'll jump before it hits, and just at that instant I'll set it afire. You understand me, Kev? The timing on this is important."

"Murder," murmured Kevin, staring at him. "You're going to murder Gramatkee—and Frank and Biff, too."

Now Curt looked his brother in the face. "Great, you finally got the point. Now start the launch."

Kevin said, "And what about Joe?"

"He stays in the boat."

"You mean you kill him, too."

"I mean that *we* kill him, too." Curt's tone was full of barely restrained impatience, as though he were trying to explain something basic to an extremely stupid person. "We can't leave a witness around to tell people what we did."

He gave Kevin a friendly tap on the shoulder. "This is graduation night for you, kid. You have to run with me now. All the kid stuff is over and done."

"And I can never come back here again." Kevin glanced at Joe, remembering the things he'd said on the trip out to the *Golden Fleece*.

He shook his head. "No, I can't do this," he said. "I can't let you kill Joe or—"

"Forget about Joe then." Curt slammed the can down, bent, and hauled the tied-up Joe to his feet. Joe tried to struggle, but the ropes prevented that.

"We don't need him for anything," said Curt, looking over the launch's gunwales. "We might as well get rid of him right now."

As soon as the dark figure leapt over the rail of the *Golden Fleece*, Frank Hardy hurled himself across the deck. He pounced on the remaining figure, then drew back in surprise.

"Biff?"

Frank rose to his knees. "So Curt Branders is the one who went overboard."

Biff Hooper shook his head a few times. "I've got to tell you," he said as he got up with help from Frank, "I've felt lots better than I do right now."

Frank searched the planks of the deck. "Here's Curt's gun," he said, picking it up. "When he lost that, he must have decided a retreat was in order."

"I'm not completely clear on what's going on," admitted Biff, holding on to the rail. "I was supposed to swipe a yachting trophy from Mr. Gramatkee's cabin. I didn't want to do it, but after they kidnapped Jeanne, they told me—"

"They don't have Jeanne anymore, Biff. She's safe." Frank moved to the rail, looking down. "I thought I heard another boat approaching."

Down below light bounced from the headlights of Kevin's motor launch off the white side of the yacht, and Frank saw Curt being pulled aboard the small craft.

Frank also saw another figure stretched out on a seat. The smaller craft was lit as bright as day.

"Joe," Frank said, recognizing his brother. "They've got Joe."

For a second he looked at the gun in his

hand. No way could he risk a shot at the bobbing boat. There was too great a chance he'd hit his brother. And if he tried a bluff—well, Curt Branders had a hostage right at hand.

Frank abruptly turned from the rail. "Biff, go into the cabin and look after Gramatkee," he said, tucking the Beretta into the waist of his pants. "You can call for help with the ship-to-shore radio."

"Got you," said Biff. "I'm real sorry I got everybody into such a mess."

"Apologies come later." Frank ran to the rope ladder that dangled over the side of the yacht. Down in the water beyond him, the motor on the Branderses' launch roared to life.

By the time Frank swung down the top rung of the swaying ladder, Kevin, Curt, and the bound Joe were heading for the mouth of Barmet Bay—out to sea?

The motorboat Frank had come in was still quietly rocking in the water, bumping against the side of the yacht. He climbed down as rapidly as he could, got in, and started its engine.

Soon he was chasing after the Branders brothers, but they had a lead that he couldn't narrow. Finally, though, the other launch stopped and Frank started to catch up, speeding across the moonlit bay.

He was close enough to make out everyone aboard—including Joe.

Curt Branders had lifted him off the seat, pressing him against the low side of the launch.

Curt gave Joe a vicious shove.

Joe hit the water and sank like a stone.

Chapter
16

JOE HARDY WAS frantically fighting two separate battles.

First, he had to break free of the line that held his arms and legs bound and useless. The knots were so tight, his hands and feet were almost numb. And the chilly water didn't help.

Still worse, his writhing, twisting, and struggling against the ropes was eating up his tiny reserve of oxygen. His chest was heaving as he struggled to keep from opening his mouth and letting out the air that was now burning his lungs.

And every second these battles went on, Joe Hardy kept dropping deeper and deeper beneath the surface of Barmet Bay. By now, the lights of the launch were only shapeless glows at the end of a dark wavering tunnel.

His struggle against his bonds was churning up the water, and bubbles and foam swirled around him. Every now and then a bubble would catch the light from far above and glisten for an instant like some strange cold jewel.

Finally Joe decided it was no use. His hands and feet were held fast—he couldn't even feel them anymore. And he knew he couldn't hold his breath much longer.

He began hearing a ringing inside his head. Then came an odd roaring hum. It reminded him of a recording he'd once heard—the strange underwater song the whales sing. The glistening bubble-jewels above him were turning beautiful colors now—gold, silver, and yellow. Then it seemed that all the gems were turning crimson. Or was that something that was happening to his eyes?

Then Joe thought he saw something dark come knifing down through the water toward him. A shark? He tried to puzzle that out, forcing some thoughts through his oxygen-starved brain. Sharks in Barmet Bay? That didn't seem right. But Joe's vision was so fuzzy now, he couldn't tell what it was.

All he saw was a diving blur, coming ever closer.

Something caught him, an arm roughly taking hold across his chest. Joe really couldn't be bothered to pay much attention, so he closed his eyes.

He was thinking about how nice it would feel to open his mouth and let out all the needles that filled his lungs and throat.

There was a reason why he couldn't do that. But he couldn't remember the reason anymore.

So Joe decided to go ahead. He let out the air he'd been storing for so long. And then he gulped in a breath.

What he got was mostly air, along with some spray.

He coughed, then breathed in and out once more.

Wait a second. Something was wrong here. Joe opened his eyes and looked around.

Slowly his surroundings came back to him and everything became less blurred. He was bobbing on the surface of the water again, his head back and sucking in the blessed air.

Joe turned to see who had saved him.

Kevin Branders had one arm around him and was treading water, keeping them both afloat. "I couldn't let Curt kill you," he told Joe.

Joe laughed, a sound that was almost a sob. "Good idea," he said. "I think—" He didn't finish the sentence, though—he had already passed out.

*   *   *

"Joe!" Frank stared in horror when he saw his brother, tied hand and foot, hit the dark water of Barmet Bay. But he was still too far away to stop Curt Branders—or to help Joe.

Frank's hands were clenched so tightly on the steering wheel that his knuckles went white. He gunned his boat's engine, counting the passing seconds under his breath.

Up ahead, he saw Kevin Branders give Curt a shove and go diving from the other launch.

"You idiot!" shouted Curt. Then he dashed to the wheel of the craft and started the engine. The boat came alive, circling away from the spot where Joe and Kevin had gone under.

For some reason, Curt seemed to be heading back to Bayport—or back toward Gramatkee's yacht. Frank hoped Biff had gotten in touch with the harbor police by now. Maybe they could give the hit man a warm reception.

Then, forgetting about the escaping Curt, Frank put his own launch into a pattern of wide circles around the area where his brother had disappeared.

He switched on a spotlight, playing it across the surface of the dark water as he moved around and around in slow, wide arcs.

It seemed to Frank that Joe and Kevin had been under much too long. Another few seconds and he'd have to dive down himself.

Then he saw bubbles and spray forming on

an illuminated patch of water. Water shot up, then the head and shoulders of a young man appeared above the surface of the bay.

It was Kevin—and he was holding Joe.

With a sigh of relief, Frank killed his engine, letting the craft drift over to where the two boys had surfaced. "Kevin," he called out, "hold on. I'll be there in a second."

"He's okay," Kevin managed to gasp. "Don't worry about Joe. . . . Just passed out."

The boat had drifted almost to them. Frank tossed Kevin a line. "Hook that around Joe— let's get him out first."

Still treading water, Kevin quickly wove the rope through the bonds on Joe's arms, then flung the end back to Frank.

Carefully striving not to capsize his small boat, Frank hauled his unconscious brother on board. Then he threw the line to Kevin, who was already swimming toward the boat. It took only seconds to pull him aboard.

Joe coughed, spat out water, and opened his eyes. "Frank?" he murmured.

"Right here." Frank pulled out his pocket knife and went to work on the ropes.

Kevin huddled disconsolately against the side of the boat. A puddle of seawater spread around him. "I guess I really didn't know the score, Joe. I thought that Curt—"

He suddenly cut himself off. "Maybe you'd

better leave the knot cutting to me," he said to Frank, "while you start up this boat."

Kevin stood, pointed after his brother's boat.

"We've got to stop Curt somehow," he said, nodding at the quickly retreating launch.

"He's covering the boat with gasoline to turn it into a huge firebomb—and then he's going to ram it into Gramatkee's yacht!"

Chapter

17

FRANK WAS AT the wheel of the motorboat again. The small craft shook as it raced along in the wake of Curt's launch. Frank shook his head in frustration. "I don't think we can catch up with him," he said.

"We've got to try," said Kevin. "Biff's on that yacht, too, isn't he?"

"As far as I know," answered Frank, watching the distance between the two speeding launches diminish all too slowly.

"Suppose we try to ram him," suggested Joe.

"That would blow us up."

"I mean if we jumped before we hit."

Frank shook his head. "Too risky."

"Come on, Frank. We can't let him kill Biff and Gramatkee without even trying to stop him."

"Joe, you're in no shape for another plunge in the bay."

"Look, I can do it if I have to," Joe insisted. "So let's get close enough to him so we can give it a try."

"That's what I'm trying to do."

Kevin cried, "Look!"

Incredibly, the launch ahead of them slowed, then stopped.

"He's too far away from the yacht," Frank said. "What's he doing?"

"Maybe he shouldn't have used that gas can to decorate the deck," Joe suggested. "What if Chad forgot to fill 'er up?"

As they came closer to the motor launch, their lights caught Curt Branders in the rear of the boat. He had the housing off the engine and was frantically working with it.

"He must have flooded the engine or something," Kevin said.

"This gives us a chance." Frank jockeyed the steering wheel. Now they were even with the hit man's launch.

Frank cut the engine. "Branders!" he called over. "Give it up!"

Curt Branders paid no attention. He stayed crouched over the engine, fiddling.

"So much for the voice of reason," Joe said.

"Curt!" Kevin yelled across the water. "You can't get away—it's hopeless." He pointed back toward the white bulk of Gramatkee's yacht, with the lights of Bayport beyond it.

"Look over there," Kevin said. They could just make out flashing red lights on the water, making their way toward the *Golden Fleece.* "That's got to be the Harbor Police, Curt. Come on—it's finished."

Curt Branders did look where his brother had pointed. He must have seen the lights, because he slammed the housing down on the engine and started it up again. But it didn't respond with a full-throated roar of power. The engine noise was decidedly ragged as the boat lurched forward again.

"He's going a lot slower," Joe said.

Frank nodded grimly. "But fast enough to beat the police cruisers to the *Golden Fleece.*" He pushed the throttle forward, and their own boat leapt through the water.

The two boats zigzagged across the bay, Frank trying to cut Branders off, the hit man dodging—but always coming back toward his target.

"Can you pull up beside him?" Joe suggested. "We could just jump aboard—"

"The water's too choppy for that," Frank objected.

"Then I don't see any way you can stop this guy," Joe complained. "Unless you decide to play chicken with him."

Frank's mouth was set in a grim line. "Maybe that's just what we'll have to do."

He pulled their boat ahead of Branders's, sweeping around in a broad circle until they faced the oncoming launch. Then Frank pushed the throttle forward, racing straight for the hit man.

"Uh, Frank, that was meant more as a comment than a suggestion," Joe said.

"I thought you were the guy who said we should ram him."

"That was when we didn't have any other chance of stopping him."

"We still don't," Frank pointed out. "Besides, I don't intend to crash into him—just slow him down so the Harbor Police can cut him off."

"Then watch your driving," Joe said, "because it doesn't look like Branders is backing off."

Curt Branders hadn't deviated an inch from his course. Frank, Joe, and Kevin stared nervously as his running lights came closer and closer.

"I don't think this is going to work," Joe said quietly. "Get ready to sheer off—"

His words were cut off by a bright flash ahead of them.

A sheet of flames marched across Curt Branders's launch, lighting up the water all around. Flaming fireballs started climbing up into the night.

"He's still a mile from the *Golden Fleece,*" said Joe. "What's he doing?"

"I don't think Curt planned this," observed Frank.

The launch was blazing, spewing flame and smoke. It was going off course, starting to zigzag.

"The broken engine," said Kevin. "A spark or something must've set the gasoline on fire too soon." They could hardly see the launch anymore. It had become a mass of fire, almost too bright to look at, staggering and lurching through the darkness.

Then there came a deafening explosion.

A cloud of roaring flame flew up across the bay. Smoke tumbled out across the bay and bright tongues of flame walked on the water.

Slowly it sank, sputtered, and was gone. The night came closing in and swallowed the last of it up.

"My brother." Kevin's voice was choked. "My brother. He's dead."

"He could have jumped." Frank turned the wheel. "We'll look for him."

"He's dead." Kevin slumped in the seat.

They circled the area, circled it twice, and then once again.

They never found him.

More and more people kept coming out on the yacht club dock, most of them in uniform. Floodlights had been set up, police cars, two ambulances, and a fire truck were parked just on the other side of the cyclone fence.

A Harbor Police launch patrolled just off the piers, and a helicopter was chuffing around up in the sooty sky, splashing its spotlight down on the water. Two different television crews were wandering around, poking their cameras and mikes into various groups and even into some shadowy corners.

"I expected this," Con Riley was saying to Frank. They stood in the small guard shack by the gate. Joe, still damp, stood by a tiny space heater. Kevin Branders was sitting outside in a police car.

"When I got the call that yanked me out of a pleasant slumber, I suspected at once that it had something to do with you Hardys." Con gave them a sour look. "Then, when I was informed that there was all kinds of trouble here at the yacht harbor, I was certain."

Frank stepped aside from the door as a paramedic came in to check over Joe. "All things considered," he told Frank, "there wasn't that much damage. And nobody—well, hardly anybody—got killed."

"Hardly anybody, huh?" growled Riley. "I'd look great saying something like that on the news tonight. 'Nothing to worry about, folks, since *hardly anybody* got killed.' Hooey."

"The point is, Gramatkee is alive."

"We've put him in that ambulance over there." Riley pointed a thumb in that direction. "He's still unconscious, but they tell me it's just a mild concussion."

"That's a whole lot better than being dead."

Con gave Frank a sharp look. "And you're sure that's what this is all about?"

Nodding, Frank said, "Curt Branders was hired to kill him. Fortunately, he failed."

"All on account of you guys?"

"We did sort of throw a glitch or two into his plans."

"While you were winding up to throw those glitches, I suppose it never occurred to you to pick up the phone and let me know?"

"There just wasn't time, Con."

"What about that kidnapped girl? Where has Branders got her stashed?"

"She's okay now. Joe found her and brought

her home. She's with our aunt Gertrude at the moment."

Riley gave him a mirthless smile. "There wasn't time to tell me about that, either?"

"No, there wasn't." Frank again looked toward his brother, asking the white-coated medic, "How's he doing?"

"He seems to be in pretty good shape," he answered, "but I'd advise you to take him to the hospital for a more thorough checkup. Being immersed in the bay can have all sorts of side effects."

"I'm okay," insisted Joe. "I'm fine."

Con Riley asked Frank, "What about Kevin Branders—whose side is he on?"

Frank frowned, considering. "He's on ours now," he replied finally. "And I'm sure he never knew what his brother was really here to do. But he was involved with the pranks and the vandalism."

"Well, he told me about that old barn where we nabbed his brother's two goons. I'm sure he'll have a lot more to tell me down at the station."

"Keep in mind that he saved my brother's life."

"I will," said the police officer. "Now, where does your friend Biff Hooper fit in?"

"He was a reluctant practical joker," said

Frank. "But he also saved Gramatkee's life *and* mine."

Riley grunted. "I should have brought some medals and trophies along with me tonight, according to you," he said. "Here I thought I was going to nab some burglars and arsonists, but you claim I'm surrounded with heroes."

"What I'm trying to get across to you, Con, is that both Biff and Kevin did some things that were wrong," said Frank. "But they both tried to make up for that. I don't know how the law will look at any of that."

"Between that and the fact that they're kids, they may be lucky and get off fairly lightly," Riley said, shaking his head. "As for our rich young arsonists and so forth, I foresee fines— lots of money going out in damages—and certainly some community service."

He grinned evilly. "Maybe they'll put them to work cleaning the gym and fixing up the Hickerson Mansion. There's nothing wrong with those rich kids that a little honest sweat wouldn't cure."

Riley's face changed as he brought up the final piece of unfinished business. "You searched for Curt Branders?"

"Yes, for quite a while," answered Frank. "We never found a trace."

"Did you actually see him on the launch once it had started burning?"

"I can't be certain. It caught fire incredibly fast. And after that, we couldn't make out anything."

"Is it possible he jumped clear?"

"He could have. It's a hard one to call."

Riley nodded over at Joe. "All right, you'd better haul him off to the hospital," he told Frank. "I'll want to get statements from the both of you tomorrow."

"Okay, Con." Frank went over to his brother. "Let's get you over to the hospital."

"I really don't think that's necessary," Joe protested.

"Fine, if you want Aunt Gertrude fussing over you," said Frank.

Joe gave his brother a dirty look as he thought over the alternatives. Then he sighed. "Okay," he said. "The hospital it is."

WITHOUT A TRACE

Chapter

1

"I HATE TINY PLANES!" Joe Hardy's face was pale under his blond hair as the small commuter plane dipped in midair. Joe looked as if his stomach had been left on the ceiling.

Across the aisle, lean, brown-haired Frank Hardy grinned. "Cool it, Joe. If you settle down and look out the window, I bet you'll see Lubbock. We'll be on the ground in minutes, and then at the ranch in a couple of hours—if our ride's waiting for us."

"Great," Joe growled. "We limp over half of Texas in this oversize eggbeater and then have to drive the rest of the way to New Mexico. A nice, big jet would have gotten us there much faster."

Frank shrugged. "Not the way the schedules run. And look how much more you're seeing than you did on the jet from Bayport to Dallas." He grinned. "And you don't get the *feel* of flying in a jet. You might as well be riding an elevator."

Just then the small craft lurched, buffeted by rising warm air.

Joe's knuckles were white as he gripped the arms of his seat. "Right—this really beats flying in a nice, comfortable jet with cushy seats." He glanced out the window. "Ever since you got your student pilot's license and started to solo, all I hear from you is flying." He turned back from the window. "At least we don't have to worry about plowing into a mountain. It's flat as a tabletop."

Frank glanced briefly out the window. "Yeah, I bet even I could make an emergency landing down there if I had to."

Joe shook his head. "I hope the scenery improves in New Mexico. Doesn't sound like it, though, does it? I'm not excited to be looking at a few dead cows. I must have missed something—why isn't the local sheriff handling this, or the vet?"

"The cows belong to Roy Carlson, and Dad owes him a favor," Frank said as if he'd told him before. "And it's more than a few dead cattle. Roy isn't a guy to lose his cool easily. Anybody who runs a ranch the size of his— fifty thousand acres—" He stopped. "They're

2

reducing power. We're on the final approach to Lubbock.''

The plane banked steeply. Joe saw the runway pavement crisscrossing a field ahead. To the west, the sky was turning a dirty brown.

"Looks like we're coming into a dust storm," Frank said. The twin-engine plane bounced lightly on the cement as it touched down, taxied down the runway, and stopped. The Hardys waited while the copilot got their bags. Then they crossed the pavement and entered Lubbock Terminal.

"Frank? Joe?" A woman's voice called out.

They turned to see a tiny, older woman, wearing jeans and an embroidered western shirt, with snow white hair piled high on her head.

Frank smiled. "We're the Hardys."

"I'm Dot Carlson, Roy's wife." She extended her small hand to grip Frank's, which to Frank's surprise was firm and strong. "Roy's sorry that he couldn't pick you up." She lowered her voice. "We've got another problem at the ranch."

"What kind of problem?" Joe asked.

"I'll tell you in the car," Dot said. Minutes later the boys' bags were in the trunk of a large white luxury car. Frank sat in the front seat beside Dot, and Joe in the rear. Almost as soon as they left the parking lot, they were in open

3

country. Ahead of them, the storm spread across the western sky like a huge brown stain.

"I don't like the looks of that dust storm." Dot frowned. "It'll hamper the search."

Frank raised his eyebrows. "Search?"

"Roy and Rudy are out looking for Jerry Greene. He didn't show up for work this morning." Dot sounded worried.

"Maybe he's just taking a long weekend," Joe suggested.

"Jerry's not like that," Dot said. "His father worked for Roy for thirty years, and Jerry's always treated the ranch as if it were his own. He's been coming up with all sorts of new ideas to run the ranch better." She smiled. "He's just a little older than you boys. In fact, he's more like a grandson than an employee. No, I'm afraid it's more trouble."

"Who's Rudy?" Frank asked.

"Rudy Castillo is our other hand," Dot replied.

"You mean, Roy ranches fifty thousand acres with only two hands?" Joe blurted out in disbelief.

Dot nodded, amused. "*You* may think the Circle C is big, but it takes hundreds of acres of this rough country to feed one steer. If we need more hands, we borrow them from other ranchers." Her smile faded. "Ranching isn't going through boom times right now. Even some really big spreads went under when the price of beef dropped.''

"This is where the dead cattle come in?'' Joe asked.

Dot sighed. ''Roy will give you the details. But it looks like somebody's trying to drive us out of business. Roy's been trying to get to the bottom of it, but so far, no luck. We hope you can help.''

The dust storm was sweeping over them now, cutting the visibility to a few hundred feet. Swirls of fine soil rippled across the road. After a while they passed a sign that read, Welcome to New Mexico, Land of Enchantment, but it was almost obscured by blowing dust.

Frank grinned. ''Do these storms happen often?'' he asked.

"Too often,'' Dot said, concentrating on the road as they continued to drive west. ''This is a hard land—no trees to break the wind, no surface water. The Spanish who settled Santa Fe over three hundred years ago called the area *La Tierra Encantada*. State boosters translate it to mean 'enchanted,' but the words also mean 'the bewitched land.' All this open territory pretty much belonged to the Indians and the comancheros—renegade whites—until after the Civil War.''

More miles passed. Finally they pulled up to a run-down gas station and parked beside a dirty, once-red pickup truck. "Where are we?" Joe asked, peering through the fine haze of dust that whirled and covered everything.

Dot laughed. "This is the 'town' of Caprock—gas station, post office, and general store. I'm going to pick up the mail. We still have some distance to go." She stepped from the car and with her head down bolted for the door.

The boys watched her disappear inside. When she started to come out, her hands full of mail, a giant of a man walked up and blocked her exit. With his broken nose and big hands, he towered threateningly over her. But all he did was give her a surprisingly sweet smile and hold the door for her.

They talked for a moment, then Dot darted back to the car. The giant headed for the pickup with a fancy gun rack in its cab.

"Who *was* that guy?" Joe asked curiously when Dot got back into the car.

Dot was smiling. "He's the new foreman at the Triple O—Nat Wilkin. I hope his boss doesn't hear about him being polite to me. We've had trouble with Oscar Owens, the owner, off and on for years—and we'll have more. Nat just warned me that Oscar's upset about a fence being down." She started the car and backed onto the road.

"Do most people carry guns around here?" Frank asked.

Dot shrugged. "There's a bounty on coyotes. You can't tell when you'll meet one."

"Why is the town called Caprock?" Joe asked as they continued their westbound drive.

"You'd see the caprock shortly," Dot answered, "if it weren't for this storm. It's a long cliff that runs for miles, north to south. On the east side of it, where we are now, is the *Llano Estacado*—the 'Staked Plains.' It's almost perfectly flat, and the story is that the Indians marked their trails with stakes because there weren't any other landmarks. To the west are the sand hills—" Suddenly a gust of wind rocked the car, and she struggled for control.

"Hey!" Joe exclaimed, staring out the window. "Did you see that guy?"

"What guy?" Frank asked. "Anybody'd have to be crazy to be out in *this*." He peered out the window. "I can't see anything."

"But *I* saw him," Joe insisted. "An old geezer with a Mexican hat and some sort of straw bag. One minute he was standing there, and the next minute he just seemed to vanish."

"Must have been Caprock Charlie," Dot suggested, the car under control again. "Some folks think he's Native American, some Mexican, but most say he's loco. You know," she said, tapping the side of her head, "touched. He appears out of nowhere at the oddest times."

Dot turned off the highway and onto a dirt

road. "Almost there," she said. Through the swirling dust they could just make out a low, white-painted stucco ranch house with a cedar-shingle roof. They pulled up beside several pickups parked in front.

A tall man with a weathered face, around sixty, opened the front door and stepped out. He wore a jacket and a light gray Stetson. "So these are Fenton's boys, eh?" he said. "Welcome to the Circle C. I'm Roy Carlson."

"I'm Frank. This is Joe," Frank told him, shaking hands.

"Any sign of Jerry?" Dot asked worriedly.

"Nope," Roy replied. "We just got back from his bunkhouse. Looks like he left in a big hurry—food on the table, TV still on, the truck out front. But his horse is gone, so he must've ridden out. I figured we wouldn't have much luck tracking him in this storm. I did call the sheriff, and he'll be out soon." He looked at Frank. "You know anything about telephone answering machines?"

Frank grinned. "A little. What do you want to know?"

"Will you excuse us?" Ray asked Dot. He led the way into a small office. An answering machine sat on the desk, its red light blinking. "Jerry set this up yesterday, but I wasn't here before he had to leave, so he didn't explain how it works. Now I'm afraid I'll make the stupid thing erase itself." Outside, a horn sounded, and Roy turned. "Maybe that's the sheriff." He hurried out the door.

Frank looked the machine over, then pressed a button. The tape whirred. "Hi, Roy," a cheerful voice said. "This is Jerry. I'm back at the bunkhouse and I thought I'd give the machine a try. See you in the morning." The message ended with a loud beep.

Then a second message came on. "Roy! This is Jerry." The ranch hand sounded worried. "It's ten o'clock, and there's something weird going on near the old homestead. I can see lights. I'm going down to have a look."

Frank and Joe stared at each other. Was this a lead to Jerry's whereabouts? Suddenly they were aware of angry voices out front, loud and getting louder.

A threatening voice cut above Roy's, shouting, "I want that fence fixed and I want it fixed pronto. I'm warning you, Carlson. The next critter—four- or *two*-legged—that wanders onto my place is going to be buzzard bait!"

Chapter
2

As FRANK AND JOE dashed to the front of the ranch house, they heard the slam of a door, the roar of a powerful engine, and the sound of tires sliding on gravel. They reached the porch just in time to see a shiny pickup speed off.

"Who was that?" Frank asked Roy, who was calmly watching the pickup disappear into the dust storm.

"Oscar Owens," Roy said. "He owns the Triple O, just south of us." He shook his head. "That old boy's got a short fuse, but he'll get over it. Always does."

"What was he mad about?" Joe asked, trailing the others back into the house.

"His foreman spotted some of my cattle on his land before the storm this morning. Turns out a section of the fence was down. He claims my bull did it. I don't believe it, but I promised to round up my stock as soon as the storm cleared. But I can't get to the fence until next week. That's when old Oscar blew up."

"Fence down, cattle loose—is this the kind of thing that's been happening to you?" Frank asked.

Roy nodded, deep frown lines cutting his forehead. "It started with gates left open, fences down—or cut—a phone line out. Then a calf or two began to disappear, and the horses showed up lame. It's hard enough making a living out here. Now I've got someone trying to bleed us dry, a drop at a time."

"So that's why you called Dad?" Frank asked.

Roy frowned. "No, I called him after Rudy went down to the south tank a couple of days ago and found eleven head dead."

"Tank?" Joe asked, looking confused.

"It's like a little lake," Frank told him. He turned to Roy. "You think somebody poisoned them?"

"I'd bet on it," Roy said grimly.

"Poisoned them how?" Joe asked.

"Salt water, that's how."

"Salt water!" the boys exclaimed together.

"Where would anybody get *salt* water around here?" Joe asked. "There's no ocean in a thousand miles."

11

"Out of an oil well, maybe," Frank suggested.

"You've got to be kidding," Joe said.

"No, Frank's right," Roy cut in. "On some wells, you hit salt water before you hit oil. They pump it out and truck it away. There's a bunch of new wells between here and Armstrong, the county seat. It wouldn't be far for someone to bring a truck full of bad water and dump it into my tank."

His frown deepened. "And the only clue we found was tire tracks—plenty of them, and plenty wide."

Frank nodded. "Like a truck's tires."

Joe changed the subject. "Had Owens seen Jerry?"

"I didn't have a chance to ask. He just yelled and was out of here."

"There were two messages on the answering machine," Frank told him. "From Jerry. The first was a test. The second time he sounded nervous, talking about lights at the old homestead. He was going to take a look."

Roy looked surprised. "This I want to hear," he said, leading the way inside. After he'd heard the message, his look changed to one of worry.

"What's this old homestead?" Joe asked.

"It was the first house in these parts," Roy said. "Not much more than a ruin, now. It just happens to be right on the boundary between Oscar Owens's place and mine."

He went to the window. "Looks like the storm's about over. I've got to wait for the sheriff, but maybe you could check out the homestead for me." He peered at Joe. "Can you handle that beat-up yellow pickup out front? It's got an old three-speed 'tranny.' "

Joe's eyes lit up. "Sure thing!" he exclaimed, catching the key Roy tossed him.

The sky was clearing, and as the boys stepped through the front door they took in their new surroundings. The ranch house was on a ridge facing east. Below, at the bottom of the slope, was a sheet-metal barn and a cluster of buildings—a garage, maintenance shop, and various other sheds. Beyond, to the east, lay a vast stretch of rolling treeless country. The lowlands were covered with shrubs and small bushy trees, broken occasionally by bare, light-colored hills. Against the horizon lay a long, curved line.

"Is that the caprock?" Joe asked.

"You got it," Roy said. He pointed slightly southeast. "The bunkhouse is a couple of miles in that direction, just off the top of the caprock." He glanced at Joe. "That's an easy place to get stuck, if you don't watch yourself."

"Where's the homestead?" Frank asked.

Roy pointed due south, along the ridge.

"That way, about five miles. If you take the road that you came in on, you'll come to a fork. Take the leg that heads south."

Frank was staring at something at the foot of the hill—it looked like a wind sock that airports use. The brush on both sides of a flat stretch of road had been cleared away, but the "runway" was too short to handle an ordinary aircraft. "Is somebody flying an ultralight?" he asked.

Roy gave him an appraising glance. "You know about that new miniplane Jerry's flying?"

"Jerry's got an ultralight?" Joe asked, surprised. "What does he do with it?"

"He runs cattle out of the bush with it," Roy explained. "He read somewhere that they use helicopters for that kind of work down south, and he reckoned that an ultralight would do just as good and be a lot cheaper."

He shrugged. "Thing looks to me about as solid as a butterfly, but he talked me into it. It's easy for him to fly, and he can spot cattle we'd never see from the ground. The thing makes a whale of a racket, so he gets behind the cattle and drives them along like a good cow dog."

"Where is it now?" Frank wanted to know.

"Down in the barn." Roy looked at them. "Either of you boys fly?"

"I'm learning," Frank said. "Can I have a look at it?"

Roy nodded. "It sure could speed up the search."

"But you only just got your *student's* license," Joe objected quietly so only Frank could hear.

Frank was already heading down the hill. "Doesn't matter," he said out of the side of his mouth. "Federal regulations don't require a license for flying an ultralight, as long as it's under a certain weight and flies less than fifty miles an hour—and as long as there are no passengers."

In the dim light inside the barn, Frank whistled softly, "She's a beauty, Roy."

The ultralight had long, red, heavy nylon wings with yellow stripes. The aluminum tubes that supported the wings and connected them to the tail and the tricycle undercarriage were also red. The engine was hung under the rear edge of the wing, and the prop stuck out behind it. There were two bucket seats over the wheels.

"These look like the controls on the trainer I fly," Frank remarked, climbing in from the left. "But it's a lot more open."

Joe grinned. "Sort of like a motorcycle of airplanes."

"This would sure help a lot in searching for Jerry." Frank looked at Roy. "Mind if we wheel it outside and try it?"

"If you think you can handle it," Roy said.

A minute later Frank was sitting inches above the dirt road, facing into the wind. The engine whined like a chain saw. He tried the hand controls to check the movement of the ailerons. "If I did this in the air, it would make the wings waggle left to right."

Then he checked the elevators on the tail. "This would make the tail go up or down." Finally, Frank worked the foot controls side to side as the rudder on the tail moved back and forth.

"Let me guess," Joe yelled over the noise of the engine as he steadied the right wing. "This is for right or left turns?"

Frank nodded and gave a thumbs-up to Joe. "I'll just take off, circle, and land," he shouted, and pulled back the throttle.

The ultralight seemed to spring forward. Frank felt the blast of the air rushing past him as he rose. Soon he was even with the ranch house at the top of the hill, at an altitude of a hundred feet or so, and he began his turn to the left, still climbing.

As he passed over the ranch house, he reduced power and began to glide, continuing his turn. The road was now directly in front of him and a little below. He leveled the wings and eased back on the elevator, slowing his descent and reducing his speed. He was sailing between the scrub on both sides of the road when he felt the wheels bounce. Carefully, he applied the brake and came to a smooth stop.

"How was it?" Roy shouted, as Frank cut the engine.

"Great!" Frank replied. "It works fine."

"So what's our next move?" Joe asked.

"You take the truck and head for the homestead. I'll shadow you from the air."

"How do we communicate?" Joe asked doubtfully. "That thing doesn't have a radio."

"Arm and hand signals, I guess. If I spot something, I'll circle and point at it."

"Good luck," Roy said.

Joe climbed into the yellow pickup. From the looks of it, the truck had lived its whole life on the ranch and had never seen a car wash or a vacuum cleaner. He turned the key and its giant V-8 engine thundered to life. He grinned. The muffler had seen better days, but maybe the cows didn't mind. He pulled down on the massive stick shift. There was an angry grating sound.

Transmission could use some work, he thought. Joe shoved into first gear, and the truck lurched off. He turned down the hill just in time to see Frank making his takeoff run.

The road forked half a mile to the north. Joe twisted the wheel to the left and headed south, down a road with plenty of washouts. Frank was hovering off to one side, at an altitude of about a hundred feet. He could easily outdistance the truck, but he was holding back.

The sun was low in the west. All at once Frank took the lead, circling about a hundred yards ahead. Joe was almost on top of the homestead before he saw it through the ferny fronds of six-foot-high mesquite bushes.

It was a single-room shack, weather-beaten and sagging. Behind it was a corral and loading pens. A few small trees had grown up around the abandoned wooden windmill.

If there had been any tracks in the sand, the wind had erased them. He stopped the truck, left it running, and opened the door to the shack. Inside was a bunk in one corner and a table in the middle, with a couple of wooden chairs. Papers, bottles, and cans lay on the cracked cement floor, around an old iron stove. But there was no sign of life—not even a footprint in the fine layer of grit that covered everything.

When Joe stepped outside, he saw Frank high above, heading east. He jumped into the truck and gunned it into pursuit.

Up in the ultralight, Frank had seen something moving up ahead, among the sand hills. He had soared over to check it out while Joe searched the house. As Frank flew closer he saw it was a horse—a horse with a saddle but no rider. It could be the horse Jerry had been riding when he went to check out the lights.

He banked, preparing to circle back to the homestead. Suddenly he felt a jerk on his right foot pedal, the one that controlled the right rudder. Then the ultralight whipped into a spin.

Frank frantically worked the rudder pedals. The right one was stuck in the stop position. Trying the left pedal, he managed to move it slightly—but then it stuck, too.

Fighting panic, Frank glanced behind him at the tail. The rudder was definitely jammed, which meant that a control cable must have broken and the control line had fouled.

The ultralight kept whirling in a tight circle—and the ground was moving up closer and closer.

If Frank didn't get control back, the ultralight would crash!

Chapter
3

STAY COOL! That was what Frank's flight instructor always said. The foot controls didn't work, but what about the hand controls? Gingerly Frank tried the control stick. The ultralight banked to the right, stopping its spin.

"All *right!*" Frank muttered. "I've still got the aileron controls and can make wide turns. But I'll be flying with crossed controls—if I don't watch it, I'll either stall out or wind up in another spin. Either way, I'll fall—and there's nowhere safe to land right here."

Using the stick, Frank carefully fought the spin to bring the ultralight shakily around. Then he leveled it out at about a hundred feet. He was heading back for the ranch when he saw Joe's yellow truck on the road below. Joe, his head out the window, was staring up at him.

Got to let Joe know what's wrong, Frank thought. He pointed to the ultralight's tail and shook his head violently. He pointed to himself, then toward the ranch. Then he pointed down at the truck and toward the sand hills where he'd seen the horse.

Joe stopped the truck and climbed out, looking up. Frank repeated the gestures. This time, Joe gave him a thumbs-up sign, got back in the truck, and started off.

Frank had a long, nervous flight back to the ranch. He still wasn't home free—landing with crossed controls would be tricky. But he'd practiced cross-wind landings, which also made planes spin. The trick was to kick in the rudder at the last possible moment to make the plane straighten out. But Frank had no rudder!

He reduced power as much as he dared, slowly bringing the ultralight's nose up. He was coming straight down the road, aiming slightly to the left, his right wing a little low. Just before touchdown, he jammed all his weight on the right brake. The ultralight landed on the right wheel, bounced, pulled violently to the right, then straightened out.

Roy ran up to the plane. "Where'd you learn to fly like that?" he asked.

Frank managed a shaky breath. "Just lucky?" he said.

*　　*　　*

Joe knew something was wrong, but he didn't know what. His first instinct was to follow Frank, in case he was in real trouble. But Frank had obviously spotted something he wanted Joe to check out. So Joe continued toward the sand hills.

When he got to the edge of the low dunes, the road narrowed to a trail and then disappeared altogether. Joe remembered what Roy had said about getting stuck, so he stopped the truck, climbed out, and started to climb the nearest dune for a look. There wasn't much vegetation, and it was slow going in the loose sand.

As he reached the top of the dune, the sun was dipping below the horizon. Twenty yards away, Joe saw what Frank must have spotted from the air—a riderless bay horse, reins trailing in the sand.

Joe approached cautiously, afraid the horse would bolt. But the animal was exhausted. It just stood with its head down as Joe grabbed the reins. "Hey, fella, where's your rider?"

Joe led the horse to the truck, tied it to a bush so it could graze the tall grass, then headed back up the hill. Trailing the hoofprints brought him to a small hollow—the horse must have taken shelter there during the storm. Joe saw no trace of the rider.

He headed back to the truck and sat down

on the tailgate to watch the gathering shadows. "Hope Frank comes back quick with rein-forcements."

Finally two sets of headlights appeared from the darkness. The lead truck slid to a stop and Frank jumped out. Roy pulled in behind, tow-ing a horse trailer. A small, wiry man with dark, straight hair and a broad, flat face got out with him as a gray dog leaped from the truck bed and trotted toward the horse, whining.

"Glad you could make it." Joe grinned at Frank. "How come you cut out back there?"

"The rudder cable broke," Frank replied. "It was some trick getting down in one piece."

"But he did it—good job, too," Roy said. He looked at the horse. "That's Jerry's bay, all right. Where'd you find him?"

"Over there," Joe said, pointing. "I didn't find anything else—no tracks."

"Rudy, take Shep and have a look," Roy told the other man. "We'll load the horse."

"Shep! *Venga!*" Rudy commanded. The dog whined and sat down beside the horse. "Come here!" Reluctantly, the dog got up and trotted after him.

"That's Rudy Castillo," Roy told Joe, pull-ing down the trailer tailgate. "Fine ranch hand. He's got a sixth sense—if there's anything out there, he'll spot it."

"And the dog?" Frank asked as they loaded the horse.

23

"Shep belongs to Jerry." Roy shook his head and frowned. "That was one funny thing I noticed at the bunkhouse—Shep wasn't there. Rudy said he showed up a little while ago. There was something else—"

Rudy came up, shaking his head. "No sign of him, Senor Roy."

Roy nodded grimly. "Well, I guess that's it for now. Let's head back to the ranch. I called the sheriff and told him to come later. I don't want to miss him. We can get some supper, too. They piled into the trucks and headed back.

"That was delicious," Joe told Dot as he polished off the biggest meal of chicken-fried steak he'd ever eaten. "If supper's always like this, I may sign on permanently." Everyone laughed.

"I want to hear more about the grazing leases you told me about earlier," Frank said to Roy. "You're renting some land? You don't own all fifty thousand acres?"

"Right," Roy said, pushing his chair back. He led them into the office and pointed at a large wall map, a section of which was outlined in red. "We actually own this part." His hand moved along the middle third of the outlined area. "This is state land." He traced out a section to the north. "We lease the south end of the ranch—the sand hills section—from the

24

federal government. In fact, our leases are up for renewal next month.''

"So you get to use the land?'' Joe asked.

Roy grinned. ''We get to use the grass on it to feed our stock. And we get the right to renew it. The leases are so cheap that nobody ever lets them go unrenewed.''

A car pulled up outside, then came a knock at the front door. ''Hi, Bobby,'' they heard Dot say. ''Roy's in the office.''

A man in a dusty khaki uniform stepped in the room. The sheriff was slender and just over thirty. He wore a badge, and a .357 Magnum was holstered at his hip. ''Evening, Roy. Jerry show up yet?''

''Not yet,'' Roy said. ''Boys, this is Bobby Clinton, our local sheriff. Bobby, this is Frank and Joe Hardy. I worked with their father awhile back. They're here to help me straighten out those problems I've been having.''

The sheriff nodded. ''Welcome to Armstrong County.'' His eyes weren't welcoming, however, as he gave Frank and Joe the once-over. Clinton turned back to Roy. ''You want me to file a missing persons report on Jerry, or do you want to wait a few days to see if he wanders in?''

''We found his horse this afternoon, out in the sand hills,'' Joe volunteered.

The sheriff gave him a thin smile. ''He must

have got bucked off," he said. "Chances are he'll come walking in tomorrow morning, complaining about sore feet."

Roy fixed his eyes on the sheriff and shook his head. "You don't believe that. I think Jerry was riding before he could walk."

"Well, what then?"

"I don't know," Roy said slowly. "We're going looking in the morning."

"Guess I could spare a couple of deputies," the sheriff offered. "And I'll talk to a few of the other ranchers."

Roy nodded. "Have them meet us by the bunkhouse up on the caprock at sunup."

Clinton left, and Roy turned to Frank and Joe, grinning crookedly. "Bobby's what we call 'a good ol' boy.' Problem is, he's still got a lot to learn about being a good sheriff."

"Maybe there's a connection between Jerry's disappearance and the other problems," Joe said.

"I don't know," Roy said. "But I'll tell you one thing. Remember when we picked you up, I said something was funny. I just figured out what it is. Why would Jerry ride his horse from the bunkhouse to the old homestead at night, in the dark? He would've used the truck. But he didn't—it was still there."

"So somebody went to a lot of trouble to make us *think* Jerry took the horse," Frank suggested.

"Maybe," Roy agreed, with a frown. "That doesn't sound good."

"Would Jerry—or you—have an enemy who'd want to get rid of him?" Joe asked.

For a moment Roy was silent. Then he said, "Jerry didn't, but I might."

"Can you give us some names?" Frank said.

Roy's voice was reluctant. "I don't like to bad-mouth a man without proof."

"We understand," Frank said. "But we've got to have some leads."

"Well, the first name that comes to mind is Jake Grimes," Roy said. "He was a hand here last year, but I had to let him go because I caught him selling off some of the ranch supplies." He grunted. "He and Jerry parted on good terms, but Jake was pretty angry with me."

"Where can we find him?" Frank asked.

"He was working in Armstrong, last I heard. For the feed lot."

"What about Oscar Owens?" Joe asked. "He didn't sound like your best buddy when he left here this afternoon."

"Oh, Oscar yells a lot," Roy admitted, "but it doesn't usually amount to anything." He straightened his shoulders. "But for right now, let's concentrate on finding Jerry. I don't think he's wandering around out there. But if he is, he won't last more than another day in this heat, without water."

"What about the ultralight?" Joe asked Frank. "Can it be repaired to help with the search?"

Frank shook his head. "I checked it out. It needs a new rudder cable."

"Not enough time for that," Roy told them. "Tomorrow we'll drive into the back country. It's easy to get lost if you don't know your way, so one of you can come with me, the other will go with Rudy."

Frank and Joe agreed.

At dawn the next day a dozen trucks and jeeps were parked at the bunkhouse, a small neat building just off the road along the top of the caprock. There were the usual barns and corrals, and out back, beside a propane tank, there was a satellite dish.

"Can we have a look inside?" Frank asked Roy.

Roy unlocked the front door. "Go ahead. But you'd better hurry. We'll get started as soon as Bobby Clinton's boys show up."

The bunkhouse had apparently once been a rancher's main home. Now, though, it looked more like a bachelor pad. In the bedroom there were posters of several appealing young movie stars, a gun rack on the wall, and a closet full of cowboy boots, work shirts, and blue jeans.

The living room was nearly bare, except for a TV and a stereo, with a rack of country and

Without a Trace

western cassettes. There was a half-eaten pizza on the kitchen counter beside the microwave. As far as clues were concerned, nothing.

Outside, Roy was talking to the group—about thirty men, including a couple of uniformed deputies who had just arrived. "Okay, boys. You all know that Jerry disappeared night before last. We found his horse yesterday afternoon, near the old homestead. So that cuts down the area we've got to search."

"Great," Joe overheard one of the searchers whisper to another. "That cuts us down to about twenty square miles of desert."

Roy broke the group up into pairs and assigned them search areas. In a few minutes everyone climbed into vehicles.

Frank rode with Roy in a green pickup with a CB radio. All morning they bounced up one rutted road and down another, leaving a trail of dust. At each windmill or water tank, Roy stopped and got on the radio while Frank pushed through a cluster of cows and climbed the tower. He then scanned the area with a pair of powerful binoculars. Actually, he was glad that he and Joe weren't out on their own. Every road, every windmill, every tank, looked exactly alike.

For lunch they headed back to the ranch house. Frank and Joe were surprised that Nat Wilkin was there, along with a couple of other searchers.

29

"Any news?" Roy asked.

Nat shook his head. "Sorry, Roy, all the groups reported the same thing—no luck."

They ate quickly, then headed out for another bone-jarring tour of dusty scenery. Just before sundown, the searchers met back at the ranch house again. They all looked dejected.

"Nothing," Nat said. "I'm available tomorrow, if you want—"

Roy shook his head. "Thanks for the help, boys." The searchers left in silence.

"They're not coming back tomorrow?" Joe asked.

Roy shook his head wearily. "No point. We covered the territory pretty thoroughly. If Jerry's out there alive, which I doubt, his only hope is to get to one of those water tanks. Rudy and I'll keep checking them out."

Frank nodded. "Joe and I would like to camp out at the old homestead," he said. "If Jerry really saw something suspicious down there, we want to know what it is."

"That's as good an idea as any," Roy said. "Dot will make you some sandwiches. Load a couple of mattresses into the green pickup, the one with the CB. That way, you can keep in touch."

It was dark by the time Frank and Joe finally made it to the old shack. Their lantern lit the single room, casting shadows into the corners. Outside, the wind moaned in the mesquite trees. Then the boys heard the sound of twigs breaking underfoot.

Joe grinned. "You think there are bears in this country?"

"I doubt it," Frank said in a low voice. "And we didn't hear an engine. Let's check this out."

The Hardys rose to their feet and headed silently for the door.

Just as silently, someone outside was lifting the rusty old latch on the door.

Chapter

4

THE DOOR OPENED A CRACK. Frank and Joe froze in their tracks as something was thrust through the door. It looked like an old gourd on a stick. An ancient hand then appeared, clutching the stick and shaking it. The gourd rattled.

Then the door creaked open all the way, to reveal an old man with stringy gray hair. He wore a straw sombrero and carried a straw bag.

"It's him!" Joe whispered excitedly. "Caprock Charlie—the old man I saw in the dust storm!"

"Hello," Frank said, nodding to their uninvited guest.

"Buenas noches." The old man looked at both boys, rattling the gourd again. "Call me Carlos. I come with a warning."

"Warning?" Joe asked. "About what?"

"There is evil here," the old man whispered. "Danger." He pointed out the window to the east. "You see?"

Joe turned to see a crescent moon rising over the caprock. "That's weird," he muttered. "I've never seen a ring around the moon like that."

Frank shrugged it off scientifically. "Ice crystals at high altitudes," he said.

The old man stepped forward to draw a *C* in the dust on the table with his finger. Around the *C* he drew a circle. *"Muy malo!"* he exclaimed. "Very bad."

"That's Roy's brand," Joe said in a low voice.

"It's also the crescent moon," Frank pointed out, "with a ring around it." He turned to the old man. "What does it mean?"

"Long ago," the old man said, "comancheros attacked settlers who came to live up there." He pointed to the caprock. "Near my people's sacred place. All the settlers but one died that night, when the moon was a ringed crescent, like now. You must leave and not come back!"

Outside, a cow bellowed. The sound distracted the Hardys, who turned to the window. As they turned back, they felt a swift, chill breeze. The room was empty.

"Let's go after him," Joe said, heading for

the door. But outside, they saw no sign of the old man.

"Forget it, Joe," Frank told him. "That guy's got some vanishing act. If we go after him, they'll be looking for us in the morning."

"Okay," Joe agreed, as they stepped back inside. "What say we get some sleep?"

Joe woke well after midnight, stirring restlessly on his mattress. He'd heard something— no, *felt* something. It was like a clap of thunder, reverberating in his bones. Through the window he could see that the moon had moved far to the west in the cloudless sky. No thunder. He must have been dreaming.

When he awoke again, it was almost daylight. Frank's alarm watch was beeping.

"Give me a break." Joe sighed sleepily.

Frank was heading for the door. "I promised to check in with Roy on the CB at seven. After I do that, maybe we can check out some dead cattle."

After Frank finished on the CB, they set off to find the stock tank. A quarter mile south of the homestead, Joe slowed the truck and pointed to a dozen large black birds circling just ahead. "Buzzards?"

"Vultures, actually," Frank said. "Scavengers. That must be the place."

Just off the road, an earth dam had been pushed up across a dry stream bed. Most of the water in the tank had evaporated, and all that was left was a puddle of green water, thick with pond scum. The edge of the puddle had a thick white crust. Deep tire ruts filled with drifted sand led from the road to the tank.

Joe sniffed. Nearby, at the edge of the sagebrush, were the carcasses of several cattle. "I thought they got rid of the dead cattle. These must have been new customers."

Frank knelt beside the puddle. "Looks like salt, all right," he said. "Why don't you collect a sample of the crust, and fill a bottle with water. I'll have a look around."

While Joe collected the samples, Frank inspected the ruts and then walked around the tank, looking at the ground. Joe saw him pick something up, sniff it, and put it into a plastic bag. "What did you find?"

Frank handed him a plastic bag with three shiny rifle cartridge cases in it. "They're fresh."

"What kind of gun?"

"Can't tell. They've got military ordnance marks on the bottom—number forty-three. Probably the year of manufacture, not the caliber. I'd say they're World War II surplus." He examined them closely. "Weird looking. The base and the shoulder are unusually short, and the base has a lot of taper. I'd guess they're about thirty caliber."

"Maybe Roy or Rudy shot some of the cattle that were too far gone to save," Joe suggested.

"Maybe. We'll ask." Frank looked at the tire tracks. "I don't think there's any point in trying to make casts of the tracks—they're too badly eroded by the wind. But I think our major clue is the tank truck that left them. Let's head for the ranch house. I've got some questions for Roy."

As they drove up to the ranch house, Roy came out to greet them. He shook his head when he saw the cartridges. "We didn't shoot any cattle. But that tank attracts game and people hunt out there all the time."

"We were thinking of trying to find the truck that poisoned the tank. Can you give us some idea about where to look?" Joe asked, as Frank stuck the plastic bag with the cartridges back into the glove compartment.

"You can try the oil-drilling services in Armstrong," Roy said. "Plenty of those companies use trucks like that—probably too many to check out."

"Well, we'll give it a try," Frank said.

They drove to Armstrong, the county seat thirty miles to the southeast. The town was an odd mixture of western cow town and modern city. The outskirts housed companies supplying the relatively new oil and agricultural economy. But in the heart of town, the courthouse was surrounded by old stores that had gone up around the turn of the century.

"Let's start here," Frank said, pulling into

the parking lot of the Acme Drilling Service Company. He parked beside a truck hitched to a huge tank trailer.

"Look at the size of those tires," Joe said, marveling.

"Big enough to fill the ruts at the stock tank," Frank said as they got out.

"Help you boys?" the man behind the counter asked.

"Are you the dispatcher?" Frank asked.

The man grinned. "Among other things."

"We're looking for a tank truck."

"We lease by the hour, the day, or the week. How long you need it?"

"What we need is information," Frank said. "The truck we're looking for was involved in illegal dumping."

"Registration number?" the dispatcher growled.

"We don't know," Frank admitted.

"What makes you think it was our truck?"

"We're just trying to figure out where it could have come from," Frank said. "How many companies lease trucks around here?"

The dispatcher barked a laugh. "At least three others I know of. Plus half a dozen independents."

"Nine companies, just in this town." Frank began to understand what Roy had meant. "Do these trucks keep any kind of a log?" he asked.

"Most don't. We've got better things to do

with our time." The dispatcher scowled. "Like make a living."

"Do you know of any trucks working up near the town of Caprock?" Frank asked.

The dispatcher seemed to relax a little. "Nope. As far as I know, there's no drilling going on there." He eyed them. "What kind of dumping?"

"Uh, nothing, I guess," Frank said, tugging on Joe's arm. "Thanks for your help." They headed for the door.

"That didn't get us anywhere," Joe said grimly as they crossed the lot.

Frank shrugged. "I guess Roy was right. Let's head back to the ranch. Maybe they've heard something from Jerry."

The sky had been clear all day, but as they drove north, threatening gray clouds began to loom against the horizon, dark and heavy. Bright lightning flickered in all directions.

"Looks like we get to see one of those famous desert thunderstorms," Frank said.

As they drove into the approaching storm, the black clouds seemed to rise like a dark curtain, then lower behind them until the horizon at their backs was only a narrow, eerie strip of pale light. No wind stirred the oppressive layer of heat that blanketed the desert, but overhead the clouds were boiling and the black had turned to a peculiar violet-green.

"I don't like the looks of this," Joe muttered, pointing at a dark mass hanging below the cloud base.

Suddenly, less than a quarter-mile away, a long, dark finger reached out of the blackness and groped toward the ground.

It touched down, bounced up, then came back down beside a roadside sign. Joe stared as the billboard disintegrated, sucked up into the darkness.

"Did you see *that?*" Frank gasped, pulling onto the shoulder and stopping.

The tornado lifted up again, pulling a stream of dirt and dust after it. Then, with the roar of an immense freight train, the twister came directly at them!

Chapter
5

"QUICK! INTO THE DITCH!" Joe heard Frank
shout, over the deafening roar.

It was so black that Joe could barely see the
edge of the road as he jumped out of the truck
and flung himself into the shallow ditch. He
kept himself flattened against the ground as the
wind worked hard to pry him loose. Minutes
ticked by as the storm roared around them, the
air thick with dirt and gravel and twisted
shrubs. Finally the noise died down.

"You okay?" Frank asked, behind Joe.

"Yeah." Joe sat up, rubbing his shoulder.
"Hey! Where's the truck?"

Frank was on his knees, looking a little gray.
"I think that's it," he said, pointing. In a field
several hundred feet away was a mass of crumpled metal.

40

"Guess we can chalk up one truck to the storm," Joe grunted, getting to his feet. He shivered. The air, which had been like a blast from an oven only minutes before, now felt refrigerated. The storm had dropped the temperature at least forty degrees in just minutes. A few chilly drops of rain began to fall.

"Come on. Let's take a look," Frank said.

The truck lay on the driver's side. The top had caved in, with the passenger door wrenched off. The glove compartment was open and empty. Five minutes of searching didn't turn up the bag of cartridges.

"So much for our evidence," Joe sighed. "Think you'd recognize those cartridges if you saw them again?"

Frank nodded. "They were pretty unusual."

Joe took a last look at the truck. It was beginning to rain heavily now. "This thing's not going anywhere," he said. "Let's head back to the road. Maybe we can hitch a ride."

They had scarcely reached the road when they saw the flashing lights of an emergency vehicle approaching at high speed. The car—a highway patrol car—slowed as it neared them. The trooper pulled onto the shoulder and rolled down his passenger window.

"The weather service just put out a tornado bulletin. You guys better be on the lookout."

Joe laughed. "We've already seen as much of that tornado as we care to." He jerked his thumb over his shoulder. "It totaled our truck."

The trooper glanced toward the wreckage and let out a whistle of surprise. "Anybody hurt?"

Frank shook his head. "Nope. We hit the dirt just in time."

The trooper opened the door. "Come on in—you're getting wet."

The boys listened while the trooper got on the radio and made a report. When he finished, he turned to them. "Which way you headed?"

"North," Joe said. "To town—Caprock."

"That's my patrol," the trooper said. "I'll give you a ride."

The trooper eased the patrol car back onto the highway. After a while, he asked, "You guys from around here?"

"We're visiting Roy Carlson, on the Circle C," Frank replied.

"I picked up a missing persons report about a Circle C hand," the trooper told them. "Has he turned up yet?"

Joe shook his head. "Not yet," he said.

"Well, it's not surprising," the trooper told them. "Young guys pack up and leave all the time, most of them without notice. He'll show up somewhere, sooner or later."

"There's been some trouble out at the ranch—vandalism," Joe said. "Do you see much of that around here?"

The trooper looked surprised. "Not much," he said. "It's too far from town for the punks to come out."

Twenty minutes later the patrol car pulled up in front of the Caprock store. The Hardys thanked the trooper for the ride and climbed out.

"I'll call the ranch." Frank headed for the pay phone. "Somebody can come and pick us up."

"Good idea," Joe said, on his way into the store. "I need something to drink. How about you?"

"Sounds good," Frank replied, dialing the phone.

The inside of the old store was just what Joe had expected. A dusty front window was the only source of light for the small room. The walls were lined with homemade shelves of boards and plywood. Stacked on them were cans and boxes, their labels faded and peeling, and lots of miscellaneous hardware.

To the right of the door was a long wooden counter with a postage scale on it. Behind the counter stood a bank of boxes with numbered glass doors—Caprock's post office. In one corner stood an ancient soda machine filled with bottles. Joe fed it some coins, took out two bottles, and opened them.

"Roy's on his way," Frank said, coming into the store. He took the bottle Joe handed him.

"You boys the ones staying at the Carlson place?"

The question came from the frail, white-haired man behind the counter. Joe had felt his gaze since they walked into the store. Not too many people get dropped off here by the state cops, Joe thought, amused. "Yeah, we lost our truck in a tornado," he said. "The trooper gave us a ride."

The little man's eyebrows shot up. "I'd say you boys are born lucky," he said.

"We hope so," Frank said. "Say, do you know an old Native American guy who hangs out around here? He's got gray hair. I think he carries a straw bag."

"Oh, Charlie. Sure, I know him. He was here when I came and that's been—well, let's see." He calculated. "Better than forty years now."

"Where does he live?" Frank asked.

The white-haired man shifted uneasily. "Here and there. Mostly in a shack below the caprock. How come you want to know?"

"We've been staying at the old homestead on the edge of the sand hills," Joe replied. "He paid us a visit last night with a crazy story about a Native American raid under a crescent moon with a halo around it."

"Yep, that sounds like Charlie." The frail man got serious. "But that's no crazy story. About a hundred years ago, a bunch of renegades hit a homesteader's cabin out on the caprock one night. Killed every last soul they could find. Then they burned the place to the ground."

"Charlie said they were comancheros," Frank interrupted. "And the comancheros weren't all Native Americans, as I understand it. Some of them were Mexicans, others were renegade whites."

The little man shrugged. "Who cares nowadays? Only one person survived—and he died years ago."

"Charlie was talking about evil and danger," Joe told him. "Do you know what he meant?"

Now the storekeeper laughed. "I wouldn't worry if I were you. Charlie's always trying to scare folks with talk about evil." He grinned, showing one gold tooth. "I think he hopes we'll all get scared, pack up and leave. Then his people can come back to their sacred place."

"Sacred place?" Frank asked curiously. "Charlie mentioned that, too. What tribe does he belong to?"

The old man looked doubtful. "I really don't know—Kiowa, maybe. I've heard that their sacred place was near where they killed those settlers."

A truck stopped outside and Roy came in. "Afternoon, Matt," he said to the little man. "Hey, you guys okay?" he asked, frowning at the Hardys.

45

"We're fine," Frank assured him. "Sorry about the truck, though. There's not much left." He turned to the little man. "Thanks for the information."

"Don't mention it," Matt said.

On the way back to the ranch, the brothers described their narrow escape from the tornado, and then filled Roy in on their lack of success in Armstrong. As it turned out, Roy and Rudy hadn't been successful either. They had patrolled the tanks all day without finding a single sign of Jerry.

"We'll spend the night at the homestead," Frank said, as they neared the ranch house. "Maybe Charlie will pay us another visit."

Roy nodded. "Might be good if you could talk to him."

"Why? You don't think he's got anything to do with what's happened, do you?" Joe asked.

"Not directly," Roy replied, hesitating. "But there's not much that goes on around here that he doesn't know about. No telling what he's seen. He might just solve the whole riddle on the spot, if he's got a mind to it."

After dinner Frank and Joe returned to the homestead. The wind had picked up and there was a chill in the desert night.

"What say we try out that old iron stove?" Joe asked. Dot had made them a thermos of breakfast coffee, and he set it on the table.

Frank set up the lantern. "Charlie will see

our light—so we don't have to worry about smoke signals."

Joe lifted one of the heavy, round stove covers. "Looks like somebody left this thing full of kindling," he said. "Did Roy give you any matches?"

Frank tossed over a pack of matches. Joe struck one, touched it to a piece of paper under the pile of wood splinters in the stove, and watched the flame grow. "That's funny," he said.

"What's that?" Frank asked, coming to stand beside him.

"This stuff is hissing like green wood—but it's burning fine. Not even any smoke."

Frank poked the kindling with a lid handle. It shifted slightly, to reveal what looked like a short length of heavy cord, sizzling hotly.

Frank jumped back. "That's a blasting fuse!" he yelled. "They use it to set off dynamite!"

Chapter

6

"LET'S DOUSE IT." Joe grabbed for the thermos of coffee on the table.

"Are you nuts?" Frank jerked his arm and towed him toward the door. "Run!" Joe sprinted through the yard just behind his brother. As he dove for cover behind a metal horse trough, a hot blast caught him from behind. Then he was sailing through the air.

A moment later Frank was shaking his shoulder. "Joe! Joe, are you all right?"

Joe opened his eyes. He lay facedown beside Frank, his mouth full of dust, his ears ringing. His right shoulder felt as if it had been hit by a sledgehammer when he struggled to sit up. Splintered cedar shingles fluttered down out of the night sky like a flock of wooden butterflies. Joe shook his head and began to laugh.

48

"What's so funny?" Frank demanded in a low voice, irritated.

"Oh, nothing." Joe gritted his teeth. Laughing hurt his shoulder and his chest. "I guess it's just good to be alive."

"You're right about that," Frank whispered. "But we'd better lie low, just in case whoever rigged that little surprise is still hanging around to check out the damage."

"They couldn't have done a better job on that cabin with an artillery strike," Joe whispered back. In the moonlight he could see that there was nothing left of the cabin. The walls and floor were scattered around the yard.

"We're lucky we didn't catch any cast iron from that stove," Frank said. "That blast must have sent pieces flying like shrapnel. Whoever's behind this just graduated from dirty tricks and suspected kidnapping to attempted murder."

"At least the blast blew out the fire," Joe said. "It would have been a real mess if it had started a brush fire, dry as it is around here."

They lay in silence as the crescent moon climbed over the caprock. The wind-blown mesquite branches painted moving shadows across the rough landscape, fooling the Hardys' eyes.

Finally Frank decided to get a reaction from anyone skulking around. He picked up a rock, tossing it at the old storage tank beside the abandoned windmill. The tank gave off a hollow boom, but that was the only sound they heard.

"Looks clear," Frank whispered. "Let's work our way to the truck and get out of here."

Joe slithered forward, trying to ignore the pain in his shoulder. "And what if they booby-trapped *that,* too?" he wanted to know.

Frank grinned. "Are you trying to spoil my night?"

"Just being cautious," Joe retorted. "If I had checked out the stove first—"

"Don't worry. We'll look before we drive."

They crawled on their bellies to the pickup. Still keeping low, they checked over the wheels, behind the seat, and finally in the engine compartment.

"Looks clear to me," Joe said at last. "I'm ready to chance it. You?"

Frank nodded. "I guess. I sure don't want to hang out here until dawn. Think you can make it to the road without any lights?" He climbed into the truck.

"Watch me." Joe slipped into the driver's seat, put the key into the ignition, and with a deep breath, turned it.

The engine roared to life. In a split second Joe had shifted the truck into low, and it was bouncing from rock to rock between the mesquite toward the road.

"Okay," Frank said as Joe expertly whipped

the truck over the ditch and onto the dirt road. "Let there be light!"

Joe switched on the high beams. On the quick trip back to the ranch house, they saw no sign of life except for one startled antelope that bounded across the road in front of them.

When they arrived, Jerry's dog greeted them with a wild flurry of barking. By the time Joe switched off the engine, lights were coming on all over the house.

Roy stuck his head out the front door. "Trouble, boys?"

"Just a little rural renewal." Joe's voice was tight. "Somebody blew up the old homestead."

After Roy had heard their story, he said, "You should be safe enough here tonight. Nobody's going to set foot on this place without Shep letting us know about it."

Frank climbed out of the truck. "I think we could use a safe night's sleep. But first thing in the morning," he added with determination, "we're heading for Armstrong. I think it's time we looked for a replacement cable for the ultralight. And we're going to look up that former hand of yours—Jake Grimes. I wonder if he's been playing with dynamite lately."

Joe's shoulder was a little stiff the next morning, but aside from that, the boys were none the worse for their narrow escape. It was

51

late morning before they were on their way to Armstrong. They drove past the spot where the tornado had slammed their truck off the road.

"Roy said he called the insurance company," Joe commented. "After they take a look at it, it'll get hauled off for salvage."

On the outskirts of Armstrong, they stopped to get Grimes's address out of the phone book. The place they were looking for was a rundown house a couple of blocks off the square.

"Grimes might be at work," Frank said, as they pulled up out front. "If he is, we'll try the neighbors—find out what they know about the guy."

An angry snarl greeted their knock. "What?"

"Mr. Grimes?" Frank said, to the closed door.

"Bug off! I can't pay you—I'm flat broke."

"We're not bill collectors," Frank said in his most sympathetic voice. "We need your help."

"Help, huh?" Now the voice was suspicious. "I wish somebody would help *me*." There was a grunt, then a noise like somebody dragging a heavy weight. "Hang on."

In a moment the door opened slowly and the boys were greeted by a scowling, round-bellied man in need of a shave. He had a crutch under each arm and his right pants leg was ripped to reveal a heavy plaster cast from his ankle to the top of his thigh. "Well? Say your business and be quick about it."

Frank exchanged glances with Joe. Obviously, Jake Grimes wasn't in any shape to go prowling around old cabins, setting dynamite charges.

"We understand that you used to work on the Circle C," Frank said a little hesitantly.

"What if I did?" Grimes growled.

"There's been trouble out there," Joe said. "We need some information."

Grimes slammed the door in their faces. "Well, you won't get it out of me," he screamed.

"Jerry Greene's disappeared," Frank called through the door on a hunch. Roy had said that Grimes parted on good terms with Jerry. They might have been friends.

There was a silence. Then the door opened a crack. "What's that about Jerry?"

"He disappeared two nights ago," Frank said.

The door swung open. "Come on in," Grimes said. He led the way into a tiny living room, littered with beer cans and old newspapers, and dropped down into a ratty-looking overstuffed chair. "I don't have much use for old man Carlson, but that kid was okay."

Frank glanced at the cast. "When did you hurt your leg?" he asked casually.

"Last week. Got caught between a fence and

53

a steer with a grudge. Looks like I'll be out of commission for a while." He frowned. "When did Jerry disappear?"

"Sunday night," Frank told him. "As far as we can tell, he went out to check some lights at the old homestead and didn't come back. We're wondering if there was any connection between his disappearance and the dead cattle—and the other things that have happened out there." He eyed Grimes. "You know about the cattle?"

"Heard about it. Bad news, if you ask me, people going around wasting good steers." He grinned bleakly. "I guess somebody else doesn't have any use for Carlson."

"Any idea who?" Joe asked.

Grimes thought for a minute, scratching his stubbly chin. "Nope. None I'd care to name, anyway. How about that old Native American?" He grinned again. "People say he can do magic. Maybe he turned that water to salt."

"What did you think about Grimes?" Frank asked Joe as they sat in a dark corner of a little Mexican restaurant where they'd stopped for something to eat.

"My gut reaction is to cross him off the list," Joe replied, taking a bite of his fajita, a soft tortilla wrapped around spicy slices of beef. "He didn't pretend to hide how he feels about

54

Roy—and he probably would have if he'd been involved in any of this."

"Yeah," Frank agreed. "With that leg, he'd need an accomplice. My feeling is that he doesn't have the money to hire one. And I'd bet he doesn't have any friends who'd be willing to go out on a limb with him just for the fun of it."

"Uh-huh," Joe replied vaguely. He was looking over Frank's shoulder.

Frank turned to see what Joe was staring at. He grinned. Might have known—a girl. She was slim and attractive, about their age. She wore jeans and hiking boots, and her long dark hair swung down almost to her western belt. Judging from her tanned face and the easy way she moved, she was the outdoor type.

"Hi, Barb," the manager called from behind the counter. "Where've you been lately?"

"Hey, Tony," Barb replied, giving him a smile. *"Cómo está?"* She sat down at the counter and took the mug of coffee that the manager pushed at her. "I've been up in the sand hills collecting samples."

Abruptly Joe got up and went over to the counter. "Pardon me," he said, with his most engaging smile. "I heard you say you'd been up in the sand hills. Was that near Caprock?"

She turned. "That's right. Not far from there." Frank could see that she was giving Joe a suspicious who-wants-to-know look.

55

"I'm Joe Hardy," Joe said. He turned and pointed to the table. "That's my brother Frank. We're staying at the Circle C, doing a study of our own—kind of." He smiled again. "Maybe you could help us."

Barb regarded him for a minute, the suspicious look turning to an amused glint in her dark eyes. Then she stood up and picked up her coffee mug. "You must be the new guys who've been wandering around town asking questions and tangling with tornadoes."

Joe nodded. "That's us."

"I'm Barbara Harris." The girl shook Joe's hand, then stepped over to the table to shake with Frank.

"How'd you figure out who we were?" Frank asked.

Barbara sat down, flicking her long hair back over her shoulders. "You *are* new," she said with a smile. "And green, too. Don't you know that gossip travels with the speed of light in a small town like this one?" She put her coffee mug down, her smile fading. "Any word about Jerry?"

Joe shook his head. "Nothing."

"You know Jerry?" Frank asked.

"Sure. We went to high school together," Barbara said. "He stayed on at the Circle C, and I enrolled at Eastern New Mexico U." She shrugged. "I'm majoring in geology, with a minor in anthropology."

Barbara grinned. "I was always interested in the Native Americans around here. Anyway, it was a good combination. It got me a great summer job with the BLM, doing a ground-water survey."

"The BLM?" Frank asked.

"Bureau of Land Management." She eyed them. "You know—the guys who handle all the federal land around here."

For the next half hour the boys listened to Barbara talk. She obviously had a detailed knowledge of the area around the Circle C— and not just the physical territory, either. She knew about its history, as well, and all the current events of the entire county.

"Speaking of current events, I see there's a dance in town tomorrow night," Joe said, pointing to the poster on the wall. It announced a dance at the rodeo on Friday.

"I hope you'll be going," Barbara said with a laugh. "We could use some extra males around here, and I could use a date."

"You've got one," Joe said.

"You know, I don't believe you." Frank shook his head as he and Joe left the restaurant.

"How's that?" Joe asked.

"You know what I mean," Frank said, giving him a sharp poke in the ribs. "You find the best-looking girl in town, who turns out to be

57

one of the best informants we've found. And you get invited to dance, as well."

"Just natural talent, I guess," Joe said with a grin, as they reached the pickup. He went to the driver's side, while Frank went to the other.

Joe reached for the door handle. "Funny. I don't remember leaving the window down."

"Joe," Frank commanded. "Get your hand off that door! It's booby-trapped."

Joe dropped his hand and peered inside. He saw a thin yellow wire leading from the door handle on his side to a large paper bag under the steering wheel. "A bomb in a bag," Joe muttered.

"I'll get in and defuse it." The muscles in Frank's arm tensed as his hand tightened on his door handle.

That's when Joe noticed there were *two* wires—the other one led to the handle on Frank's side. If he opened the door, *Frank* would set off the bomb!

"FRANK—DON'T!" Joe nearly leaped across the hood to keep his brother from opening the door. Frank sucked in a deep breath and joined Joe on the driver's side.

"I didn't figure they'd *double* booby-trap it," he muttered.

"Looks like they didn't care which door was opened—as long as it would blow us both away."

Frank stuck his head and shoulders through the open window, careful not to touch the frame. In the crevice between the door and the seat was a half-sprung rat trap, with a wire connected to the cross bar and another to the base. If Joe had opened the door, the cross bar would have snapped shut onto the base, and the two wires would have made contact.

"A simple but effective firing switch," Frank said. On the seat he spotted a couple of squares of discarded cardboard. "That's what the bomber used to keep the contacts open," he realized, picking them up.

"If you'll take about twenty giant steps back," Frank told Joe, "I'll disarm this monster."

He glanced back to see that Joe was safely behind cover, took a deep breath, and firmly grasped the trap. As he slowly let the bar down, he slipped a piece of cardboard between it and the base. "That's one," he muttered to himself.

Carefully, he opened the driver's door and reached across to roll down the window on the passenger side, being careful not to jar the truck. Then he went around and repeated the process on the second trap.

"That's two," he announced out loud, as he opened the passenger door very slowly. "I'm going to have a look in the bag."

"What if it's booby-trapped, too?" he heard Joe ask, behind him.

"Doesn't look like it," Frank said, easing the mouth of the bag open. Inside, he saw four large flashlight batteries and seven sticks of dynamite taped into two neat bundles, a network of wires running from the batteries to the dynamite. Gently, he lifted the bundles out of the bag, studied the wires for a minute, and then began pulling them loose. At last, he pulled a small metal cylinder out of the dynamite.

"That's it," he said, holding up the two bundles for Joe to see. "We're clean."

"Maybe," Joe said. "But let's make sure, huh?"

After searching the truck for any more surprises, they climbed in. "All set?" Joe asked. "If we're going to locate that ultralight cable, we'd better get going."

"All set, except for one thing."

Joe raised his eyebrows. "Which is?"

"I wonder," Frank replied reflectively, "whether Barbara Harris had any intention of keeping that date."

The boys spent several unsuccessful hours trying to find a piece of stainless steel cable to repair the controls on the ultralight. Finally, they stopped at a pay phone and Frank called the ultralight's manufacturer.

"Sky Streak Aviation," a woman's voice said on the other end of the line.

"My name is Frank Hardy. I was flying a Sky Streak One-oh-seven the other day, and the rudder cable broke. I need—"

But he didn't get to finish. "That's impossible, sir," the woman said confidently. "Our control cables *never* break!"

Frank chuckled. "Maybe not. But this one did, I assure you. I need a replacement."

On the other end of the line, he could hear the murmur of voices. Then the woman came back. "We hope that the break didn't cause you any inconvenience," she said. "The cable is covered by our warranty, of course. We can ship you a replacement by overnight express." She paused. "Would you mind returning the original? Our engineers would like to examine it."

Frank couldn't help smiling. "It's a deal. I'll pick up the cable at the express package depot in Armstrong, New Mexico, and return the one that broke."

It was late afternoon by the time the boys got into the truck and headed back to the Circle C. They stopped at the store in Caprock for a soda.

"Glad to see you boys," the frail little man greeted them. "Got a message for you."

"A message?" they said together, eyeing each other. What now?

"Old Charlie was in here a little while ago, looking for you."

"What did he want?" Frank asked.

"He seemed to think it was real important that you come to see him, at his place."

Joe's eyes narrowed. "How do we get there?"

"Best I can remember, after you come down

62

off the caprock you hit an old survey road."
The storekeeper squinted, trying to think.
"Take a left and go south about half a mile,
and you'll come up on some ruins. That's
where he's got his shack."

Just after the highway reached the bottom of
the caprock, Joe spotted a rutted road, not
much more than a pair of dusty tracks, leading
off to the left through the mesquite. It looked
as if it hadn't seen a vehicle all summer.

"That must be it," Frank said.

Joe turned down the road. Within half a mile,
the caprock to their left and above them
changed dramatically from a gentle slope to a
high, rugged cliff. The narrow road, wide
enough for only one vehicle, hugged its base.

"Some road," Joe grunted, swerving to
avoid a big rock that looked as if it had tumbled
off the cliff face.

Frank laughed. "I don't imagine Charlie has
a whole lot of visitors," he remarked. He
frowned, peering ahead. "Wonder where that
dust cloud's coming from?"

Joe glanced up from the road. Up ahead, not
too far, he saw a rolling dust cloud. Another
storm?

No—this cloud was on the road, coming
straight at them. Joe made out the front of a
huge truck in the swirling dust.

Then chrome grillwork filled the whole windshield as the truck barreled straight for them.

Chapter

8

JOE SWERVED SHARPLY to the right, praying they could scrape past the huge truck. Shrub branches screeched against the sides as the pickup careened on two wheels off the road. Joe fought the wheel, gritting his teeth as they bounced around.

The pickup settled back onto four wheels, unhurt by the passing truck. When Joe looked in the mirror, all he saw was a cloud of dust.

"What was *that?*" he gasped.

"It sure wasn't the tooth fairy," Frank said, looking behind them. "Looked like a Mack truck cab without a trailer. The driver was pushing that rig at a pretty good clip."

"I wonder if that's the kind of truck they use to pull the tank trailers?" Joe asked.

"Maybe." Frank glanced over at him,

frowning. "I don't like this. It's almost as if it were waiting for us to come along."

"Let's try to follow it." Joe restarted the engine and shifted into reverse. The wheels spun, showering sand, but the pickup didn't move.

Frank climbed out and looked under the truck. "Forget about following them—we've bottomed out."

After a half hour of digging in the loose sand, the boys could finally see under the truck again. "Okay," Frank said. "Let's give it a try. I'll push."

With Frank putting his shoulder against the front grill, Joe eased out the clutch and felt the truck lurch backward onto the dirt road.

"Next stop, Charlie's place," Frank announced, hopping in. He grinned at Joe. "Let's stay on the road, huh? I'm not crazy about doing any more digging."

Joe laughed. "Tell that to the big Mack."

A half mile later, by a streambed, the boys spotted a low adobe hut with whitewashed walls and a roof made from scrap sheet metal. They parked in a dirt yard that had been swept clean. But the only signs of life were a couple of chickens and a scrawny-looking goat tethered to a post beside a battered, rusty bucket of water. The door to the hut open invitingly.

"Charlie?" Frank called through his cupped hands. "Hey, Charlie!"

THE HARDY BOYS CASEFILES

Joe put two fingers to his mouth and whistled, but the only answer came from the goat, who bleated at them with a woeful sound. The boys went to the door and looked into a small, spotless room. The floor was packed dirt. Along the far wall was a blanket-covered cot. In one corner was a set of narrow shelves.

"Everything in its place," Frank said.

Joe found himself lowering his voice. "He may not have a lot, but it feels so—peaceful—in here. Almost like a church."

Frank nodded. "You're closer than you think. Those shelves over there must be Charlie's shrine," he said quietly. "Should we go in?"

"Well, he invited us," Joe said. "And the door's open. Maybe he wanted us to *see* something."

The boys stepped inside. The shelves were full of candles and handmade pottery bowls. The bowls held dried herbs, or colored sand and powders. A bundle wrapped in white goatskin took up the lowest shelf. Beside it lay a heap of rattlesnake fangs and a half-dozen snake rattles. A snakeskin hung beside the shelf.

"Looks like old Charlie had a real thing for rattlesnakes," Joe said.

"It may be a totem, or some kind of spirit guide," Frank said. "A lot of Native American beliefs deal with animals and how they can lend people their strength. Animal spirits can also teach people and protect them."

Joe's curious gaze went from the rattler fangs to the goatskin bundle. "And this?"

Frank shook his head. "That's Charlie's medicine bundle. I don't think we ought to mess with it. Whatever's in there is sacred to him."

Joe pulled his hand back. "Thanks for telling me." He was about to turn away when he saw something else. "Hey, what do you make of *this?*" he asked excitedly.

Behind the medicine bundle was an old pine board, painted with three sets of symbols. On the right was a circle with a *C* in the middle. Slightly above it were three squiggly lines, one on top of the other. On the left were three interlocking circles.

Joe frowned and pointed to the three circles. "This looks a lot like the Olympic symbol."

Frank leaned over, studying it. "If I remember my rules for naming brands, I'd say that's the Triple O."

"And that's a Circle C!" Joe exclaimed. "And that stack of squiggles—"

"They look like sound waves to me," Frank said.

"I don't think that's what Charlie means," Joe said. "Maybe he's trying to show the conflict between the two ranches."

Frank raised his eyebrows. "It's possible,"

he said. "I'd give a lot to know what Charlie really knows." He turned and started out the door. "Well, I guess there's no point in hanging out here any longer."

Outside, the goat gave them another forlorn bleat as they climbed in the truck and drove off.

At the bunkhouse on the caprock, Joe took a pizza out of the freezer and put it into the microwave, while Frank called Roy and went over the day's events. "We're going to spend the night at the bunkhouse," he said. "We've got a lot to do tomorrow."

"We do?" Joe asked as Frank hung up the phone. "And I noticed you didn't ask Roy about those symbols."

Frank shrugged as he sat down at the table for pizza. "So far, Roy hasn't been willing to say much about his relations with Oscar Owens and the Triple O. We know there are bad feelings between them." He took a bite and chewed. "I think we can find out why and how much by checking the records in the courthouse."

At nine the next morning Frank and Joe were parked on the square in the center of Armstrong. Under the stately cottonwood trees were several granite memorials and war souvenirs, including an olive-drab artillery piece and a ship's anchor. The boys climbed the steps of the impressive dome-topped courthouse. Inside, there was a three-story rotunda with a mosaic floor. On the far side of the rotunda was a glass door with County Clerk on it in gold letters.

Behind the marble counter of the county clerk's office, a grandmotherly woman greeted them. "May I help you?" Then she gave Joe a startled look. "You look *just* like my grandson," she said. "Isn't that a coincidence?"

Joe ducked his head and gave her a shy, embarrassed grin. "Yes, ma'am," he said, sounding interested. "Does he live around here?"

In a minute the woman had treated them to a description of her whole family. She had obviously taken a liking to Joe. Then, suddenly, she remembered that they might be there on business. "Now, what can I help you find this morning?"

Frank leaned forward. "We'd like to examine the deeds to a couple of ranches up near Caprock—the Circle C and the Triple O. We'd also like to see copies of their grazing leases."

"Mineral leases as well?" the woman asked helpfully.

"What? Oh, yes, please," Frank replied.

In a few minutes she returned with a pile of folders. The deed to the Triple O was a simple document, certifying that the land had been deeded to the Owens family eighty years ago by the government. The other files concerned the Circle C. Roy had begun purchasing the land about twenty years ago. There were some grazing and mineral leases dating back before that time, but many were much more recent.

"It looks kind of complicated," Joe remarked, while Frank began to copy the dates of the leases.

"But that's the way people around here acquire land." The woman smiled at Joe. "In fact, Mr. Carlson has been very successful with his ranching operations."

"What about these mineral rights?" Frank asked. "Are they worth anything?"

The woman shrugged. "Not much, probably. Nobody's located anything in that area. Mr. Carlson probably picked them up to prevent exploration, which can be pretty destructive. The oil companies have to pay damages, but some ranchers don't think it's enough."

Joe smiled at her willingness to answer questions. "I'll bet you get all the land gossip," he said. "Have you heard anything about the Circle C and the Triple O—you know, problems, anything like that?"

The woman hesitated. "Well, of course, it's not a matter of public record, and I probably shouldn't say anything. But I heard that Mr. Carlson and Mr. Owens banged heads a few years back, when they shared some leased

70

pasture where the two ranches join." She smiled. "My husband worked at the auction barn that spring, and he said that everybody was talking about how many Circle C mama cows had calves with Triple O brands."

"You mean, Owens put his brand on Circle C calves?" Joe asked, sounding shocked.

"Of course it wasn't ever proven," she added hastily. "But I know for a fact that after that, Mr. Carlson wouldn't have anything to do with Mr. Owens."

Frank closed the folders. "Is any of the land around here owned by Native Americans?"

The woman shook her head. "No, the reservations are all west and north of here."

"We heard that some of them consider part of the caprock to be their sacred territory," Joe said.

"Oh, you probably mean Lawson's Bluff." She turned to the topographic map on the wall behind her and pointed to a section that jutted out from the ridge of the caprock. "Actually, it's on the Circle C, just north of the boundary with the Triple O. It's called Lawson's Bluff because the Lawson family was killed there in an Indian raid." She shook her head. "But the Indians don't have any legal claim to it."

Frank folded his notes and put them in his pocket. "Thanks for your help," he said.

Joe leaned forward, giving her a special

smile. "Tell your grandson 'hi' for me," he said.

"I'll do that," the woman promised.

"Why don't you give Barbara a call," Frank said to Joe as they left the courthouse. "See if she can join us for a cup of coffee."

Joe frowned. "You still think she might have had something to do with that booby trap, huh?"

"You've got to admit that it was quite a coincidence." Frank watched the annoyed expression on his brother's face. Joe liked to trust pretty girls. Sometimes that got him—and Frank—into trouble. "At least she can explain some of this stuff about land leases and dirty tricks. We could use a clue or two."

With a sharp nod, Joe agreed and headed for a pay phone. Joe reported that Barbara would meet them in an hour. The two boys walked down the street to the express package depot to pick up the cable for the ultralight.

They strolled into a clothing store and each of them bought new boots and a western hat.

"We've still got some time to kill," Frank said after they left and were passing a combination pawn shop and sporting goods store. "Let's take a look in here."

"Hey," Joe said as they stepped inside, "this place could arm a banana republic." The shelves were filled with surplus military equipment.

Frank went to the counter. "Do you handle army surplus ammo?" he asked the clerk.

"Got some M-sixteen and some forty-five." The man opened a glass case. "What are you looking for?"

"Just trying to identify some empties I found," Frank said, scanning the case. The M16 ammo was a .223 caliber, much smaller than the casings he'd found at the stock tank. Then he spotted some larger, tarnished, bottle-neck cartridges. The bullet tips were painted black.

"Armor-piercing three-oh-three British," the clerk said, following Frank's glance. He took one out and handed it to him. On the base was the number forty-three.

Joe looked over Frank's shoulder. "Seems to me that the shells we saw were tapered like this, but the shoulder was shorter," he said.

The clerk nodded. "Yep, it was a three-oh-three. Looks that way after it's fired. Packs quite a punch, too—armor-piercing bullets have a steel core." He smacked his fist hard into his open palm. "Designed to smash right through armor plate. It fits the Lee-Enfield rifles the British used in World War Two." He pointed to a heavy-looking, old warhorse of a rifle hanging on the wall. The unfinished wooden hand guard and stock extended almost

73

to the end of the barrel, while the magazine was sharply tapered.

Frank handed back the cartridge. "Sell many of these?" he asked casually.

"Not a whole lot," the guy said, putting it back. "But a fella came in the other day and bought a couple of boxes." He shut the case.

"Somebody you knew?" Joe asked.

The clerk shook his head. "Never saw him before." He studied the boys. "Got a reason for asking?"

"Just curious," Frank said. He lifted his hand in a wave, and they left.

"Well, now that we know the gun we're looking for," Joe said with satisfaction, "it shouldn't be too hard to find."

Frank gave a short laugh and pointed to the dusty pickups parked in a row along the curb. Each one had a gun rack in the back window, and every rack held at least one rifle. "Knowing what we're looking for is one thing," he said. "Finding it is another."

They'd been at the restaurant only a few minutes when Barbara came in. She'd pinned her hair up and traded her jeans for a denim skirt.

"Hi, guys," she greeted them, sliding into the booth beside Joe. "What's new?"

Joe smiled at her quick laugh and easy, open western way. He wouldn't mind making friends

74

with her, but what they needed right then was information. Barbara grinned at him, her eyes crinkling when she smiled. No way could Joe believe she had anything to do with the bomb in the truck.

Frank started leading the conversation, telling Barbara about their visit to Caprock Charlie's place.

"I'm jealous," she told him. "Charlie's always friendly to me but never talks much. Too bad. He'd be a term paper in anthropology. I've heard that he's the last of his tribe, and it would be a shame to lose the knowledge he has."

"Do you think he's angry at the people around here?" Frank asked. "Maybe he thinks Roy Carlson shouldn't be ranching around the holy place on Lawson's Bluff."

"You don't mean you think *he's* behind all the trouble on the Circle C?" Barbara showed that she knew about the Carlsons' problems. But she mentioned no more than she might have heard on the county grapevine. Joe breathed a sigh of relief.

Then Frank changed the subject abruptly. "We were over at the courthouse this morning, looking at the mineral leases," he said. "Do you suppose that minerals—gold, oil, uranium—might have something to do with this?"

Barbara's mouth tightened. "Maybe," she said guardedly. "And maybe not." She pushed her coffee cup away. "Time to get back to work." She glanced at Joe. "You're picking me up for the dance tonight, right?"

"At eight," Joe said, but he didn't give her his usual grin. He didn't *feel* like grinning. Obviously, Barbara knew something. But what?

When Barbara left, the boys headed out for the pickup. This time, they inspected it carefully before they opened the doors and climbed in.

"Well," Frank said, eyeing Joe, "what do you think?"

"I don't know," Joe said glumly. He'd still bet on his hunch that Barbara was okay, but maybe he wouldn't be willing to go with long odds. *What* did she know?

The boys made a quick trip back to the ranch. Frank removed the damaged cable from the ultralight, while Joe went over the rest of the aircraft.

Frank had pulled the cable out and was studying the broken end when Joe interrupted him. "Looks like you've lost a rivet here," he said.

Frank turned. Joe was pointing to a perfectly round hole in the bottom of the tail strut tube, through which the control lines passed.

"That's funny," Frank said. "There shouldn't be any rivets there."

He explored the hole with his fingers and

76

then reached around the tube. There was a matching hole on the other side. It was rough-edged and something was stuck in it. He worked it loose, then took it to the barn door, where he could examine it in the light. What he was holding was a small flake of copper.

With a frown, he took another look at the tip of the cable he'd just removed. Then he turned to Joe, his face bleak.

"This cable didn't break on its own," he said. "It was cut—by an armor-piercing bullet!"

Chapter
9

"A BULLET?" Joe exclaimed, staring at the frayed steel strands with a smear of metal on the ends. "A bullet made of copper?"

"That comes from the jacket of that armor-piercing bullet. The steel core, of course, passed through and kept on going."

"Talk about a lucky shot." Joe's face grew grim. "This means that the guy who did this was on to us from the minute we got here."

"That's what it looks like," Frank agreed. "Maybe the shot was meant as a warning—but if that's the case, they were wasting ammo. I couldn't have heard a shot over the racket that engine makes."

Joe turned back to the ultralight. "I haven't spotted any other damage."

Frank was looking at the hole. "And I don't

think the shot did any structural damage to the strut. If you'll give me a hand, I'll route the new cable and take this thing for a test flight." His eyes narrowed. "And after that, I think we ought to give Oscar Owens a visit."

The new cable worked perfectly, and the test flight was beautiful. The boys stopped at the ranch house to ask directions to the Triple O.

Roy wasn't very enthusiastic about their plan to talk to Owens, but he finally agreed. "If you go a couple of miles past the old homestead," he told them, "you'll come to a fence and a cattle guard. That's the boundary with the Triple O."

"So you can drive from one ranch to the other without going onto the highway," Joe mused.

Roy shrugged. "The road's maintained by the county," he said. "Anybody's free to use it."

"Then the tank truck could have been driven here through the Triple O," Frank said. "Or from there?"

"I suppose," Roy replied. "But it could just as easily have come in from the highway, or down one of the old survey roads."

The boys got into the yellow pickup and headed south. "Well, what do you make of all this?" Joe asked, steering to avoid a huge pothole in the road.

"We have too many loose ends to suit me."

Frank sounded frustrated. "But the worst of it is that we're still short of a motive. If it's revenge, the main suspect—Jake Grimes—is laid up with a broken leg. If it's greed, Oscar Owens is a good candidate. But what could he be after? Marginal grazing land and worthless mineral leases hardly justify kidnapping and three counts of attempted murder."

He shook his head. "If it's a desire to get back a hunk of sacred territory, our suspect is an old man whose only weapon is a gourd rattle. To round things off, we've got a couple of suspects who don't seem to have any motive at all—an attractive young lady and a reliable ranch hand who might have engineered his own disappearance."

"Speaking of suspects," Joe said, "look over there." He pointed to a sand dune several hundred yards away. At the top of the dune stood a lone figure, wearing a straw sombrero. Between them and the figure was a sea of waist-high sagebrush. Joe pulled over and the Hardys got out and stood beside the truck. The figure on the dune didn't move.

"Looks like Charlie's keeping tabs on us again," Joe remarked. "It's really weird how he always seems to be in the right place at the right time—like he knows what's going to happen."

"The people who study ESP have a name

80

for that," Frank told him. "They call it precognition."

"Suppose we ought to hike over there and have a visit?"

"I don't think there's much point in it. If Charlie wanted to talk to us, he'd make an effort to come down here by the road. Anyway, we'd never get the truck through that sagebrush, and he'd be long gone by the time we could get to him on foot." He grinned. "My guess is that he'll show up again—when *he* feels like it."

As if to confirm Frank's guess, the figure vanished just then behind the dune.

The boys got back in the truck. After another twenty minutes on the rough road, they came to a cattle guard, a metal grid buried in the ground that they had to drive over. Joe slowed. A white sign fastened to a post announced that they were entering the Triple O ranch, and that trespassers would be prosecuted.

"We're not trespassing, we're visiting," Joe muttered, shoving the accelerator down. The truck leaped forward.

Three or four miles beyond the Hardys could see a ranch complex up on a ridge. The main house was large and single storied, Spanish style. Its whitewashed walls gleamed in the afternoon sun, under the neat geometry of an orange clay tile roof. As they got closer, they could see a large man standing on the veranda, looking in their direction.

"I guess they're expecting us," Joe said.

By the time they pulled up the big man was standing in the front yard. Frank recognized him—Nat Wilkin, the foreman who'd helped search for Jerry.

"What's up, guys?" he asked. "Anything new on Jerry?"

"Afraid not, Nat," Frank said. "We'd like to see Mr. Owens."

At that moment the door behind Nat opened and an older man stepped out. He wore jeans and a work shirt, with a bandanna tied neatly around his throat. "Well, now you're seeing him," he said. "Nobody can call me unneighborly."

Oscar Owens smiled at the Hardys. "So you're the guys asking all those questions all over Armstrong County." He opened the door and led the boys down a wide hall and into a spacious room furnished with several leather armchairs and a large oak desk. "Now, what can I do for you two?" he asked, settling into the chair behind his desk.

"You know that Jerry Greene is still missing, of course," Frank began cautiously.

"Sure, I know," Owens said, with what sounded like genuine sympathy. "Too bad. My guess is that he got thrown, wandered around, and then the next day lost his bearings in that dust storm." He shook his head. "It was a bad one—one of the worst in a couple of years."

"But why would he still be wandering the next day in the storm?" Joe wanted to know. "Also, Ray says Jerry was a good rider."

Owens nodded. "Even a good rider can get thrown if his horse gets spooked. He was like his father—a good man. It doesn't seem likely that he'd wander off, the way some do."

"The Circle C has been pretty well searched," Frank said. "We wondered if you'd mind if we had a look on the Triple O."

Owens lost some of his good humor. "I don't see any harm in it. But you'd better let me know so I can have one of my hands go with you. It's awful easy to get lost around here if you don't know the country." He gave them a measured look. "No point in us having to go on another search—for you two."

Frank wondered briefly whether that was a threat, but the man's eyes still seemed friendly. "Maybe we could start in the morning."

Owens nodded. "No need to hurry," he said regretfully. "If Greene's out there, there's not much chance that he's alive." He pushed the chair away from his desk and started to stand up.

"Have you had any truck traffic down here lately?" Joe asked, carefully casual.

Owens sat back down, giving Joe a long, hard look. "As a matter of fact, my hands say they've seen some tracks. Maybe a stock truck took a wrong turn. Why do you ask?''

Frank shrugged, his eyes on Owens's face. "It was a big truck that dumped salt water into that tank," he said quietly.

Owens just nodded. "You know, I've had some trouble with Roy Carlson," he said. "That nonsense with the fences is just the latest. But things have been going worse for Roy. His horses pulled up lame, and after that came the dead cows."

He shook his head. "I can't see Roy hauling in a tanker load of salt water to kill his own stock." A slow, angry red flush moved up his face. "And I know *I* had nothing to do with it."

The silence was thick. "Well, I guess we got what we came for," Frank finally said. He stood up.

Owens didn't even show them to the door.

On the way out Frank spotted a gun rack on the wall by the door, filled with a variety of shotguns and deer rifles. Something about one rifle caught Frank's attention. The gun had a polished wooden stock that extended halfway down the shiny black barrel—and an odd magazine. It was wedge shaped, tapered sharply from the back to the front.

Frank stepped over and picked up the rifle. As he hefted it, he saw a stamp, just in front of the bolt action. It was the broad arrow, the British governmental sign.

"What are you doing with that?" a sharp voice came from behind them.

Owens came up to the door and snatched the gun from Frank. "I brought this home from the war," he said angrily. "It's my favorite gun—and I'm not going to have some kid steal it." He raised his voice. "Nat!"

The foreman appeared in the doorway as Owens pointed at the Hardys. "See these two off the ranch."

Joe glanced at Frank curiously as they were escorted to their truck. "What's the story about that gun?"

"I guess you didn't get a chance to see it clearly," Frank answered in a low voice. "It's a British Three-oh-three, Mark Three Lee-Enfield." He glanced over his shoulder to where Owens was standing on the porch, holding the rifle.

"That's the gun that shot me out of the air."

Chapter
10

"GUYS, I DON'T KNOW what happened in there," Nat Wilkin said as the Hardys got into their pickup. "But I do want to apologize for Mr. Owens. He just hasn't been himself lately."

"It's his ranch," Joe said, starting the engine. "And we're getting off it."

As the Triple O ranch house disappeared behind them, Joe shook his head. "The way Owens blew up over that rifle—he'd have to be a complete nut case to call attention to it if he'd used it on you." He swerved to miss a steer that had wandered onto the road and stood watching them with what looked like antagonism. "On the other hand," he added, "how many of those souvenir guns would there be in this area?"

86

Frank looked out the window. Nat Wilkin was following them in another truck. "Yet the man's reaction to the dirty tricks sounded genuine. I can't see him taking target practice on the ultralight." He sighed. "It just doesn't jibe—all we really know about Owens is that he has a violent temper."

Joe was momentarily distracted by a roadrunner, big as a rooster, that jumped out of the ditch. It zoomed down the road ahead of them, going as fast as the pickup. "What would Owens's motive be? Drive Roy out of business? Get control of the federal land?"

"A grazing lease for near-desert? That doesn't wash," Frank said thoughtfully.

"What about the mineral leases? Suppose Owens knows something nobody else knows?"

"It doesn't seem likely," Frank said doubtfully. "The big oil companies must have surveyed this area years back." He frowned. "Although—maybe Barbara knows something about those mineral leases. She cut the conversation off when I brought them up."

Joe glanced at his watch, then pushed the accelerator down. "Speaking of Barbara, we'd better head back and change—if we want to get to the dance tonight, that is."

Barbara's house was a small, yellow-painted frame house in a well-kept, older part of Armstrong. As the Hardys drove up the quiet street, they saw a red four-wheel-drive pickup parked in front.

"Well, looks like she's home," Joe said, turning off the ignition. He gave his brother a slow smile. "So, do we kick in the door and interrogate her?"

Frank grinned back. "What are you asking me for? I'm just riding shotgun. *You're* the one with the date." He settled back in the seat and settled his new cowboy hat over his eyes. "I'll wait here. But if you're not out in ten minutes, I'm calling the sheriff."

Joe laughed. "Ten minutes, huh? I guess I can handle that." He got out of the truck, giving his boots a quick rub, and started up the walk.

"I'm coming," a voice called in response to Joe's knock. The door opened and Barbara stood there, giving him a look. "Just like a real cowboy," she said, grinning at Joe's clothes.

He looked down at his fancy plaid shirt, fresh jeans, and new cowboy boots, then at Barb's plain T-shirt and comfortable jeans. "A little overdressed, huh?" he asked.

"Oh, you'll be fine. Every girl in town will want to dance with you."

Barbara's excited face showed she had something more important on her mind than a dance. "There's something I want to show you—" She looked around. "Where's Frank? I want *him* to see this, too."

"He's out in the truck, waiting for us," Joe said, puzzled. "See what?" He glanced past her. On one side was the living room, which seemed empty. At the end of a short hallway was the kitchen, empty, too, as far as he could tell.

"But he'll want to see this," Barbara insisted, sounding impatient. "Really, Joe, I think this is something you *both*—"

"Why don't you show me first," Joe suggested, beginning to feel faintly uneasy. He *knew* this couldn't be a trap, but if it was, it was better to have Frank out in the truck.

Barbara stood back and opened the door wider. "Okay," she said, sounding resigned. "Come on. I'll show you." She reached for his hand and pulled him quickly into the house.

Nervously, Joe threw a quick glance behind the door as she shut it. Nothing. And definitely nothing in the living room, either.

Barbara pulled him down the hall and into the kitchen, where the table was piled with yellowing chart paper, like the kind he'd seen used in a polygraph machine. The paper was covered with rows and rows of weird-looking squiggly lines.

Suddenly Joe had a flash of the strange symbols he'd seen at Charlie's shack. Stacks of wiggly lines—these were very similar to the ones Charlie had painted.

"What's all this stuff?" he asked.

"This is what I want to show you," Barbara said, sounding excited again. "I've been working all afternoon on them, ever since I left you and Frank at the restaurant."

She spread out the papers. "After Frank asked about the mineral leases, something clicked. So I went down to the basement at the Bureau of Land Management office and dug out these old logs. Most of them date back to the 1930s. From the looks of them, I'd guess that nobody's examined them in years." She gave him a modest smile. "You can call me brilliant, if you want to."

"Brilliant?" Joe laughed. "Maybe I'd better call you cross-eyed. What's this mess of old paper? And what are all these squiggles?"

"This 'mess of old paper,' " Barbara told him with a little annoyance, "is a batch of ancient *seismograph* logs." She ran a finger along the wavy lines. "And those squiggles are records of soundings that indicate where certain mineral deposits are located."

Joe shook his head. "I still don't get it."

Barbara's dark eyes were dancing with excitement. "Unless I'm dead wrong, Joe, the Circle C is floating on an ocean of oil!"

Chapter

11

"THIS IS INCREDIBLE!" Joe wrapped an arm around Barbara's shoulder and gave her a huge hug.

Suddenly he remembered that Frank was waiting in the truck.

"Hang on a sec," he said, and hurried to the front door. He stepped outside and closed the door behind him to show Frank that nobody had the drop on him. Then he beckoned his brother to come in and stepped back inside, leaving the door open. In a moment Frank had joined them in the kitchen.

"Look what Barbara found in the basement of the BLM." Joe pointed to the piles of paper on the kitchen table. He shot him a triumphant what-did-I-tell-you look. "She thought of them when you mentioned the mineral leases this morning.''

''What are they? Old seismograph logs?'' Frank asked, picking up one of the long sheets and studying it. His face was expressionless, but Joe could tell that it was excitement that was tensing the muscles in his brother's jaw. ''Somebody's already explored for oil in the area, then?''

''Yes.'' Barbara nodded. ''These logs were made in the Caprock area, back around 1930. I'm not exactly sure of the coordinates, but as far as I can tell, the exploration took place on the south end of the old Circle C, near the sand hills.''

''Can you read these?'' Frank asked, still studying them.

''I took a geology course last year, and we did a lot of work with seismograph reports.'' Barbara pointed to the set of squiggles that Frank was looking at. ''Those wavy lines, for instance—they indicate a big salt dome.''

''What's salt got to do with oil?'' Joe asked.

''A lot,'' Barbara told him. ''Under great heat and pressure, salt deposits ooze around, sort of like molasses. When the salt finds a weak spot underground, it rises up like a giant bubble until it's stopped by harder rock. As the salt bubble heads upward, oil can flow up too, collecting around the top of the dome. So when you find a formation like this, you'll often find a pool of oil at the top."

Frank grinned. "As I recall, Spindletop was a salt dome."

Joe frowned. "Spindletop?"

Barbara nodded. "The first—and the biggest—oil field discovered in the Southwest, back in 1901. It was a salt dome formation."

Joe thumped the pile of yellowing logs. "But if they found *this* dome back in 1930," he asked, "why didn't they sink any wells?"

"Look at these notes," Barbara said, pointing to a faded pencil scribble in the margin of the log Frank was looking at. "The top of the dome is about eleven thousand feet below ground level."

Frank whistled. "There's your answer, Joe. Back in the thirties, nobody could drill that deep. The technology was still pretty primitive."

"Right," Barbara chimed in. "And even if they could've sunk a well that deep, the price of oil was so low that it wouldn't have justified the cost."

"But the price of oil is a lot higher now." Joe leaned back thoughtfully against the refrigerator.

"And they're drilling that deep, and deeper, if the formation looks good enough," Barbara said. "Especially in the U.S., with this push to find domestic oil."

THE HARDY BOYS CASEFILES

"These seismographs"—Frank tapped the log on the table—"they're made by exploding subsurface charges and measuring the shock waves. Right?"

"You mean, bombs?" said Joe.

"These logs were probably made that way," Barbara told them. "Nowadays, geologists generally use large, specially equipped trucks. They drop heavy weights that cause the vibrations."

With growing excitement, Joe looked at Frank. He could see what his brother was getting at.

"But they could still use the old method, couldn't they?" Joe asked. "And the people who were setting the charges would have to know how to use dynamite, wouldn't they?"

Barbara nodded. "If you didn't have the new equipment, I guess you'd *have* to do it the old way." She looked puzzled. "Why?"

Joe grinned triumphantly. Barbara couldn't be faking this kind of innocence. Whatever dirty dealing was going on, she wasn't involved in it.

"Oh, we've just been getting a lot of dynamite lately," he said casually. "Somebody stuck some in the stove at the old homestead on the Circle C, where we were camping. Then they wired it to blow up our pickup when the door opened."

Barbara's dark eyes widened in horror.

"You mean, somebody's been trying to *kill* the two of you?"

Joe laughed. "Either that, or they just like the noise dynamite makes when it blows up."

"Speaking of the noise dynamite makes," Frank broke in, "do you remember the thunder we heard that first night at the homestead shack? I'll bet we were hearing somebody setting off an explosive charge."

Barbara let out her breath. "Somebody must be looking for oil!"

"Sounds that way," Joe said. He frowned. "What would a seismography site look like? A bunch of big holes blasted in the ground?"

Barbara shook her head. "Not at all. The bore holes are only about three inches in diameter, maybe a hundred feet deep or so, and about a hundred feet apart. But on the surface, all you'd see is the hole, with a small pile of drill tailings—dirt the drill rig brought up."

"What about the drill rig?" Frank wanted to know. "Would they need to bring in a big one?"

"Not to drill small test holes—they can drill them dry, with a rig that can be hauled on a truck."

Joe scratched his head. He could see that they were getting somewhere. But there was a big hole in their logic. "But what good would it do somebody to find out about the oil?" he asked. "It would still cost them a fortune to get it out, wouldn't it?"

"But you could get plenty rich without drilling," Barbara pointed out. "Once you've got reliable evidence that the oil is there, you buy the mineral rights or leases for next to nothing. Then you take your evidence to any big oil company and watch the value of your leases shoot sky-high."

"That explains the secrecy, but it still doesn't explain all the nasty tricks," Joe said. "Roy owns the middle part of the Circle C—that's where you're saying most of the oil is. He leases the northern end from the state—"

"And the southern end from the federal government," Frank finished for him. "All the trouble has been on the federal land—to keep him from renewing his grazing lease."

"But why?" Barbara said. "Oil drilling isn't like strip mining. There'd be lots of room for the cattle to graze around the oil wells."

"Unless"—Joe snapped his fingers—"they don't *want* Roy to know about the oil wells!" He swiveled around to face Frank and Barbara. "Try this out. Part of the oil deposit extends onto the federal land. If nobody's grazing out there, who'd know that somebody was drilling for oil?"

"And maybe sucking it up from someone else's land!" Frank nodded. "That would finally nail down a motive. I think we'd better check this out. *Pronto*".

"Right," Joe said.

"Hold on, cowboys!" Barbara said, grabbing them both by the arm. "If you're running around out there in the desert tonight, who's taking me to the dance?"

The brothers exchanged reluctant looks.

"You won't find anything out there in the dark, except for a few coyotes," Barbara said, bullying them good-naturedly. "And, anyway, you're going to need *my* help."

"Your help?" Frank asked. "Hey, wait a minute. I don't think—"

Barbara planted her feet firmly. "You don't know your way around that desert. *I* do. You'd get lost in a minute. *I* won't." She gave them a pitying look. "You've never even seen a seismography site. *I* have. *I* know what we're looking for, and you don't."

"The girl's got a point," Joe admitted to Frank, trying to keep from laughing.

"Sounds like blackmail to me," Frank muttered.

Barbara gave them both an angelic smile. "It's called compromise," she said sweetly. "Tomorrow we search. Tonight we party! You guys haven't lived until you've danced the cotton-eyed Joe."

Frank grinned in mock surrender. "Okay,"

he said. "Tonight we party. First thing in the morning we look for bad guys."

It was just before dawn when Joe heard the sound of a jeep outside the bunkhouse. The horn honked twice.

Frank lifted the curtain. "She's here," he announced. "Right on time, too."

"She *would* be," Joe grunted, trying to overcome his sleepiness with a second cup of coffee. He wiggled his toes. His feet were *still* sore from dancing the cotton-eyed Joe.

While Frank called the Circle C ranch house to tell Roy where they were going, Joe stepped outside into the chill, predawn dark. He rubbed his eyes, wondering if he was still dreaming. Barbara's jeep was painted a bright candy-apple red, with fancy black stripes and a black roll bar. Barb herself looked as if she were dressed for work, in a khaki jumpsuit and hiking boots, with a soft hat mashed down over her hair. A pair of binoculars were slung around her neck.

She already had a map spread out as the Hardys climbed into the jeep. "We'll be heading across the caprock, then down into the sand hills." Barbara traced the route with a finger.

"I took another look at the logs this morning before I left," she said. "And I think this is where they tested back in the thirties. It seems like a good spot to start our search—then we can work our way east. The road peters out at this point—" She jabbed at the map.

"The old homestead isn't far to the west, but it's all loose sand. No way to get across in a vehicle, so it's not likely they were doing seismographic blasting in that direction. It would be murder to cross it during the day, on foot."

She grinned, proud of her detecting. "So, buckle up and hang on. The road gets a little rough from here on out."

She gunned the engine and headed off fast down a dirt track that Joe hadn't noticed behind the bunkhouse. Boy, she wasn't kidding about it being rough, Joe thought, waking up in a hurry as he grabbed for something to hold on to. At the edge of the caprock, the trail turned south and then dropped over the edge, angling steeply, doubling back a couple of times as it zigzagged down. It was rocky and badly rutted.

Barbara downshifted but she didn't slow down, and Joe, bouncing in the front seat, gritted his teeth and held his breath as they plummeted toward the bottom. At the foot of the cliff, the track wound through the sagebrush and then intersected with a hard-packed gravel road. Barbara pushed the accelerator to the floor.

"That detour saved us about twelve miles," she shouted over the roar of the jeep. She patted the dash affectionately. "Tinkerbell *loves* to fly down cliffs. It's her favorite thing."

"Tinkerbell?" Frank blinked.

Barbara laughed. "Isn't that a great name? It's definitely *her*."

Great, Joe thought wryly. Tinkerbell had saved thirty minutes—and only scared about five years of life out of him. But his admiration for Barbara reached even higher. She was some driver.

For the next thirty minutes, they rocketed through a maze of roads and dirt trails, through the scrubby mesquite trees and low sand hills. At each intersection, Barbara twisted the wheel without hesitation. Joe couldn't help being glad they'd left the driving to her. All the roads looked alike to him. He wouldn't have known which way to turn.

At last the jeep slowed to a reasonable speed and they could talk comfortably.

Frank leaned forward and tapped Barbara on the shoulder. "Stop!" he commanded. Seconds later he was vaulting out of the jeep and scrambling up the sandy slope beside the road.

Joe saw what had caught his brother's attention. A little way up the slope were a series of wavy marks, like squiggles traced in the sand by some unseen finger.

"Hey, that looks like the symbol we saw in Charlie's shack!" Joe opened his door and jumped out.

"What symbol?" Barbara asked, standing up in the jeep and putting her binoculars to her eyes. "What's Frank looking at?"

Right then, Joe became aware of a strange buzzing noise somewhere down at his feet. It sounded like a clock radio alarm buzzing, and he glanced down, puzzled.

The next thing he knew, someone was hitting him in a flying tackle.

Joe tried to turn in midair, tried to grab for his attacker. Instead, he found himself going facedown into the gritty sand.

Chapter

12

JOE LANDED HARD, but in a second he was on his feet, glaring at Barbara and spitting sand. "What's the big idea?" he demanded. "Where I come from, they call that clipping!"

Barbara chuckled as she looked down at him. "Around here, they call it saving your hide, cowboy. That sidewinder almost got you."

Barbara pointed under a sagebrush, where a pale, leathery tail with a rattle on it was just wriggling out of sight. "Only a greenhorn goes messing with sidewinder tracks without looking for the sidewinder."

Frank joined them. "So that was a rattlesnake track I was looking at, huh?"

"Give that man an A in herpetology." Barb bent over and traced out a wavy track in the sand. "Somewhere back in its evolution, the sidewinder rattlesnake learned how to get around in loose sand. It throws its body in loops out to one side, turns its head that way, and literally moves sideways. That's how it got its name."

Joe brushed sand off his jeans. "Those tracks look like the symbol on Charlie's wall. And we guessed he's really into snakes." He quickly told Barbara what they had found in Charlie's hut—the snakeskin, the rattles and fangs, and the crude sketch on the old pine board.

"I wouldn't be surprised if it was his symbol for a sidewinder," Barbara said, nodding.

They got back in the jeep and Barbara spun it around. As they drove, the boys kept watch for any sign of recent traffic.

Frank pointed to a trail of tire tracks that led off through the mesquite. "These had to be made after the storm. Let's check them out."

Expertly Barbara shoved the jeep into low gear and headed in the direction Frank was pointing. The tracks wound into the sagebrush for about fifty yards. Then they ended in a clearing.

"Hey, look," Joe shouted, jumping out. On the ground were several pairs of thin yellow wire strands—like the wire they'd found in the truck bomb. These were partly buried in the sand, but Joe could see they led off in several directions.

Barbara pulled up on one end of a wire. "This must have been the firing position," she said. "Let's see what's on the other end of this."

The three of them followed the wire through the thorny vegetation. With its feathery leaves, mesquite might be pretty to look at, Joe decided, and it might even be good to eat, if you were a goat. But it definitely wasn't fun to get scraped by the long, sharp thorns. He winced and muttered as one of them made a deep scratch on his arm.

Barbara was pulling up the wire where it was partly buried under drifted sand. Following it, they came across a small pile of fresh red clay powder. The wire disappeared down a three-inch hole beside the pile.

"That, gentlemen," Barbara said in an authoritative voice, "is a bore hole. If we traced out the other wires, we'd find one of these at the end of each of them."

"Well, I guess we've found the evidence to back up our motive," Joe said. "What now?"

Before the others could answer, a horse's whinny pierced the air—from very close by.

"We've got company!" Frank whispered.

Quickly the three of them slipped behind the cover of some dense mesquite bushes and crouched close to the ground. A minute or two passed. There was only the sound of the wind. The air, which had been chilly when they set out, was beginning to warm up as the morning sun climbed higher in the sky.

"Maybe we shouldn't have left the jeep alone," Joe said. "This far from civilization, we'd be in trouble if somebody took it out."

"Right," Barbara whispered. "It'd be a long walk to *anywhere* from here."

Frank nodded, agreeing. "Let's swing out wide and double back to the jeep."

The going was rough. They hunkered down, trying to keep to the cover of the low mesquite. It was hard to keep their footing on the drifted sand. By the time they crept back to the clearing where the jeep was parked, Joe was covered with sweat. His eyes ached from straining for any sign of movement that might give away the presence of their uninvited guest.

"No sign of horses or riders," Barbara whispered as they lay on their stomachs on a sandy rise, surveying the clearing.

"Looks okay to me, too," Joe said, wiping the sweat out of his eyes with his sleeve. He started to get to his feet. "I'm tired of this creepy crawly stuff. Let's—"

Ka-bam! A shotgun blast raked the clearing, kicking up geysers of dust. Joe dropped to the ground, shielding his head with his arms. He waited for another blast, but nothing happened. A half minute later they heard the snort of a horse and muffled hoofbeats. It sounded as if whoever had fired at them was heading away at a fast clip. Joe decided to stay put for another minute, just in case.

He glanced at Barbara. "You okay?" he whispered.

"I'm fine," she answered, then turned her head. "Frank?"

There was a silence, and Joe raised his head, suddenly scared. Had Frank been hit?

"I'm fine." Frank had slithered down the small hill. "But Tinkerbell isn't. They blew away her radiator."

Joe saw a stream of green liquid spurting from several holes in the front of the jeep. A growing pool had already formed under the jeep's engine.

"Poor Tink!" Barbara exclaimed. "How can we plug all those leaks!"

Frank's voice stopped her. "Forget it. Even if we could stop the holes and there was enough coolant left in the radiator, the plugs would never hold under pressure. Tinkerbell's had it. She's not going anywhere without a new radiator."

"Looks like we'll be stuck here for a while," Barbara said calmly. "But I always carry an extra couple of gallons of water in the back of the jeep, and we still have the CB. So let's have a drink and call for help."

"Okay," Frank agreed. "But just in case

we're not alone, I say that only one of us checks it out. You two stay here.''

Before Joe could protest, Frank headed for the jeep, bent over in a half crouch. Cautiously, he circled the vehicle, then, confident that their attackers had gone, he straightened up, reached into the back of the jeep, and grabbed two plastic jugs.

"Empty," he said, tossing them on the ground.

"Impossible!" Barbara exclaimed in dismay. "I filled them before I left!"

"Then somebody must have emptied them." Joe scrambled hurriedly to his feet. "And if they got the water, maybe they also got—"

"Right." Frank's voice was quiet, but Joe could hear the underlying tension in it. He held up the microphone cord for the CB. The cord was there, but the mike was gone.

Joe wiped the sweat from his eyes and glanced up at the sun. It was already burning down on them and noon was still hours away. "What do we do now? We're at least fifteen miles from help, on foot in the desert. It's going to be murder out there in a couple of hours."

"That," Frank said in a grim voice, "is exactly what our attacker had in mind."

13

"THEY REALLY DID a number on us." Frank's face was worried as he started back up the slope. "We're stranded, with no way to call for help, and our whole water supply is sinking into the sand."

Barbara glanced up at the blazing sun. "They might as well have shot us dead."

"Oh, no," Frank said grimly. "If someone found us dead of thirst, it could be an accident—especially if they come back and wreck the jeep. That wouldn't work if we had bullet holes."

"How did these guys know where we were?" Joe asked. "Did they follow us?"

Barbara looked embarrassed. "All they needed was a lookout up on the caprock with binoculars and a radio. The dust we were kicking up would send them a smoke signal. They'd know just where we were going and radio a warning ahead."

Joe felt his anger rising—mostly at himself. "These guys have been one step ahead of us ever since we got here." And one reason they'd kept their lead had been the way he'd let himself get distracted with Barbara. If he'd thought about the case instead, they might not be in this fix.

Barbara patted him on the shoulder. "Loosen up, cowboy. You don't know this country. I guess it should have occurred to *me* that somebody might not want us poking around, looking for seismography sites. I might have been a little more careful about the dust I was raising."

Frank nodded. "We got what we came for," he reminded Joe. "Now we have a motive for what's happened at Roy's place. And even if we *never* find out who's behind it, we've got enough to sink their plan. Once Roy hears about the oil, he can protect his ranch—and what's under it."

Joe sat back on his heels. "Not only that, we have a very solid suspect. I'd like to ask Nat Wilkin if Owens has been out using his three-oh-three lately." He frowned. "Unless I miss my guess, Oscar's got an accomplice we haven't met yet—somebody in the oil business."

"That's all great," Barbara said. "But you're forgetting something."

The Hardys looked at one another. "Forgetting what?" Joe asked.

"Jerry Greene." Barbara's face was somber. "It's beginning to sound to me as if Jerry might have stumbled onto their game. And if he did . . ."

Joe completed the sentence for her. "If he did, they probably finished him off." He stood up, too. "We've *got* to get back to the ranch and warn Roy. With this much at stake, there's no telling what these guys will do next."

Frank snapped back to their present bad situation. "Without water," he commented wryly, "one murder could easily turn into three more."

Barbara stood up. "Maybe we can still find some—yiii!" She slipped on a ridge of loose sand, sliding down hard into the ferny branches of a half-buried mesquite bush.

Joe followed her—more carefully—and helped Barbara back to her feet. But she limped as they stumbled over to Frank. "Oh, great," Barbara said, pointing at her leg with a grimace.

Joe looked—and sucked in a quick breath. Four ugly red blotches marred her khaki trouser leg—and sticking out of them were two-inch-long mesquite thorns.

"Broke my fall on a branch," she said in a

shaky voice. "But it got its revenge. I don't know how far I can walk just now."

Joe knelt down beside her. Together, they gently pulled the thorns free. Barbara rolled up the leg of the jumpsuit. The bleeding was already beginning to stop, but the areas around the wounds had turned an angry-looking red. They were also beginning to swell.

"Does it hurt?" Joe asked.

"Not too much yet," she said. "But it will." She stretched her leg out in front of her. "I won't be able to search—but one of you should check out the area for water. If we don't find any, I suggest that we just cool it here in the shade until the sun comes down." She glanced up at the sun again. "We'll stand a better chance of survival if we don't move around in this heat."

Frank and Joe flipped a coin, and Frank got the job. Half an hour later he returned from the search, looking hot and sweaty. Joe didn't envy him—the weather forecast had called for a high of 115 degrees.

Frank squatted down beside them. "I lost more water than I found," he said. "Looks like we don't have any other choice—we'll stay put until sunset." He shook his head.

An hour passed, then another, and another. The sun, burning orange in a sky of molten brass, crossed the zenith and began to fall toward the west. Even in the dusty shade of the mesquite, the temperature must have been well over a hundred. It felt like the inside of a kiln, a fierce, dry heat that seemed to warp the roof of Joe's mouth.

Even the flies were off somewhere taking a nap, Joe noticed almost in a daze. He saw lots of ants, though, and he could hear the erratic *click-click-click* of a locust on the bush above him. Far overhead, buzzards soared in expanding spirals, never in a hurry. Joe began to wonder if that wasn't quite a flock of them overhead, their wings like coal black *V*'s against the sky. What were they waiting for?

Suddenly Joe sat up. A movement in the brush had caught his eye.

"Ss-s-t." He leaned over and tapped Frank on the shoulder, pointing.

A figure lean and gaunt as a scarecrow stepped into the clearing. He wore homespun cotton pants and shirt. There was a straw hat on his head.

"It's Charlie!" Joe whispered. Beside Joe, Barbara stirred, sat up, and rubbed her eyes.

"What did I tell you?" Frank asked with a grin. "Didn't I say he'd show up again?"

The old man looked directly at them, beckoned slowly with one upraised hand, then turned and vanished into the brush again.

"I think he wants us to follow him," Frank said.

"But it looks like he's heading east," Joe

said uneasily. "We want to go *west*, toward the ranch."

Painfully, Barbara pushed herself up. "I'd bet on Charlie," she said. "His people lived on this land long before any of us got here. We can count on him to get us out of this fix."

Frank nodded. "Let's go," he said. With Barbara hobbling along, leaning on Joe for support, they made their way slowly after Charlie.

He glanced back at them, and motioned for them to stay low. A second later they saw a brief glint of light up on the caprock far to the east.

"I'll bet that's either a pair of binoculars or a rifle scope," Frank said, as they crouched down. "Our friends must be keeping an eye on us."

"That flash came from just south of Lawson's Bluff," Barbara said, a little breathlessly. "That's down on the Triple O."

"How come I'm not surprised?" Joe muttered.

A little farther on Charlie led them into a dry stream bed that wound eastward, toward the caprock. The gullied sides were just high enough to hide them from the bluff where the flash had come from. The ravine floor was littered with rocks and rough gravel, and in places it was crusted with white, sun-baked alkali. It was slow, hard going, but Joe had to admit it was better than being shot at.

He marveled at Charlie. The man's thin, wiry body moved effortlessly. He never glanced at the ground. Yet he put each foot down firmly and surely, without pausing, without stumbling, his sandals never leaving a print in the dusty sand. How did he do it? For a second Joe wondered if he were following a mirage. Then he grinned. "The heat must be getting to me," he told himself. "The three of us wouldn't see the same mirage."

To keep himself going, Joe began counting steps. When he reached a thousand, he glanced at Barbara. "How're you doing?" he asked. She'd managed to keep pace with him, but she was limping and leaning on him more and more heavily. He knew that leg must be giving her real trouble.

"I'll make it." She smiled bravely, but her dry lips had little cracks. "But I sure could use a drink of water. Anybody have a Popsicle?"

Joe laughed. He knew what she was talking about. His mouth was as dry as parched shoe-leather, and he was beginning to feel a little lightheaded. Somewhere close by, a raven gave a loud, raucous laugh, and a minute later, a couple of other ravens joined him in a chorus of mad laughter.

Joe didn't blame them. There had to be something pretty funny about two greenhorns and a girl following a little old man down a bone-dry canyon under a blast-furnace sun. If his mouth weren't so dry, he'd laugh, too.

But he realized they were getting somewhere. Now the caprock cliff towered above them. Ahead, the dry stream bed they were following made a sharp bend around a heap of big gray boulders, fragments of the cliff face that had broken off and tumbled down. Beyond, Joe could see the green shadow of what looked like a cottonwood tree.

"I guess the heat's getting to me," Frank said. "I'd swear I just heard running water."

Joe and Barbara stopped and listened. The sound of the wind rose and fell, eerily, and Joe could hear the faraway call of a mourning dove. But beneath those sounds was an unmistakably melodious note—the sound of water dripping into a deep pool! Without a word, they redoubled their efforts to catch up with Charlie, who had never broken his effortless pace.

"Look!" Frank exclaimed, as they rounded the heap of boulders.

A clear ribbon of water oozed from a thin, crumbly layer of sediment in the cliff. It trickled over harder rock, then dropped six feet into a deeply sculptured basin in the rock below. The water hold was surrounded by monkey flowers and clumps of maidenhair ferns. Overhead the wind stirred the cool, green canopy of cottonwood.

Seconds later, as Charlie watched, the three of them lay flat on their faces, drinking the cool, sweet water. After he'd sipped enough, Joe dunked his head and shoulders under, staying a long time, letting the water cool him off.

"Watch out," Frank cautioned Joe when he finally came up for air. "You don't want to drown in the stuff."

"Drown?" Joe laughed, giving his head a shake. He took another loud slurp. "When I finish drinking, there won't be enough left to drown in."

"It's funny," Barbara said. "I've been all over this part of the cliff, and I didn't know this spring was here. It must be seasonal."

"I'm for staying until it dries up." Joe stretched out in the shade of the cottonwood.

"Where do you think we are?" Frank asked Barbara.

Barbara grinned. "You're not going to believe this, but I'll bet we're almost directly below the bunkhouse. It's on the caprock, up there."

At that moment Charlie stepped forward and said something to Barbara in what sounded to Joe like Spanish. She replied. Joe couldn't make out anything but the urgency in Charlie's voice.

"He says we have to go now," Barbara told them. "If we don't hurry, we'll be late."

"Late for what?" Joe demanded without

stirring. He opened his eyes. "Is somebody giving a party?"

"I couldn't quite make out why," Barbara replied. "But it's got something to do with getting to the top of the caprock."

Joe blinked. "Up *there?*" he asked. The top of the caprock was straight over their heads. "What does he think we are, mountain goats?"

But Charlie had already set off, taking a narrow path that clung to the side of the cliff.

Joe stood up with a sigh. He could take the climb, maybe. But what about Barbara?

She caught his look. "I can make it."

They climbed for a half hour. The sun was much lower in the west now and not so hot. But the loose limestone made the footing treacherous, and at its widest, the trail was only a foot wide. Ahead of them, Charlie moved along steadily, never wavering. Behind him, Barbara faltered, clinging to the rock with both hands. Joe and Frank brought up the rear, moving carefully, one foot in front of the other. Joe didn't want to look down.

When they finally reached the top, they were only a hundred yards from the bunkhouse. Bringing up the rear, Frank breathed a sigh of relief and took a quick look around. Everything was quiet. More importantly, the pickup truck was still parked beside the house, still in one piece.

Charlie picked up the pace now, heading

straight for the house. When they'd gotten almost to the back door, Frank turned to Joe. "You don't suppose we're walking into another trap, do you?"

Joe looked around carefully. "He could have left us out on the sand," he said. "But he got us here safely. I'd trust him a little further."

Charlie was saying something to Barbara.

"He wants us to go in," she said. "He says we've got to hurry."

Frank stepped to the kitchen window, checking the inside of the small house. "Everything seems okay," he said. "Just the way we left it this morning." He opened the back door.

"I still don't understand," Joe said as he stepped in. "Why all the hurry? What's—"

"Telephone!" Charlie said in a low voice, raising his hand to his ear as if he were picking up the receiver.

Pick up the phone? Was that what Charlie wanted? Frowning, Frank reached for the receiver.

"Careful!" Charlie whispered, putting his finger to his lips.

Gently, Frank lifted the receiver, keeping a hand over the mouthpiece.

"Told you . . . never use . . . party line . . . risky!" The line crackled with static, and the angry voice was too low-pitched to make everything out.

"Relax, relax," another voice said. Maybe it

was nearer, because it came through a little more clearly. Frank wished the line were better—he almost recognized the speaker. "The only other phone on this line is Carlson's bunkhouse. And I left those kids in a bad way. The sun's probably finished them off by now." A blast of static cut him off in midlaugh.

Frank picked up the conversation again. "Greene kid played his part well . . . wait for the two of you up here on the caprock."

Another blast of static wiped out the response. "Reach the old windmill to pick up our other friend. Look for us after dark."

Frank had to strain to hear the next part. But what he caught made his stomach turn over. "Have two bodies to get rid of instead of one."

Chapter

14

FRANK HEARD A LOUD CLICK, and the connection was broken. He put the receiver down and faced the others. "I wish that line had been better. I knew the voice, but couldn't swear it was Owens. At least it confirms part of our suspicions—there is an accomplice involved." He shook his head. "But from the sound of things, Jerry's mixed up in it, too."

Barbara shook her head firmly. "I can't believe that Jerry's part of this," she protested. "He's just not the kind of guy to—"

"Look!" Joe exclaimed. "He's done it again!"

Frank turned. Joe was pointing to the open door. Charlie was nowhere to be seen.

"We turn our back on him for one second," Joe said, "and he goes into his vanishing act."

"I guess he figures we can take it from here." Frank grinned crookedly. "I hope he's right."

"Listen," Joe said, leaning forward, "I'm with Barbara on this Jerry bit. She knows him—we don't."

Frank nodded. "It did sound as if the guy on the other end was on his way to pick somebody up. And if they're planning to kill two people, that must mean Jerry and this other person. We need to get to Roy," Frank said urgently. "They talked about an 'old windmill,' and maybe Roy knows what they might have been talking about. It sounded as if they were on the caprock somewhere."

"We don't dare phone him, though," Joe said. "The bad guys might pick us up on the party line. We've got the old yellow pickup, but it doesn't have a CB." He looked at Barbara. "We used the ranch road to get here. Is there a faster way back to the Circle C ranch house?"

"The long way round, by the highway," Barbara replied. "It's probably ten miles farther, but it's a lot faster and there's less risk of being spotted."

Frank and Joe checked out the pickup in record time.

"It looks like you guys have had a lot of practice at this," Barbara said as Joe rolled under the pickup and Frank crawled under the dashboard.

"You bet," Joe told her. "As of a couple of days ago, we don't drive *anything* we haven't checked out first."

"Clear here," Frank called.

"Let's go," Joe said, sliding into the driver's seat. "Roll 'em!" He shoved the gearstick into first, scattering gravel, and they were off.

They were a mile and a half from the ranch house when a sharp *bang* came from the right front. The truck pulled hard to the right. Wrestling the wheel, Joe managed to keep the truck from skidding and bring it to a smooth stop on the shoulder.

"Of all the luck!" Joe thundered. "A blowout! Just what we need!" He thumped the steering wheel.

Frank peered around cautiously. There wasn't any good cover nearby. "You don't suppose somebody took a shot at us, do you?"

Joe was already out of the truck, studying the flat tire. "Doesn't look like it to me. I think we just got unlucky." He stood up, scowling. "Now what?"

Frank looked in the bed of the truck and gave the spare tire a thump with his fist. "Looks like the spare's good, and there's a jack behind the seat. I'll take off on foot, and we'll see who's fastest."

"I'd race you, but . . ." Barbara gave a wan smile at her injured leg.

"I'll need someone to cheer me on with this tire fixing," Joe said with a grin.

Frank set off at an even, steady trot. It was much cooler now that it was almost sunset, and the sun was falling into a cloud bank of crimson and orange and blue. A nighthawk, high above, folded its wings and plunged straight down through the still air, pulling up just above Frank's head, where it plucked an insect out of the air and soared away.

Fifteen minutes after he'd left Joe, Frank panted the last hundred feet up to the ranch house. The only vehicle he could see out front was the white car that Dot drove. Shep came running out to greet him with a storm of excited barks. Dot came out on the front porch.

"Frank!" she exclaimed. "What are you doing on foot? Where's Joe?"

"Fixing a flat," Frank gasped, catching his breath. "They'll be along in a minute." He stepped up onto the porch. "Where's Roy? I need to talk to him right away. We've solved the case! Now all we have to do is find Jerry and—"

"Find Jerry?" Dot broke in, looking confused. "But I don't understand. Roy's already left, to meet *you*. Right after he got the phone call, three-quarters of an hour ago."

Frank stopped dead still. "To meet *us?* Who called?"

Dot's confusion was turning to concern. "Roy didn't know who it was. Anyway, whoever it was said that Jerry was still alive and that you and Joe had found out where he was. Roy was suspicious—he insisted on talking to Jerry in person."

"What happened then?" Frank asked. He could see a cloud of dust on the road, the yellow pickup barreling in front of it.

"Then Jerry came on the line and said he was okay. Roy was sure that it was Jerry's voice, even though he sounded like he was sort of in a daze." She stopped, her voice beginning to fill with panic. "After that, the caller came back on the line. He said—he said that he had you and Joe and Jerry, and that if Roy wanted to see any of you alive again, he had to meet him. Right away. Alone."

"Meet him *where?*" Frank demanded. But he already knew the answer.

"At the windmill," Dot replied. "Down on the old homestead."

Frank kept his face still. How was he going to tell Dot that Roy's appointment was a setup for murder?

Chapter
15

"BAD NEWS!" Frank shouted as Joe drove up. "They're after Roy. He left for the old homestead nearly an hour ago."

"Roy Carlson!" Barbara exclaimed. Then she nodded. "That figures, I guess."

"What are we waiting for?" Joe demanded. He put the truck into reverse and got ready to back up. "Let's go! Maybe we can get there in time."

Frank shook his head. Whatever was planned at the old windmill had already happened. Joe cut the engine in disgust. But from the look on Frank's face, they might have another plan.

"It'll be dark in half an hour," Frank told them. "Owens said that he and Jerry would be waiting up on the caprock. So that's where this other guy will be taking Roy. They've counted us out. So if we can get up there, maybe we can catch them off guard—and save Roy and Jerry."

"But *where* on the caprock?" Barbara wondered.

Frank wheeled to face Dot. "We're looking for a place that's on the same party line as the bunkhouse," he said.

Dot's face was drawn with worry. "Then you're looking for the old shack at the north end of the Triple O, just south of Lawson's Bluff. The place is a wreck—I thought that phone line had been down for years."

"Well, that explains the great connection on the call we overheard," Frank said.

"And that must have been where we saw the flash this afternoon," Barbara added.

"How's the land there?" Frank asked. "Flat and fairly open, like around the bunkhouse?"

Dot frowned. "As best I can recall, it's mostly open pasture with some mesquite bushes. There's an old shed and a corral out back. And it's quite a distance from the highway."

Joe leaned against the truck. "They're bound to be keeping an eye on the road coming in from the highway," he said, "so we can't surprise them that way." He shook his head. "Too bad we don't have more time. We could cross the sand hills and climb the caprock, the way we did this afternoon."

"Yeah, sure," Barbara said skeptically. "In the dark, without Charlie to guide us."

"Anyway, there's no time for that, even if we could," Frank said. He grinned. "What I had in mind was dropping in on them."

Without waiting to explain, he strode into the house and headed for the office, where he studied the wall map for a minute, and then got a ruler out of the desk and began to measure distances on the map. Finally, he sat at the desk and began to punch numbers into the calculator. "It should work," he muttered to himself, satisfied. When he came back out onto the porch, Barbara and Dot were talking in low voices, confusion on their faces. Joe was wearing a big grin.

"Drop in on them?" Dot asked. "What in the world are you talking about, Frank?"

Frank pointed toward the east. Above the caprock, slightly to the north, they could see some blinking red lights.

"Those lights mark three tall radio towers a couple of miles beyond the caprock," he said. "If Joe and I fly directly toward them—"

Barbara gave Frank a withering look. "And just where are you planning to get your wings, Peter Pan?"

Frank ignored her. "If we fly directly toward them in the ultralight, we'll get to maximum altitude just as we cross the caprock. From that point, we should be able to reach our objective."

"But that contraption makes too much noise," Joe objected. "They'll hear us coming and shoot us out of the sky."

Frank grinned. "There won't *be* any noise. When we cross the caprock, we cut the engine and glide the rest of the way. I figured it out on the calculator. At maximum altitude, and with the ultralight's glide ratio, we can make it to the shack where they're holed up."

Joe stared at him. *"Glide?"* He gulped.

Frank paused, testing the wind. The crescent moon was just rising to the south of the radio towers.

"Unfortunately, this south wind isn't going to help. It'll cut our ground speed. But the moon should give us enough light to spot the shack from the air, even if they don't have any lights on."

"Assuming you find it," Barbara asked worriedly, "what then?"

Frank squared his shoulders. "The tough part is the landing. We'll have only one try. If we have to restart the engine, they'll hear us. And then we might as well forget rescuing Roy and Jerry."

"What can *we* do?" Dot asked.

"You and Barbara can get ahold of Sheriff Clinton and seal off the road," Frank said. "In fact, you might even catch the guy who's bringing Roy in." He chewed his lip. "I just hope he hasn't got there yet with Roy. I have the feeling that Roy and Jerry won't stay alive very long once they're up there."

"What if you need reinforcements?" Barbara asked.

"We'll signal. Three of anything—shots, honks, flashes," Frank said. "That'll be your signal to close in."

While Dot began to dial the phone, Frank, Joe, and Barbara headed for the barn and rolled the ultralight outside.

"We'd better top off the tank," Frank told Joe. "Running out of gas tonight could be embarrassing."

Barbara picked up a gas can inside the door and followed them as they pushed the ultralight onto the dirt road. She was still limping. Frank took the can and filled the small fuel tank.

"I think that does it." He stepped beside the pilot's seat.

Joe looked at the light craft. Suddenly, it seemed pretty puny looking.

"What did you say the maximum altitude is?" he asked, trying to keep the uneasiness out of his voice.

"About five thousand feet," Frank replied carelessly, climbing in. He was grinning. "Come on. No guts, no glory!" He turned on

THE HARDY BOYS CASEFILES

the ignition, and the little engine screamed to life.

"Take care, cowboy." Barbara gave Joe a quick hug. Then Joe climbed in beside Frank, trying not to look as reluctant as he felt.

"Are we legal?" he shouted, over the shrill whine of the engine.

"Not until I get my license," Frank replied, testing the controls. "If we run into an FAA inspector, you'll have to get out and walk." He stared into Joe's unhappy face. "Look, it's the only way we can get there to save Jerry and Roy."

The yellow pickup rolled to a stop beside the ultralight and Barbara ran over to it. Dot took a shotgun out of the gun rack and handed it to Barbara through the window, saying something Joe couldn't hear.

"Dot says you might need this," Barbara reported, handing Joe the gun. "Just in case you run into varmints or something."

Joe gave her a thumbs-up as Frank pushed the throttle to full power. The ultralight gained speed very slowly, it seemed to Joe. Finally, Frank eased the controls back and slowly, laboriously, they rose into the air.

"Anybody ever tell you that you're a lot of dead weight?" Frank shouted as they sluggishly climbed above the scrub.

"I just hope you did those calculations

right," Joe said with a worried glance ground-
ward.

He could see the lights of the pickup already
heading north at top speed toward the highway.
Ahead of them in the darkness were the three
radio towers, their red lights blinking. Frank
turned the ultralight to bear directly on them
and leveled the wings. Slowly they gained altitude, climbing through the chilly dusk, the
laboring engine shrieking in Joe's ears.

"With this load," Frank shouted, "we won't
make much better time than they will in the
pickup, even if we are cutting cross-country."

Joe nodded. The ground below them was
rapidly losing its landmarks in the darkness.
Here and there a light patch of sandy dune
stood out. The moon still hung low on the
horizon. Somehow, those three strings of red
lights straight ahead gave Joe a lot of comfort.
Then, after a little while, he saw the caprock
cliff below, a long, chalk-white thread that
wound across the darkness below. From five
thousand feet, it looked tiny—nothing at all
like the frightening cliff they'd climbed just that
afternoon.

At that moment Frank pulled back on the
throttle. The engine cut off, leaving a high-
pitched ringing in Joe's ears. The only other
sounds were the rush of air over the surface of
the wings and the eerie whistle of the wind
through the struts.

"Here goes." Frank banked the ultralight to the right, heading south.

Now they were slipping effortlessly through the darkness, losing altitude in a long, smooth glide. Frank leveled the wings. "Five minutes to touchdown," he said. "Watch for the shack—and keep your eyes peeled for a good landing zone."

So this is what the glider troops in World War Two felt like, Joe thought. There was a knot in the pit of his stomach and his mouth was dry. He remembered reading that some of those night operations had been real disasters—gliders piling up against trees and fences. He'd always trusted his brother to get them out of tight spots—but *this* was a killer!

They were near enough to the ground so that Joe could begin to make out surface features in the dim moonlight. There were open areas which appeared to be covered with grass, broken with shadowy spots that might be mesquite. Occasionally, the shadowy splotches seemed very dense. Joe shuddered as he thought of those mesquite thorns, sharp as needles, hard as nails.

"Lawson's Bluff coming up," Frank said, pointing ahead and to the right, where the caprock jutted out. It was bare and open but not level enough for a landing, Joe saw. On its far side was the line traced by a barbed wire fence. Briefly, he wondered what the Native

Americans would have thought, the night of the raid, if a strange machine like this one had dropped in on them from the sky.

"Hey, a light!" Joe exclaimed, pointing to a single pinprick of yellow, two hundred yards ahead of them. Then, in the moonlight, he began to pick out the structures—a small cabin, with corrals and a shed behind it.

"We need a landing spot, in a *hurry*," Frank said, his voice grimly urgent.

Joe was suddenly aware that every inch of ground beneath them was covered with dense growth and the shadows it cast.

Off to the left he spotted a patch of what looked like open pasture. "How about there?" he said, pointing.

Frank banked the ultralight and headed for it. But then Joe could see that the shadows were lengthening out ahead of them. The open patch had disappeared behind clumps of brush and trees.

Frank's voice was tight. "We're not going to make it."

Chapter
16

THE DARK, SCRAWNY SHAPES of bushes seemed to rush up at them. "Hang on tight," Frank said. "We're going in!"

As they began to slice through the feathery tops of the mesquite, Frank pulled back on the controls. The nose of the ultralight rose, almost hanging in front of them. Then the craft seemed to drop out from underneath them. Joe felt it shudder as the limbs caught at it, then gave way under its weight, crackling sharply. The front tire hit the ground, but the steel tube that supported it bent. They thumped to the ground.

Joe was tossed forward to bounce against his seat belt. The ultralight leaned crazily, its rear wheels still caught in the bushes. The shotgun fell out.

"You all right?" Joe asked, turning to Frank.

"Somebody said any landing you can walk away from is a good landing," Frank replied, undoing his seat belt. "Let's see about that."

As Joe gingerly climbed out, he stubbed his toe against something. He looked down to find the missing shotgun. Its butt stock was snapped at the neck. The gun was worthless.

The Hardys made their way through the mesquite to the clearing where they'd seen the light. A shadowy figure stood on the rickety front porch, looking toward them. At that moment, a bull in the pasture behind them gave a loud bellow. The figure on the porch turned back into the house.

"Think he heard anything?" Joe whispered.

"Probably. But he must have thought it was the cattle, crashing through the brush." Frank shrugged. "I guess we're lucky there's a lot of mesquite between here and where we landed."

They waited a couple of minutes, but there was no move from the cabin. The sounds of country and western music drifted out of a window into the cool night air.

"Well, if we want something to happen, looks like it's up to us to *make* it happen," Frank whispered. "Here's what I suggest."

Joe listened, then nodded. "Gotcha."

A moment later Frank darted across the dusty, rock-littered yard, keeping low and in the shadows. He reached the porch and crouched down.

"Hey, Jerry!" he heard Joe shout, from his concealed position.

The radio suddenly clicked off and the light went out. Frank heard the sound of heavy feet running across a wooden floor and a screen door screeching open and slamming shut. Footsteps pounded the porch and the wooden steps as a figure with a drawn revolver charged past.

Frank lunged in a diving tackle. Smashing into the guy, he was a little surprised—Oscar Owens was fairly short. The figure that toppled to the ground was huge. At least the gun flew from the guy's hand to land with a thud in the soft dust several feet away.

The man made a quick recovery, scrambling to his feet to face off against Frank. It was Nat Wilkin! Frank froze in an instant of surprise—and Nat took advantage of it. A giant fist came like a pile driver toward Frank's jaw. Frank managed to divert the blow but not the momentum of the charging figure behind it. Nat ran full into Frank, knocking him flat on his back, then he crashed down on top of him.

A blow from that iron fist slammed into the side of Frank's head. He shook his head, trying to clear his eyes—and wished he hadn't. A large hunk of limestone in two giant hands hovered over his head. Nat knelt over him with an evil grin, ready to smash the rock into his face. Frank could hardly move, much yet fend him off.

"Freeze!" The command seemed faint, far away.

But the rock hesitated over him.

"Don't even think about it." The voice came closer. "Put it down. Very gently." The voice was harsh. "This is no time for a mistake."

The rock came to rest on the ground, inches from Frank's face.

Now Frank saw the barrel of a very large pistol jabbing Nat just behind his right ear. The pistol was held in Joe's strong, steady grasp.

"Lace your fingers behind your head," Joe commanded. "Get up—slowly."

Nat was red-faced with rage. "I'll have you punks tossed into the pen!" he snarled, glaring at Joe. "Trespassing and assault!"

Joe faced him calmly. "I'll see that and raise you two counts of kidnapping and three counts of attempted murder."

"That wasn't my idea!" Nat whined. Then he checked himself.

Frank got to his feet. "Maybe you'd like to tell us whose idea it was," he suggested, brushing himself off.

"I bet you'd like that," Nat growled. "But the game's not over."

Frank nodded. "The rest of the players haven't shown up yet, have they?" He stepped onto the porch. An ancient bell hung there—

rusty, but loud enough when he gave the warning signal.

Bong! Bong! Bong! The three deep notes reverberated through the still night air.

"Let's have a look inside." Joe prodded Nat forward at pistol point.

Frank turned on the light inside the door. A young man lay on a bunk, his eyes glazed. Frank knelt beside the bunk to check Jerry's pulse. "What did you do to him?" he demanded.

"Hey, nothing," Nat said, shifting nervously away from Joe. "Nothing a little sleep won't cure, anyway." He shuddered. "Be careful with that gun, kid. It's got a hair trigger."

Frank heard the sound of the two vehicles coming up, and glanced out the window. "Here comes our reinforcements," he confirmed to Joe. Two pairs of parking lights bounced swiftly through the pasture to the east. In the moonlight Frank recognized the yellow pickup, leading a squad car. He stepped to the porch and waved.

"Frank! Where's Joe?" Barbara called, jumping out of the truck even before it rolled to a stop.

"He's inside." Frank grinned. "Keeping tabs on Nat Wilkin, of all people. And we've got Jerry, too," he added as Dot came running up. "I think he's going to be okay."

Dot was followed by a stern-faced Sheriff Clinton. "What's going on here?"

"Kidnapping, for starters," Frank told him.

The sheriff stepped past Frank, into the room. While Joe still kept the prisoner covered, Clinton pulled Nat's hands down, one at a time, and deftly handcuffed them behind his back.

"What about Roy?" Dot asked worriedly.

"We haven't seen him," Frank said. "What about you? Did you see anything out there?"

"Not a thing." Dot sounded scared. "Oh, Frank, what if Roy's already—"

"Well, Nat," the sheriff said, pushing Wilkin out onto the porch. "What have you got to say for yourself?"

Nat didn't reply. He seemed to be listening. Then an unpleasant smile spread over his face.

Barbara turned, looking toward the west. "What's that sound?" she whispered, as Joe came out onto the porch behind her.

They all heard it now—a roaring rumble like a monster engine, protesting under a heavy load. The sound came from below the cliff.

"I'd say," Frank remarked, "that it's a very large truck, in very low gear."

The noise grew rapidly louder, and the engine wound itself into a high-pitched whine. A squat, heavy shadow lumbered like a tank over the edge of the cliff. Frank recognized it immediately—it was the giant Mack truck cab that had nearly driven them off the road. Its lights were off. The moonlight reflected off the broad windshield and tall chrome grill. Then the headlights flashed twice and the engine was switched off.

"That must be some kind of signal," Joe said to Frank. "He must be expecting a countersign. But what?"

"The bell, maybe?" Frank replied.

They all turned to look at Nat. He just grinned at them.

"Well, now," he drawled. "It looks like you boys have run smack into a Mexican standoff!"

Chapter

17

NAT SQUARED OFF against them. In spite of the handcuffs on his wrists, he acted as if he were holding all the aces.

"Look, Sheriff, be reasonable," Nat said smoothly. "There's no point in anybody getting hurt, is there? We can do a deal here—you get Roy, and my friend and I get on our way."

"No way," Joe snapped.

"If anybody gets hurt," Frank said grimly, *"you're* an accomplice."

Their voices were drowned out as the truck engine started up, bringing the cab closer. Sheriff Clinton brought up a six-cell flashlight, shining it toward the truck.

"Wilkin! What do you think you're doing?" a furious voice came from the truck cab. Then everyone on the porch was blinded as the truck's huge lights came on, dazzling them.

"Looks like you really fouled things up, huh, Nat? Sheriff, you've got Nat, and as far as I'm concerned, you can keep him. I just want to get out of here."

"What makes you think we'll let you get away?" the sheriff shouted.

The voice chuckled. "Because I've got insurance, that's why." The truck door slammed open. "His name is Roy Carlson!" Against the glare of the high beams, they saw the shadowy form of a tall man, hands crossed in front of him. A shorter, stockier figure prodded him along with a long-barreled weapon.

"That's Roy!" Dot whispered. "What are we going to do?"

Nat spit into the dust. "That no-good double-crossing snake," he muttered. "I knew he was crazy, but I thought I could trust him."

Abruptly, the short, stocky man pushed Roy forward a few paces. Roy stumbled and caught himself.

"Look, people, what's it going to be?" the voice demanded. Against the lights, they saw the rifle come up. "You've got ten seconds! Let me go, or I'll blast good old Roy!"

Frank and Joe stared at each other helplessly. Silence hung over the scene, while the crescent moon cast long, strange shadows over the pasture, the corral, and the bluff beyond.

"One," the shadowy figure called out. "Two—three—"

"You think he means it?" Sheriff Clinton asked Nat.

"He's got nothing to lose," Wilkin said worriedly. He'd just realized that he was the one who'd be paying if Roy got killed.

"Five—six—seven," the gunman's voice counted out.

Beside them, Dot Carlson began to whimper.

"Eight—"

"Stop it! Stop it!" Dot screamed. "Let my husband go!"

Clinton looked helplessly from Dot to the two figures outlined against the lights.

"Nine—te—"

The voice cut off as another sound broke in—a rattling that was quiet, but grew louder. The stocky figure in front of the truck whirled around.

"Hey-hey-hey-ya! Hey-hey-hey-ya!" A thin, wavering chant rose rhythmically into the moonlight, bone-chilling, bloodcurdling. Beyond the truck, on the other side of the fence that ran beside the promontory of Lawson's Bluff, a skeletal apparition rose up, arms extended to the open sky. "Hey-ya-hey-ya-hey!" The apparition turned several times, bending and bowing in a slow dance.

"You there! You stop that!" the stocky man commanded. He stepped toward the dancer, his attention momentarily diverted from Roy and the group on the porch.

"Come on," Joe whispered, grabbing Frank's arm. "Let's circle around behind the corral!" The two boys slipped into the cover of the shadows and began making their way silently toward the corral.

"Hey-hey-hey-ya!" The thin, tuneless chant came again, fading, then growing louder.

"That's got to be Charlie out there," Frank whispered. "Boy, he sure turns up at the weirdest times."

Charlie's chanting was obviously getting on the stocky man's nerves. "Knock it off!" he yelled, backing that demand up with a wild shot.

The boys reached the corner of the corral and peeked around it. The stocky man had turned his back on Roy. He was concentrating on the dancing figure, now beginning to circle on the rock, with a slow, shuffling step.

The pitch of the chant rose and the speed picked up as the figure swayed and turned, faster and faster. Joe had to admit that the dance was eerie, frightening. It was like a ghost dancing out there—the ghost of the long-dead Native Americans who had once ruled this cliff, this desert.

"Hey-hey-hey, hey-hey-hey, hey-ya, hey-ya!"

"Stop!" The stocky man had vaulted the

fence that separated him from Charlie. He was advancing on the dancer, the barrel of his gun pointed menacingly.

Roy took advantage of his captor's distraction, stumbling as he ran for the safety of the corral.

"Over here, Roy!" Frank called, in a low voice. In a second Roy was beside them and they were untying his hands.

"Boy, am I glad to see you guys," Roy said, rubbing his wrists. "That guy—the guy driving the truck—he's nuts. I thought I was a goner for sure." He peered in the direction of the dancer. "What's going on out there?"

They were close enough to make out the scene clearly. Charlie was moving faster and faster, his chant rising in a wild wail. His long hair was woven into braids, and he held something in his hand, something that twisted and writhed.

"It's a *snake!*" Joe gasped. "He's got a live snake out there!"

Frank shook his head. "Risky business, if you ask me."

"Hey-ya-hey-ya-HI!"

Facing the man with the gun, Charlie suddenly stood tall and flung his arms wide.

"Get it away!" the man shouted, his gun sailing as he leaped away. A second later, he was on his knees. "My leg! Help! I've been snake bit! A rattler got me!"

In an instant Frank and Joe were over the fence. They seized the man and dragged him to his feet, searching him quickly. He had no weapons, but in his pocket Frank found a handful of blasting caps.

"Like to play with these, huh?" Frank murmured.

"I need a doctor," the man said. There was panic in his voice. He looked down at his leg. "I need a doctor, *bad!*"

Frank and Joe sat him down. Joe removed one of his shoe laces and began tying it tight around the leg, just above the bite. "You'll live," he said. "Probably."

Frank nudged Joe. "Hey," he said, "he's done it again."

Joe straightened up, pulling the stocky man upright. "Who?"

"Charlie."

Frank pointed. All of Lawson's Bluff lay still and empty. Charlie and his snake had vanished.

Chapter

18

"BARBARA'S LATE," Joe complained with a look at his watch. He was sitting on the tailgate of the old yellow pickup, parked in front of the Circle C ranch house.

Frank stood beside their luggage. "I can't believe you're in such a big hurry to get out of here." He grinned at Joe. "I thought you'd miss Barbara."

Joe shrugged, a little embarrassed. "You've got to admit she was pretty nice, offering to drive us all the way back to Lubbock Airport."

"It was the least she could do," Frank pointed out, "after we sweated all morning in the mesquite, changing Tinkerbell's radiator." He laughed. "We saved Barb a humongous towing bill—and Tinkerbell a very uncomfortable trip."

Roy Carlson came out of the ranch house, a happy smile on his face. "Sorry I wasn't able to say goodbye before. I was on the phone to the hospital—just talked to Jerry, and he sounds super. The doc doesn't think he'll suffer any permanent effects from that stuff those guys doped him with. But he wants to keep an eye on him for a couple of days."

"How about Nat and his partner?" Frank asked. "Have they started talking yet?"

"It's amazing how a night in jail—or in the hospital—can make a fella talk," Roy said. "I got an earful from Bobby Clinton while you boys were out fixing Barbara's jeep."

"Do we know who that guy in the truck was?" Joe asked.

"His name is John Hicks," Roy said. "That sidewinder bite made him pretty sick—and scared. He told Bobby his whole life story. Apparently, Hicks worked for a few oil companies, long enough to pick up some of the basics about oil exploration. He learned how to handle explosives in the army."

Roy shook his head. "Believe it or not, his people came from around here."

The Hardys stared as the rancher went on.

"The Hicks family homesteaded in this area, back when the original oil survey was made, more than fifty years back. They went bust, but there was some kind of family legend about

148

their being cheated out of the land and the oil under it.''

Roy sighed. "Seems Hicks was telling the story one night in a bar and Nat overheard. He figured if the story turned out to be true, there was a lot of money to be made. So they formed a partnership of sorts.''

Joe shook his head. "I think Nat got more than he bargained for. Hicks is more than a little crazy.''

Frank nodded. "From the way they acted last night, those two looked ready to kill each other.''

"Nat's already talked his head off," Roy agreed. "So Bobby's got a pretty good idea of what happened. Old Nat went off and got the mineral leases for the federal land. But they wanted me off so I wouldn't find out what they were up to. Wilkin and Hicks set out to make ranching that land real unprofitable—they figured I'd decide not to renew my grazing lease.''

"That was probably after they'd started the seismographic tests, and figured out about the salt dome," Frank said. "They knew most of the oil was on Roy's property, so they were doing the final tests to figure where to drill and siphon off the oil.''

"And Jerry caught them in the act," Joe said.

"That's right," Roy told them. "They

grabbed him, then panicked and stashed him in that abandoned shack. Turned his horse loose in the sand hills to make it look like he was thrown.''

"I guess they were afraid I'd see their test holes when I flew over in the ultralight that first day, looking for Jerry,'' Frank said. "That's when Nat took a shot at me with the three-oh-three, cutting the rudder cable."

Roy nodded. "After that, they decided to lay low for a couple of days, until the heat was off. But they were pressed for time—Hicks was setting up a deal with a wildcat oil company to get in there and start stealing the oil."

"So, when Nat heard that the search was called off, they set off their last test?'' Joe said.

"Right,'' Frank said. "We heard the blast, and thought it was thunder, but Hicks got it into his head that we were onto them and decided to eliminate us."

"That explains the dynamite in the stove, and the bomb in the truck.'' Joe shuddered. "He came pretty close, didn't he?"

"Let's not forget that near miss in the truck, on the road to Charlie's,'' Frank told him. "What I'd like to know, though, was how Charlie figured in all this."

"His main concern seems to have been that sacred place of his up on the caprock,'' Roy said. "Well, he doesn't need to worry about that as long as I'm alive. I plan to fence it off and leave it to him and his people.''

Frank gave him an appraising look. "And what about the oil? What are you going to do about that?"

Roy stroked his chin. "Haven't decided yet. It's been there millions of years. And as far as I'm concerned, it can stay there a while longer." He scowled. "I don't like the idea of a bunch of oil patchers running all over my land, digging it up, fouling what little water we've got, scaring the cows, busting down the fences." He grinned crookedly. "Speaking of fences, I've got a few to mend myself—with Owens.''

At that moment, Joe heard the blare of a jeep horn and a cloud of dust appeared over the ridge, trailing a candy-apple-colored jeep.

"Here comes Tinkerbell," he said with a grin.

Roy stuck out his hand. "Come back during hunting season if you like. Give my best to Charlie if you run into him, and tell him he's got nothing to worry about. And thanks again for everything. Have a good trip home."

The boys loaded their luggage into the jeep, and the three of them took off.

Barbara's long dark hair was flying in the breeze as she drove along the road. "Sorry I'm late, guys," she said.

"I didn't much mind," Frank said. "But Joe was getting a little antsy."

The look Joe gave his brother could have reduced him to a cinder. He still hadn't come up with anything to say when Tinkerbell rolled quietly into Charlie's yard. The old man was dozing in the sun near his front door, his hat pulled down over his eyes. When he heard the jeep, he rose slowly to meet them.

"Tell him what Roy said about the sacred land," Joe urged Barbara.

In a warm and gentle voice, Barbara began to speak to the old man in Spanish. His face remained expressionless, but there was a light in his eyes. When she finished, he replied with a few soft phrases.

"He says to thank Senor Roy for his understanding," she said. "He says it is good when people understand one another."

"I guess you can't expect him to say, 'thank you' for something that's already his," Joe said with a shrug.

"But we can say thanks to him for all the help he gave us," Frank said. "We wouldn't be around if it weren't for him.

Barbara translated, and Charlie gave them a slight smile.

"Ask him why he didn't tell us more the first night," Frank asked. "He could have saved us some digging."

Barbara spoke to the old man briefly, and he replied.

"He says he didn't know who you were at first. You might have been evil."

"How did he know about the other things?" Joe demanded. "The telephone call, for instance." He shook his head. "That was *weird*."

Barbara spoke to him again.

This time, the old man only smiled broadly.